WAYLAID IN BOSTON

ELLIOT PAUL

WAYLAID IN BOSTON

Elliot Paul

COACHWHIP PUBLICATIONS

Greenville, Ohio

CONTENTS

1

A Wager Laid in Boston

ABOUT THREE YEARS had passed since Homer Evans had left his comfortable apartment in Paris on the pretext that he wanted to hear an unusual concert in San Francisco. Actually he had decided to help his young Irish-American protégé, Finke Maguire, get established as a private detective in Hollywood. Knowing how touchy Finke was, Homer had tactfully found a plausible excuse for making the trip and remaining on the scene, and Finke, who enjoyed and valued every moment in Homer's company, had made no objections. In fact, he was grateful and relieved. Evans had found for him his ideal secretary, Kay Cougar. He had made him acquainted with the proper persons and familiar with the right places. And when Finke had got out of his depth in his first important murder case,* Evans had flown to the rescue.

The solution of the Black Gardenia murders had required only a few days (and subtropical nights), but since, in the interest of science, Homer had decided to complete the nearly finished work of the murdered Dutch toxicologist, the late Sprouls Van Vleeck, months and seasons had elapsed while Evans was deep in the study of meat-eating plants and Oriental poisons. And when, near the conclusion of that fascinating work, Homer had found it necessary to consult with Dr. Hendrick Holz, a director of the Arnold Arboretum, that world-famous tree park on the fashionable outskirts of Boston, Finke Maguire had left his Hollywood practice in

* *The Black Gardenia*, Random House, 1952.

the competent hands of Kay Cougar to attend to some legal affairs. These had to do with an unexpected bequest to Finke, contained in the will of his father's life-long partner in the contracting business, which had prospered under various Boston political regimes before and after Finke's parents had died.

A cosmopolitan like Homer Evans has in each key city throughout the world a favorite hotel, one which suits his discriminating needs and offers a nice balance of privacy and congenial companionship. In Boston, he stopped at the Dorsetshire, and Finke, who in his boyhood had given a wide berth to the Back Bay while he roamed the toughest streets of East Boston, strung along. If he got bored among the bluebloods, he could easily flag a taxi.

The Dorsetshire is located on Commonwealth Avenue, near the Fenway. It was substantial and roomy one hundred years ago, and in the boom of the Gay Nineties grew vast and almost labyrinthine. The lobby is spacious but not flamboyant, and includes a well-stocked newsstand, with magazines and periodicals, paperbound books, and a fine tobacco counter. The writing room is quiet and well-appointed, and is flanked by a series of small reception rooms. The Anne Hutchinson Room is a decorous night spot, where guests wear formal clothes and the floor show is refined, the cooking standard and the service impressively venerable. Downstairs is a grill room where steaks and chops are served with sharper knives than in the main dining room. Above the ground floor, the suites and rooms are large and airy, with conservative modern furniture and decorations. The kitchens, storerooms, pantries and galleys seem to occupy at least an acre, and the parking lot, out back, takes up a third of the block, along the Newbury Street side.

Having been established before Civil War days, the Dorsetshire has held its own and, somehow, prospered through two world wars, with prohibition and depression years between them. Positions on its staff have been handed down from father to son, and new acquisitions have been made with care. So many of the guests are familiar with the corridors, and the accommodations are in such steady demand that, day and night, there is a comfortable flow of people moving this way and that. Only for a few hours, around dawn, are the passageways and elevators relatively deserted and even then someone is likely to be in sight, from whatever point of view.

To Evans, who knew his way around the building and the neighborhood, checking in at the Dorsetshire was like getting back to a seldom visited New England home. Finke, a native of a very different section of Boston, was astonished by the exits and entrances.

"God help the house dicks," Finke said. "There must be forty ways in, and a hundred out."

"I doubt if even the architects have counted them," Homer agreed. Then he sighed. "Well, who cares? We're both here on peaceable errands."

Finke grunted, and tightened his jaw muscles in a way that caused Homer to smile. Finke looked around the lobby uneasily. "This joint gives me the creeps. I've got one of those damned premonitions—hunches, to a guy like me. If anything's due to break wide open, 'twould be just my luck to have it happen here."

"Think nothing of it," Homer said. "This has always been a peaceful, respectable hotel. I shall spend happy hours at the Arboretum, learning of pitcher plants, skunk cabbages and Jimson weeds. You will linger in the offices of your late father's attorney, St. Clair Endicott, of Endicott, Endicott, Walpole, Winthrop and Swig, signing whatever documents are offered you. We shall have a farewell dinner, say at Locke-Ober's. I shall fly eastward to Paris, you shall return to Hollywood. No?"

Finke had been listening, but his eyes were straying in the direction of the main front entrance, where the doormen were stationed, incoming guests arrived, and a line of taxis waited just around the corner, at easy beck and call. One hundred yards down the avenue was a twin entrance as blank as the other was animate. It seemed to have been built expressly to allow anyone with furtive intent to enter or depart at will, completely unobserved.

"Shall we have a drink?" suggested Homer. "You'll like the Lantern Room. It was named to commemorate the exploits of a working silversmith, one Paul Revere."

The Lantern Room, as Homer had predicted, was very much to Finke's liking. Many others, Bostonians and discriminating transients, found it agreeable and soothing. At that hour, between 9:30 and 10 o'clock in the evening, the dim room, and the main bar adjacent, were only sparsely occupied. The lighting was dim and indirect, and all the doors and windows, except the doorway connecting with the bar, were draped.

As Homer stepped in, followed by Finke, the head waiter and another stationed nearby nodded recognition. Evans responded pleasantly and selected a table against the wall opposite the bar, where he and Finke, side by side, could see all the doorways, the platform on which stood a Hammond organ and an upright piano, and the large tables ranged around a cluster of rubber plants near the center.

"Ah, there's Jellyroll Morton," Homer said, *sotto voce*, indicating a lanky, slow-moving, moonfaced man, neither young nor middle-aged, who was sitting alone at a wall table nearest the Hammond organ and eating his late dinner with obvious distaste. "He's the piano player, and a good one," Homer added, and Finke knew the pianist must be very good, indeed. And surely this one was not the long-haired kind. He was nicknamed for one of the all-time "greats" of jazz, and he had Missouri or Iowa written all over him, before he said a word.

Having ordered their drinks—plain old fashioneds, double, without fruit or bitters—both Homer and Finke were content to sit passively and get the feel of the place. Homer exclaimed again, softly and with satisfaction, when a man in dinner clothes came in and took his place at a large round table, nearest the platform.

"That's Leverett Bengay. I've known him here and in Paris. One of the best," Homer said. And Finke, realizing that this, from Homer, was high praise, understood that later, after a decent interval, Evans would approach the well-dressed newcomer and observe the amenities. Meanwhile the piano player, dutifully munching his chicken sandwich and swallowing milk from a tall glass, slapped the open magazine he had been reading and said, to himself but aloud, "You're damned right!"

That brought a well-mannered laugh from Bengay, who had just taken his seat, not three yards away.

"Good evening, Mr. Bengay. Read this!" the piano player said, leaning over and tossing him the magazine, a popular detective-story monthly.

Good-naturedly Bengay re-opened the magazine to the page Jellyroll had dog-eared so thoroughly.

"That letter from the guy who signs himself 'G. Sharpe,'" Jellyroll said.

"G. Sharpe," repeated Finke, involuntarily, causing Bengay to glance in his direction and discover Homer. Everybody rose, introductions were effected, and at Bengay's invitation, Homer and Finke had their drinks shifted to the large round table at platformside, while Jellyroll, after shaking hands, went back to his instruments and started vamping chords on the Hammond, apparently listless and detached.

As Bengay looked down at the article he motioned for Homer to sit closer and join him in the reading. "This is more in your line, Homer," Bengay said.

"Uh, oh," grunted Finke, with instant misgivings. Homer, seated between Bengay and Finke, took the magazine, and the others read with him, from their separate angles.

> Dear Editor,
> The stuff most writers hand out about victims and suspects being shadowed I say is the bunk. It is all too easy, and untrue to real life. When Perry Mason wants to know what some man or woman is doing, for days or nights at a stretch, what does he do? All that he needs is to telephone Paul Drake on a private wire and say, "Tail him, or her, and report. Don't let him or her out of sight." I claim this can not be done. Rex Stout pulls the same old hokum. If Nero Wolfe wants to see inside somebody's house, or brain, and Archie Goodwin has other things to do, then a guy named Saul Panzer is always on the end of a wire, and observes all, learns all and reports it. I am not a complicated guy, but I could not tell where

I go, myself, and what I do and say the way Paul
Drake or this Saul Panzer report about strangers.
I said to myself before sitting down to write this
letter, "Come to think of it, what has the wife been
doing all day? Housework? Neighborhood shopping?
Was she downtown, looking at articles in stores? For
all Paul Drake or Saul Panzer, or that punk, Donald
Lam, or an op like Sam Spade could find out, she
could have had chop suey with Fu Manchu, and a
sleigh ride with Waxey Gordon. She might have
bought poison or sold it, under the name of Carrie
Nation, acquired blunt or pointed instruments, or
been untrue in almost any style."

In Europe, I hear, the police keep a record of
where everybody lives, even transients, and if anybody moves without turning in their new address,
he or whoever harbors him suffers plenty. Abroad,
with a whole city full of officials keeping records like
that, and the people afraid not to co-operate, a smart
operator might trace a fellow's movements, or even
a woman's, which are harder because women are
born and built for intrigue. I would like to see you,
Mr. Editor, try to tail the first stranger you come
across, here in the U.S.A., and see how much you
find out. I claim you'll learn nothing, unless it's
about yourself and these writers you print.

The contribution was signed "G. Sharpe," who gave an address
in St. Louis, Missouri.

Bengay, turning the question over in his receptive mind, looked
to Homer for guidance.

"Well?" he asked. "How about it?"

"I'm really unqualified to judge," said Evans. "My methods are
usually inductive or deductive, based on established or obtainable
facts."

Sardonically Finke touched his own forehead with extended forefinger. "The cerebral type," he said, drily. "It's men like me who do the leg work. We're a dime a dozen, and worth it."

Homer corrected Finke's own modest estimate of himself. "Mr. Maguire's done some fine jobs of shadowing—not the kind you read of in books. The hard way."

As they had been reading and making their comments, several other members of the group who sat habitually at that table, evening after evening, had entered and taken their places without interrupting. To bring them up to date, Bengay handed the magazine to Mirak Mirakian, a dapper young Armenian who always looked as if he had just stepped out of a barber's chair—a middle Eastern barber's chair, although he had been born in Boston, on Kneeland Street. Mirak was a feature writer for the Boston *Herald*, specializing, as so many sons of immigrants do, in the wealth of local historical material the Bostonians of longer standing neglect.

Next in line to read the piece was Angus Ferguson, a wool broker of Scottish descent. Having read only the books prescribed in school, Ferguson did not know Perry Mason or Donald Lam from Joe Palooka. He liked to spend his evenings with congenial friends, to listen to whatever they talked about, and above all, to drink Haig and Haig, for which his capacity was astronomical. He glanced at the text and expressed disapproval. Being a canny, uncommunicative man by nature, he looked with abhorrence on the idea that one man should violate another's privacy, and make notes on his intimate acts.

"Now what is it that you're so anxious to hide?" Bengay asked Ferguson, with a glint of mischief in his eye. "Your life pursues an even tenor. Your business is stable and conventional. Being a bachelor like the rest of us, your home life, thank God, is nonexistent. You are prosperous—within the law, I trust. Love, if any, leaves you placid. Your only vice, good Scotch whiskey, you indulge with dogged perseverance. You haven't changed your lodgings in years, nor the style of your haircut and clothes."

Homer Evans smiled questioningly. "If your sketch of Mr. Ferguson is just, he's the kind of man who's likely to be full of contradictions. Supposing Finke, for instance, was put on his trail, with *carte blanche*. . . ."

"That means a big expense account," Finke explained.

Bengay brightened. "What would you do, professionally, Mr. Maguire, to unravel Mr. Ferguson? At fifty or a hundred dollars a day?" he asked.

"Well," Finke replied, with a kind of diffident casualness. "A businessman, we'd tackle first in his office. That's the vital spot, for a commercial type. In some cases it's a front. How much money has he got? Just how does he make it? How fast, and who from? Does he level with the revenue boys?"

"Outrageous," growled Ferguson.

Homer took up the gag. "You see, Mr. Ferguson and gentlemen, a private investigator has an advantage over the police, in any land. Government authorities, as you can readily understand, are obliged to keep within bounds. In the process of upholding the law, they have to preserve the appearance, at least, of abiding by it. Whereas a young man like my erstwhile colleague, Mr. Maguire, whose ingenuity is perverse, combined with physical courage that seems to be absolute, can—how shall I express it not too crudely? He can cut corners, as it were. For example, were he investigating Mr. Ferguson it would be mere routine for him to gain entry into his office building by night and rifle the files."

Seeing that the Scot was about to explode, Bengay objected, "Oh, come now. Breaking and entering."

"Mostly entering. With our knowledge of locks and alarms, these days, breaking is seldom necessary," Homer said.

Finke's face showed his contagious grin. "There are other ways of getting keys," he said. "These tired businessmen have secretaries. You'd be surprised what happens when an experienced detective makes a pass at a guy's secretary."

At that, Ferguson really roared, but not with rage. He was laughing. "Miss Appleby," he gasped, and held aloft his glass quite gaily. "I'd like to see the man who tried to get a key from her, or anything else."

Finke was unimpressed. "Now and then, they're pushovers, those cranky virginal kind."

The harassed wool man was indignant again. "This has gone far enough," he said.

The pleasantries about detective work were interrupted momentarily by the entrance of Ephraim Poole, a massive rotund accountant who wore thick-lensed glasses and weighed close to three hundred pounds. What Poole liked best was scientific speculation, and only when pressed for funds did he accept a commission, if the fee was large and the problem difficult. The accountant had with him a medium-sized, reluctant man in a cheap but neat summer suit of some paperlike material, whose attitude expressed disquiet, while he uttered no words.

"This is Elbridge Gerry—Messrs. Bengay, Mirakian, Ferguson. . . . Why, hello Evans!" the big accountant said. "Gerry was lurking in the lobby. When I surprised him, he hesitated about coming in for a drink. He has a steady job and is married. Most likely owns a house."

The plain man with the job and the home had a certain aplomb, almost like resignation. If ne'er-do-wells who scorned steady employment liked to look on him as an example, he would submit, for just one drink. Then he would have to check in with the wife. That was how he expressed it. And so Homer Evans was somewhat surprised when the self-effacing Gerry nodded familiarly to Jellyroll, although to all appearances he was paying no attention to the latter's rendition of "The Wabash Blues." In fact, Gerry stepped over to the platform and exchanged a few words with the piano player, then rejoined the group at the round table when the waiter, Primitivo, brought his drink, a glass of Fundador.*

Meanwhile, the subject of shadowing and the gist of the previous conversation had been relayed to Poole, who blinked and reflected.

* Pedro Domecq, 1927.

"It would seem to me," the accountant said, "if you gentlemen were considering a wager, based on Maguire's ability to expose our friend, Ferguson, the victim is forewarned, therefore disqualified. Maguire fills the bill. He's a professional. The letter that started this argument refers to top-flight professionals, not tyros."

"What would be so hard about tailing someone?" asked Bengay. He was far from aggressive by nature, but no one knew better than Poole or even Ferguson that it was hard for Leverett Bengay to let a challenge go by. Finke saw his out, and made the best of it.

"I'm not available, just now. Not for any inducement," he said. "Why not let Mr. Bengay try his hand?"

"For Pete's sake, use your heads! Bengay, or anybody who tried a fool stunt like that, might get into serious trouble. The victim could sue him and take his last dime. He's never earned a dollar, I'll grant. Still, he's rich, and everyone in Boston knows it," Ferguson said.

"I'm sure Bengay wouldn't prove too clumsy. There's a chance he wouldn't get caught. Perhaps he'd like to risk it—for, say, five hundred on a side," Homer suggested.

"Let's make up a pool, in that case," the accountant said.

Mirakian was nervous, but tempted. Ferguson, aware that he was outvoted and outnumbered, reversed his attitude. "All right! If you want to act like chumps, you ought to pay for it. Raise your pool, and I'll cover it. On specified terms. My money says that Bengay can't follow a perfect stranger for forty-eight hours, and make a report that would satisfy . . ." Looking for a suitable referee, he hit at once on Homer Evans.

"Sorry," Evans said. "I want a part of the bet. So I can't be the judge."

"Your word's good enough for me," Ferguson said. "If you decide against me, I'm the one who has to pay. I'll take your five hundred, along with the rest. If you decide, after Bengay has been on the job forty-eight hours, that his report would satisfy a police commissioner of a big city, or the head of an insurance company, or the F.B.I., Scotland Yard, the Sûreté Générale, authorities like that, I'll come across."

Now that he saw the prospect of teaching his companions a salutary lesson, at a handsome profit, the Scot was determined and defiant.

"Who's going to pick the victim?" asked Finke.

Everyone around the table was having such a good time that a slightly jarring note was struck when Elbridge Gerry, the meek man in seersucker, rose uneasily.

"Excuse me, fellows," he said. "I really ought to go. I—I can't afford to bet, and if I could, I wouldn't know which side to take. This is all Greek to me." He looked distressed. "Frankly," he added, "I don't like to think about such things. It—if you won't take offense— isn't healthy, for anyone who has to keep his nose to the grindstone."

Homer was reluctant to let the shy man go. "You're practical, Mr. Gerry. Your feet are in the grassroots, even if your nose abuts the carborundum. Couldn't you stay for another drink of brandy—an excellent Spanish brandy, by the way—and choose Bengay's quarry?"

"I couldn't do it, Mr. Evans. I'm not acquainted with these gentlemen. I wouldn't know who is or is not strange to them." Gerry glanced experimentally toward Jellyroll, and Bengay caught on, approving at once.

"Of course. Let Jellyroll select our party." He beckoned to the piano player, who continued to the end of a riff, then took a vacant chair.

"Have you followed our colloquy?" Bengay asked.

"I catch a few words, now and then, when I'm playing, but not on purpose," the lank musician said.

Prompted occasionally by Poole or Ferguson, Bengay explained to Jellyroll the terms of the bet. "When you go back to the piano," Bengay said, "look over whoever is here, and those who come in. Pick your candidate, look his or her way casually, and play some tune we all know."

"'What Is This Thing Called Love,'" suggested Mirakian, think-ing of glamorous secretaries.

"I get you. 'What Is This Thing Called Love,'" repeated Jellyroll. "That's a wonderful tune—with the Spanish theme hanging fire in the middle, and the tempo of a rumba."

"That's really not the rumba. It's the old Spanish *danson*, or *son*," Gerry said. His Fundador had made him slightly giddy, but not quite so bashful, for the nonce. He got up again to take his leave and Finke simply reached over with one open hand, and reseated him gently, summoning the alert Primitivo with the other. Finke had an elusive hunch that he was carrying out Homer's unexpressed wishes. His first evening in the Back Bay district was not going too badly for Finke. He was not at all bored.

"There's one thing about this proposition that's not quite right," Bengay said. "The stretch of forty-eight hours, on duty, all by myself. After all, private detectives have the privilege of calling for help. If I take over tonight, about tomorrow noon I might need a few hours of sleep, or an extra hand to give me a lift."

Looking around the circle, Bengay was aware that Ferguson was following sharply the course of his eyes. He thought he saw the Scot's attitude relax ever so slightly when he looked at Mirakian.

"Would it be all right if, at twelve o'clock noon, Mirak spelled me, until six, let us say?" Bengay asked.

"How much is Mirak betting?" Ferguson asked, warily.

"I can't go higher than a C," Mirak said, apologetically, since Poole, Bengay, and Homer Evans were each putting up five hundred.

The Scot winced. "Don't refer to one hundred Yankee dollars as a C. That amount will keep the average American family two weeks."

"With bare necessities," Homer added. "But why not agree that Mr. Mirakian will be available from noon until six tomorrow evening? I assume we'll all get together here, between nine and ten, to hear about progress."

Ferguson nodded, and about that time Jellyroll got into what jazz addicts call "the groove," that is to say, he lost himself in his improvisations, and felt inventiveness and spontaneity take possession of his mind and flow through his arms and fingers. The talk around the big round table was suspended for a while.

And then, from the haze of music Finke saw that Leverett Bengay was acquiring a rapt look on his face, as if an angel with

the countenance of Marlene Dietrich had descended in the bright-
ness. Finke had been dimly aware of the well-dressed people, perhaps a dozen or as many as twenty, who had come trailing into the
Lantern Room before midnight, and others who had left to see the
second show in the Anne Hutchinson Room. More table lights
around the rim of the room had been turned on, the soft babble of
talk had heightened, and the adjacent barroom had been comfort-
ably crowded. Perhaps half the patrons were in evening dress, and
the rest were in mufti, whatever to hell that might be. Some of the
women were exotic, others were severely tailored. The best families of Boston were well represented by both sexes. A few of the
women were of the roguish kind. Actually, the New Haven railroad tracks were not far away. The ensemble was not like Maxim's
in Paris, the Stork Club in New York, or Ciro's in Hollywood. In
Boston, at the Dorsetshire, the Puritans and also the wild Irish had
left traces in the melting pot.

"Well, all right then," thought Finke.

Next, he noticed that Ferguson was also reacting to a vision of
some sort, with something approaching Scotch consternation. And
before Finke turned, in spite of Homer Evans' placid smile, he made
note of the music in his ears. The tune was not "What Is This Thing
Called Love" but, unless Finke was way off, Jellyroll's ominous
obbligato stemmed from the "St. James Infirmary." The bright-
eyed, hook-nosed little Armenian, Mirakian, was fairly bubbling
over. "Impossible!" Finke heard him gasp.

Finke shifted in his seat and craned his neck to look back over
his shoulder. The head waiter and Primitivo were ushering from
the entrance to a most select wall table set for one a woman in
black who must have dropped from the starlit sky outside to the
lonely bank of the Fenway, like the heroine in the play *The Unknown Woman* by Alexander Block. Or was it a reincarnation of
the fateful Mata Hari, of whom it took a cruel war to deprive the
world? Her hair was soft blue- black and richly piled. A lace scarf
seemed to accentuate the perfection and whiteness of her shoulders. Her eyes were large and dark. Her cheeks were pale. Her chin
was compassionate. As she adjusted her black lace skirt, her hands

were slender and poetic. Still, she was not timid. Even the head waiter was respectful, somewhat in awe of her. That neither he nor anyone around had seen the woman before was evident, unless someone were dissembling. Not one of the men who beheld her could place her in any earthly category.

The reactions of the companions around the table were varied. Finke saw that Bengay and Mirakian were eyeing Jellyroll expectantly, that Poole, with the fervent acquiescence of Ferguson, was murmuring "Won't do at all. Too easy." Elbridge Gerry, sipping his Spanish brandy glanced toward the woman in black without more than a fleeting interest. Silently excusing himself, he slipped from his chair and headed toward the barroom and the haven for gents beyond. As he brushed by, Finke noticed that the copy of the magazine which had set things in a kind of planetary slow motion was in Gerry's jacket pocket.

They all saw that Jellyroll had spotted the woman in black, but for purposes of the wager, such a spectacular dame was out of the question. Simple Willie Stevens could tail a pip like that, in the dark. And why was this woman alone? Somehow, her advent did not make sense, and Finke recalled all too well an admonition Homer Evans had given him when he was passing up a clue in Paris.

"According to Gertrude Stein," Evans had told him, "when she and Alice encountered a genius, she heard a little bell ring somewhere in the back of her head. The ideal detective, faced with the incongruous, has a similar subconscious response."

Finke looked back toward the filmy lace-clad phantom, then bit his lip and sighed. He might have known, he told himself. For Homer Evans was rising and proceeding, with gallant ease, toward the resplendent lone female, as if fate had conspired through years, if not generations, to bring them by incalculably separate courses to the Lantern Room this night.

What followed was easy for Finke to interpret, knowing Evans as he did. He saw Homer bow with just the right degree of deference. On closer inspection, the woman in black looked quite as lovely and mysterious as at first glance. A few words were exchanged as Homer introduced himself and invited the lady to join the group of male companions at the large round table. She responded without hesitation. With an explanatory nod to Primitivo she rose and walked gracefully, in step with Homer, until the passage between two tables was too narrow. When, with a pretty smile, she preceded her escort and glided through the opening, Finke grunted to himself a piquant line from Balzac, whose *Droll Stories* he had read: "Like an adder into a bowl of milk."

Again a complicated series of introductions and the lovely lone woman was seated between Poole and Bengay, with Homer and Finke across the table.

"Mademoiselle de Lassigny is not a spy or an optical illusion," Homer said. "She has a department store."

Mirakian, who had an involuntary habit of letting out, orally, what was uppermost in his volatile mind, exclaimed, "French?" The word had an interrogatory, almost fearful, intonation.

"Canadian," she replied. "From Montreal."

No one asked her any more questions at the moment, and neither she nor Homer offered further explanations. She settled among them contentedly, diffusing her fragrance, accepting their joint hospitality and comradeship and for a while was the focus of the light conversation which, at base, was a kind of subtle test. Her wit and charm were equal to the occasion.

"Just think of me as the Mademoiselle from Montreal," she suggested.

Only Ferguson looked mildly distressed. But Finke noticed that Elbridge Gerry, with the Colonial name, odd traces of Iberian tastes and information, and routine way of middle-class life, on his way back from the men's room, paused at the doorway between the bar and the Lantern Room, and, seeing that the mysterious woman in black was in the seat which formerly he had occupied, turned back into the barroom throng. He was not seen again in the Dorsetshire that night.

Surely, Finke was thinking, he must somewhere, sometime, have run across a better-looking and more agreeable dame than this de Lassigny number, but offhand he couldn't recall the name or the occasion. He was pleased to see, also, that Bengay,

the sophisticate, was hit rather hard, and the two outstanding mis-
anthropes, Poole and Ferguson, were trying their damnedest to find
something wrong with the lady and succeeding not at all. As for
her, she played the field, impartially, except that she acted as if
she had known Homer from childhood, which was not the fact, and
when she looked directly at Finke himself, her eyes took on a glint
of merriment. She made sure that on whatever topic the conversation lit, Finke had an opening to express his opinion.

"Hell," he thought. "She's playing up to me, to hold off the rest
of the wolves."

All in all, the big round table seemed to have isolated itself from
the rest of the room, as the eyes and ears of the occupants were
turned inward and the bachelors were adjusting themselves to the
vibrant element of femininity introduced in their midst.

The strains of "What Is This Thing Called Love" brought them
all, excepting Mlle de Lassigny, back to reality, or another kind of
unreality. Bengay, as soon as he was sure what Jellyroll was playing, was visibly regretful. He would have liked to stay close to the
woman in black. But he was a man of his word, and it was clearly
up to him to act in accordance with the terms of the wager. The
others, inversely as to the degree of their preoccupation with Mademoiselle, recognized the significant *motif* of the music. Again
Mirakian expressed a thought he had intended to keep silent. He
seemed to have read Bengay's mind.

"Cheer up, Lever," the Armenian said. "If the party's just come
in, he or she may stay a while. You don't have to tear yourself away
just yet."

It was natural that Mlle de Lassigny was somewhat puzzled.
She waited and watched, as well as listened. The others looked up
at Jellyroll, on his platform, and, without attracting undue attention with their group display of curiosity, identified the chosen victim by following the direction of Jellyroll's eyes.

The man in question had a sharp, fixed face. His long, pointed
nose and his steady, almost too steady, eyes gave the top half an
expression of concentration which stopped abruptly at the level of
his Dewey-type moustache. Below, his mouth was petulant and his

chin sloped away. A man with such a face could surely be capable of almost anything. His posture, as he leaned on one sharp elbow and stared into space, could be distrait or coldly deliberate. He was fairly tall, but not tall enough so that his head would conspicuously top the others in a crowd. Of course, he had to be wearing blue, but his suit was of presentable cheviot and expertly tailored. The shoulders were padded nattily and the double-breasted coat snugly buttoned, all the way down.

"May I ask what you make of him, Evans?" Bengay inquired.

Homer was purposely noncommittal. "He's not over-sociable. Too aloof for a professional man."

Grumpily Ferguson said, "I suppose you think he's a businessman? With files."

"I'd be surprised if he was in business for himself," said Homer.

Finke nodded. "Other people's money," he suggested, tersely, and looked at Homer as if he dared him to say he was wrong. Instead Homer sighed and acquiesced.

"Think he's American?" asked Mirak. As a son of immigrants, he was ultra-conscious about nationalities and races, and their local implications in Boston.

"Most likely from the South. He ties his bow tie with a droop," Homer said.

Mlle de Lassigny could contain herself no longer. "What's so intriguing about this man?" she asked. "Or mustn't I be inquisitive?"

Eyeing her through his thick convex lenses, Ephraim Poole said, as if he were kidding on the square, "Ah! Suddenly the attention shifts from you, Mademoiselle. You find that disconcerting?"

"We must explain," said Bengay, protectively.

At that instant the sharp-faced man seemed to notice Mademoiselle, let his eyes rest on her, and bowed, with a kind of reservation. She did not freeze, exactly, but neither did she respond. As if the man had made no overture, she turned back to Poole, to take up the thread of her defense against his unflattering suggestion. "I'm not vain," she said. "Only bewildered."

"You know that individual?" Poole asked, brusquely, indicating the man with the nose and Dewey brush.

"I never saw him before in my life, as far as I can remember," she said. "Does it matter?"

"A little," said Homer, softly. "May I inquire if you visited a bank today?"

"Why, yes," she said, a bit startled. "But why do you ask?"

"In ruminating about that man's possible occupation, it came to me that he might work in a bank. As cashier, or something like that. If that were the case, he might have seen and spoken with you, and, of course, would remember your face, no matter how you were dressed. Had he, at the time, been standing in a cage, with a visor obscuring his eyes, he would know who you are, and you might have had no chance to get a good look at him."

"But why should you care where he works?" she asked.

It was then that Poole explained, step by step, how the pointed-faced stranger had become so important to them. Mlle de Lassigny was delighted and thrilled. But she turned to Ferguson with a sympathetic pout.

"You mean," she said to Bengay, "that poor Mr. Ferguson is betting all alone, that you others have, as you say, ganged up on him." She opened her handbag and took from it a sheaf of crisp new hundred-dollar bills.

The effect of her gesture on Ferguson, who before that had seemed to be melting somewhat, can more easily be imagined than described.

"That's currency, madam," he snapped. "U.S."

"Mademoiselle," she corrected, provocatively. "I know what you're thinking. In times like these, one should respect its value. I remark, nevertheless, that you, yourself, don't hesitate to profit at your comrades' expense."

That did not pacify Ferguson at all. He grew less censorious, but more suspicious. "You think my end's a sure thing, I suppose," was his comment.

"So do you, *cher monsieur*, or you wouldn't be covering the pool. I'd still consider it a favor if you'd share the spoils with me," she said.

"And if you lose?" asked Bengay.

"I'll loathe it, but I'll pay," she assured him. "So, I presume, will Mr. Ferguson. To see that alone would be worth what I'm risking."

The question was settled in her favor and her gaiety on that account further piqued Bengay. "What makes you so sure I can't follow that fellow, and find out how he ticks, in forty-eight hours?"

She smiled mischievously. "You are not Mr. Finke—or Mr. Homer Evans."

"Lady! You got the order wrong," said Finke. "I only do the hatchet work, to spare the master mind."

"Achievement needs two wings," she declared.

On his new Hammond and beat-up piano Jellyroll was vamping again. Mademoiselle announced that her name was Solange. Since the others all used first names, she would be happy if they addressed her that way. One of the reasons might have been that, while Homer with his perfect French pronounced de Lassigny correctly, the others rendered it with halting variations.

"I adore that piece of music Monsieur Jellyroll was playing," Solange said.

"'What Is This Thing Called Love,'" said Mirakian.

"Would he mind playing it again?" she asked.

Bengay promptly relayed the request to the rostrum. So Jellyroll, in his Missouri drawl, announced that he was repeating the number by request, and indicated Solange as the petitioner. Everyone in the Lantern Room already had noticed and admired the woman in black, and applause broke out spontaneously and swelled until she was becomingly confused by the volume and extent of the tribute. An outburst like that, evoking a kind of unity throughout his domain, brought out the best in Jellyroll. He started the melody simply, without too much emphasis, then elaborated with more and more freedom. He must have played six or eight choruses. As the hand-clapping broke out again, and eventually diminished, Bengay was stung with sudden misgiving. He looked fearfully toward the table near the entrance. The man who had sat there was gone.

2

In Which Finke Is Taken for a Ride

FINKE COULD NOT HELP chuckling when Bengay, in the course of his first half-hour as an amateur sleuth, had let the man he was supposed to be tailing walk quietly away. Nevertheless he was impressed by the way the elegant Bostonian behaved. Bengay simply rose, bowed regretfully to Solange de Lassigny, said, "Sorry," and started toward the doorway. To avoid any show of panic he paused, halfway to the exit, and turned to wave a nonchalant farewell to Jellyroll. That failed to come off. The platform was vacant, except for the instruments. Jellyroll seemed also to have left the Lantern Room.

Near the pointed-faced man's table, Bengay accosted Primitivo, who had waited on the fellow, but the waiter, to his own discomfiture as well as Bengay's, did not know the customer's name. Neither had he seen him before. Furthermore, he had been in the pantry, in line of other duty, when Pointed Face had vanished. Bengay observed that his quarry had left a dollar bill on the plate beneath the glass which contained an unfinished highball. That would be the right amount. The drink cost 75 cents.

From the exit of the Lantern Room a plush corridor led straight to the lobby. Bengay glanced at his wrist watch, which said quarter-past 12. At that hour, if the fairly tall stranger in blue cheviot, with pointed nose and brush moustache, had gone out that way, he might have been noticed by Daisy, the Swedish blonde who had the hat-and-coat checking concession, either of the two elevator operators, the night clerk or his assistant, the night bell captain or any of the bellhops, of which there were three. All the night staff knew Bengay and liked him, as an amiable, generous patron of the place. None of them had seen the party he was asking about. The only item slightly out of the ordinary was the presence, in the door of the elevator nearest the desk, of an employee relatively new to the hotel in place of Bozo Shafter, the irrepressible near-midget who was practically a fixture there.

"Where's Bozo?" Bengay asked. He was told that Bozo had shifted, for the evening, to another distant elevator, to take the place of a colleague who was ill. That cheered Bengay a little, since Bozo never missed anything, and if the party in question had turned right, instead of left, on quitting the Lantern Room, he might have passed Bozo's station in the middle group of lifts. Pointed Face had been hatless and coatless in the Lantern Room. And Daisy was positive that no such party had checked his things with her. The night clerk could not say, one way or another, with only Bengay's description to guide him, whether such a man was registered at the hotel. So Bengay retrod the plush of the corridor toward the Lantern Room again, passed the draped entrance, and found Bozo, hands behind his back, pacing his cage like a dwarf Daniel Webster. Seeing Bengay approaching, Bozo paused, held up a restraining hand and said: "Don't ask me. I haven't seen no tall man, not so very tall; blue cheviot suit, neat, double-breasted; long schnozzel; haddock eyes; with a smudge above his kisser."

"You've heard about the bet? Whoever told you must have unusual powers of description," Bengay said.

"I've got to be neutral. I've got friends on both sides of the fence," said Bozo. Bengay took a ten-dollar bill from his pocket.

"Withholding routine information isn't neutral. That would work against me," said Bengay, stroking the ten.

The dwarf, one eye closed in a wink, the other fixed on the greenback, said, "That's different."

"You saw him, then?"

"I might have," Bozo conceded.

Suddenly it was clear to Bengay that someone else had asked about the highly describable stranger. He asked severely who it

had been. Bozo, on that point, was not saying a word. So Bengay
reasoned that the first inquiry had come from someone Bozo would
protect, even if it cost him money. That would not be another
esteemed client, but a pal on the staff. The answer flashed of its
own accord into Bengay's active mind. Of course! Jellyroll! Jellyroll
had absented himself from the Lantern Room about the time
Pointed Face had made himself scarce.

"To which floor did our stranger ride?" asked Bengay.

"The sixth," Bozo said.

"No coat or hat?"

"No."

"Which way did he turn, when he quit your cage?"

Bozo's reaction to this question was such that Bengay surmised,
correctly, that the dwarf had heard and answered it before.

"To the right," Bozo said.

"And Jellyroll rode up, just afterward?"

"What makes you think so?" Bozo asked.

"Where did Jellyroll get off?"

"I can't tell you that, Mr. Bengay," said the dwarf.

"Bozo, don't misunderstand me," said Bengay. "I'm a friend of
Jellyroll's. If he tried to follow this other party, he might have been
acting in my interest."

"O.K. Then ask him all about it."

"Does he ride up often, as high as the sixth? He doesn't sleep
in the hotel."

"I wouldn't know where anybody sleeps, outside of my elevator," Bozo said.

"All right. Did the stranger ride down again?" Bengay asked.

"Not in my car."

"In anybody's car?" demanded Bengay. The dwarf was getting
on his nerves. Still, there was some justice, even integrity, in his
contention that, with friends on both sides, he was bound to be
neutral. He was hired to transport passengers up and down, not
divulge details concerning them. For ten dollars, Bozo would
reveal whatever he could about strangers, but nothing about
Jellyroll Morton. What could there be about Jellyroll, outside of

his excellent jazz and poor digestion which for weeks had kept him on a diet of chicken-breast, lettuce and cold milk? Bengay should have a talk with him. But first he ought to inquire at the parking lot. Dozens, if not hundreds, of guests and patrons of the Dorsetshire would have autos within the big enclosure on the northeastern corner of the block. Perhaps Pointed Face, bound for the Lantern Room, had parked his car, got a check from one of the night attendants, left his hat and topcoat behind him to dodge the cloak-room tip, stopped for one highball, then taken Bozo's lift to the sixth, where he might be playing cards or calling on a woman, or, for that matter, a man, or men, a couple, mixed group, or *ménage*.

The senior attendant on the parking lot, who worked the night shift from choice, was known as Clothhead Muldoon, and his "partner," a North End Italian, was called simply "Wallyo." When activity was slight, they played two-handed stud in the small boarded shack with tar-paper roof referred to as "the office." Bengay made his way thither by means of a twisted network of corridors. When he stepped outdoors, to the concrete pavement, stained with oil, and breathed the summer night air, mixed with gasoline fumes, the sky was heavy with stars. Facing him, on the far side of Newbury Street, stood a row of residential apartments the front sections of which were desirable, because of the good location, and the rear of which were rented less dearly because they abutted the railroad. The practiced parking-lot attendants had placed in a rear section the cars that would not be used until morning. Those of the transients, who would be leaving between midnight and dawn, were more accessible. A truck from somewhere in the country, loaded with fragrant produce for the kitchen, was backing into position for unloading, and Wallyo, the No. 2 attendant, was supervising the operation. So Bengay, filling his lungs with air, such as it was, proceeded diagonally across the broad lot and found Clothhead in the shanty.

"Muldoon," Bengay said, amiably, "I've laid a little bet."

Clothhead grinned. "So I heard," he said. "I'd like to see the day when such a flyer seemed little to me."

"If you can help me, I'll make it worth your while," Bengay said.

Clothhead had much faith in the effectiveness of Irish blarney. "Shucks, Mr. Bengay," he said. "You don't have to pay me to do what I can for you. But what would it be?"

"Do you know who I'm supposed to be shadowing? What he looks like? How he's dressed?"

"Not yet," Clothhead said. He beckoned and called out, "Hey! Wallyo. Front and center!"

Wallyo joined them, touching his rakish cap to Bengay. Wallyo believed in exploiting class distinctions. Bengay described the man he sought, and asked if any such had parked a car on the lot. Both the attendants were regretful, and no mistake. They would have given much to have seen such a guy, and had they not been together, with one to keep tabs on the other, either of them might have made up a comforting story, just to please Bengay. Clothhead kept the prospect open by admitting that they could not always remember every face that passed across their line of vision. If any man, fairly tall, with a long nose, poker eyes, and a double-breasted blue suit showed up, the parking lot boys would spot him, and Bengay would be informed. While they were talking, Wallyo pointed suddenly to a dim section of the lot.

"Who's that?" he asked.

A fairly tall figure, that of a man without coat or hat, was standing alone in an open space, his back to the shanty, his face turned toward the bank of transient cars. He might have been thirty yards distant. But he was strangely immobile. His posture indicated doubt and inner conflict.

"Could that be your weenie? The guy that you're after, I mean?" asked Wallyo.

"No. It's Angus Ferguson," Bengay said, and moved cautiously toward the space in which Ferguson was standing.

"Now what brings you here?" Bengay asked. Ferguson, startled, turned around.

"I hoped you might be out here."

"Any message?" asked Bengay.

"What do you mean by that?" Ferguson asked, unmistakably anxious. His voice grew earnest, quite jittery, in fact. "Lever, why not call this whole thing off? I like it less and less, the farther it goes. This fellow Evans—he thrives on notoriety, however self-effacing he seems. His confederate, Finke, has admitted he'll stop at nothing. And now this adventuress."

"Oh, come now. Miss de Lassigny owns and operates a Montreal department store. She's having a lark."

"You'll notice she's into us for $800 already."

"Into us? Not both of us, surely," Bengay objected.

"Yes. Both of us," insisted Ferguson. "If you should win—and there's not a chance—she'd take your money. And when you lose, which is certain, she'll cash in eight hundred that otherwise is mine."

"I'll raise you eight hundred, if that's how you feel," Bengay said, quite fed up with Ferguson's assumption that he was sure to make a hash of the undertaking. He did not fail to take note when Ferguson ignored the suggestion, and let slip a hint of what was really on his mind.

"The whole hotel is talking. Suppose this affair got into the papers. You others don't care. But I'm in business. Wool business. I have to think of my credit and reputation. I can't have my linen washed in public, with international spies, mysterious women, peephole detectives, gambling. . . ."

"Ah. You'll acknowledge we're gambling. You're not just taking money from fools," said Bengay. "You ought to know a lady when you meet one, a gentleman, too, when it comes to Evans and his man Friday. For my part, I'll guarantee to say nothing for publication, if you need my pledge on that. And since you brought up the subject of linen, don't act like an old stuffed shirt. You made your bet, now lie in it."

"I might have known," Ferguson said, disconsolately, but he stiffened, turned on his heel, and started back toward the hotel.

Waiting a few moments, to give the Scot a fair start and himself a little time to cool off, Bengay watched the unloading of the produce truck a while, then made his way toward the Lantern Room. Before he reached the doorway he could hear that Jellyroll was back on his platform, and that bolstered up his spirits, somewhat. He stepped between the parted drapes and was jolted by Surprise No. 1. Pointed Face, the man he had lost and failed to find, was sitting at the same table, leaning on the same elbow, with a half-consumed highball before him, exactly as before. One of the quickest mental switches Bengay had ever accomplished enabled him, by the time he reached the big round table, to act as if he had known his quarry's whereabouts and had returned on that account.

Surprise No. 2 came hard on the heels of the first one. Ferguson, who had been given ample time to resume his place, was nowhere to be seen.

"Where is my partner, Mr. Ferguson?" asked Solange.

"I saw him last on the parking lot," Bengay replied.

"The parking lot?" she repeated. "He can't have abandoned us without a word, intending to go home," she said. "Someone called him to the telephone."

"Indeed!" said Bengay. He was trying to figure out whether Ferguson had left before Pointed Face had returned, or if the Scot had known that the quarry had come back, as it were, to the web which the spider had abandoned. Besides, Ferguson received few phone calls at night. None at all, that Bengay ever knew about. In his somewhat strained and baffled state of mind, he found himself wondering whether spiders had one web, or a string of them which they tended like traps around the rim of Hudson Bay. He must go up there for the trapping, sometime soon, by way of Montreal. Anyway, although he had not been able to track down his man, his luck had run high. Pointed Face was giving him another chance. That was a bright omen. He ventured to hope that the others, criminologists or not, were unaware that such a break had come from a clear sky, so that his first tally would be scored as unearned.

When the others had lingered long enough to convince themselves that Ferguson was not likely to return, and Pointed Face showed no sign of immediate departure, Homer proposed a nightcap and asked Solange if he and Finke would drive her to her hotel. He had noticed, when previously she had opened her hand-bag, that she was carrying a key with a tab. Bengay sighed enviously as she accepted the offer. Mirakian shrugged with Near Eastern resignation. He, of all the group, was a fatalist.

"My car is on the lot," said Solange.

Rising, Homer said, "I'll ask the doorman to send it around front."

Finke stood up. "I'm being taken for a ride," he said.

"I'll meet you both in the lobby," said Solange, then wishing the best of luck to Bengay and Mirakian, and promising to be on hand when they reported progress next evening, she made her exit in the direction of the powder room.

As soon as Homer and Finke were alone, Homer accelerated his stride, veered out of the plush corridor and headed for the parking lot. Finke trailed along.

"What's cooking?" demanded Finke. "You need me like a hole in the head."

"Forbearance. Philosophy," admonished Homer.

When they came to the lot and were met by Muldoon, Evans said to the Celt, "Miss de Lassigny's car, if you please."

"Come again, Mr. Evans," said Muldoon. Then, by intuition he put two and two together. "Oh! You mean the Canada license?"

"That's the one," Homer said. He pretended not to notice what Finke remarked at once. The "Canada license" was not among the transient cars, of which at that hour there were not many. It was with those that Muldoon had figured would stay in his care all night.

"I'll drive," Evans suggested. "Why don't you sit with our lady in black?"

"Our Lady of the C's," grunted Finke. "Could you tell me what's the pitch?"

"She's taken a fancy to you."

"You wouldn't be passing me the buck, by any chance?" Finke asked.

That Homer did not deign to answer. Instead, as he tipped Muldoon and took his place in the driver's seat of the neat convertible, he asked the attendant when Mr. Ferguson had called for his car.

"Not yet. It's right there," Muldoon replied, thumbing toward a '41 Dodge.

"Thanks," Evans said. He reflected a moment, then stepped out of the convertible. "I wonder, Finke, if you'd mind taking Mademoiselle for a drive, before retiring. I'd like to check on a trifle or two."

"Mine not to reason why," Finke said. "But can't we stay out of this mess?"

"Nothing shall divert me from my research about weeds, I assure you. Or you from Endicott, Endicott, Walpole, Winthrop and Swig. Especially Swig. Convey my apologies to the fair one. You'd better not explain in detail," said Homer, and, with an easy gesture of good night left Finke muttering.

At a distance of about six paces Homer turned. "By the way," he said. "You can select your own route for the drive. Our lady has a suite in this very hotel."

Finke jammed down on the starter, and drove away with a reckless address which caused Muldoon and Wallyo to gasp and whistle. Bringing up sharply at the curb in the exact center of the front entrance, Finke stepped out and was met by Solange, who had somehow acquired a cloak of cloth of gold and a black lace headpiece which had the effect of a holiday mantilla.

"The brains got unavoidably detained," he began.

She let out a soft silvery laugh. "Such a tactful, considerate man, your Monsieur Evans," she said.

"Shall I leave your key at the desk?" Finke asked, to show that he was not entirely dense. "And what's so courtly about a man's dating you for a drive to your hotel, which you're already in, then standing you up?"

Meanwhile they were seating themselves in the roadster, Finke at the left, and Solange beside him. "Monsieur Evans gave me a chance for a graceful exit, so none of the others could possibly feel slighted, and he must have sensed that I'm not quite tranquil about my partner's—Mr. Ferguson's—disappearance. Most likely, when

I get back to the hotel desk, I shall find a note in my box, with reassurance. Meanwhile, Mr. Finke, you are what Americans term 'the goat.' *Pas?*"

"Who's complaining," Finke said, "if not you?"

"Not I," she said, and leaned a little closer. "I've never met a detective before, in either the cerebral or the hatchet category. Now, if it were you who had been assigned to follow that long-nosed specimen I'd be supporting your side."

"Bengay's no dope. He might have beginner's luck."

"I noticed that you didn't bet," she said. "Isn't that unusual, for you to fail to take a chance?"

"'Twas too tough, making the decision. On the amount, I mean. You see, tomorrow I go to my lawyer about some dough a friend of my father's has left me in a will. I don't know how much. I can't even guess. It wouldn't be respectful."

"This is fabulous," exclaimed Solange, with delight. "You may be poor, you may be rich. You don't really care."

"To tell the truth, I don't know how I'll feel."

"I'm sure you've had whatever you wanted, up to now," she said.

"Maybe," Finke agreed. "That doesn't mean that if I find myself filthy with money I might not get mixed up about what I want from now on. Living from hand to mouth, it's been easy to decide what to go after."

"Your instinct has told you, I suppose."

"A guy's instinct gets him into more trouble than anything else he's got," he said, with feeling.

"Long live trouble," was her retort, and she spoke with feeling, too. She was so lovely, in black lace. Her fragrance was enchantment itself. Still, under the surface she was vibrant with refined discontent. "I'm going to confess," she continued, impulsively. "It's true that I own a department store, and thus far have managed it well. The hundreds who are dependent on its profitable continuance are secure, I believe."

She adjusted her cloth of gold wrap around her perfect and delicate shoulders. She was young, but far from naïve. Her character, like her body, had an appealing shape that would lose nothing as it matured. Finke knew better than to interrupt, or urge her to continue. She resumed, of her own accord.

"You mustn't tell this to Mr. Ferguson," she said. "He might be shocked. But occasionally, when I feel that I must, I leave my business to carry on of its own momentum, drive or fly to Boston, New York, Paris—but usually Boston. I don't know why. This city, which many find stuffy, or passé, has a fascination for me, perhaps illogical. In a Boston bank I keep a personal account, distinct from all other accounts. I like to take whatever amount pops into my head, and spend it as I please, regardless of arithmetic. This afternoon I asked a cashier for 25 C's." She hesitated, then asked eagerly, "Tell me, Mr. Finke. If you learn tomorrow that your fortune is colossal, shall you have the impulse to do things like that? To free yourself of all responsibility? Not mere drunkenness. That's banal."

Finke grinned. "I didn't notice you tossing any of those cognacs over your shoulder tonight," he said. "You've got a head for hootch. And what you do makes sense. So all right, then."

Her gentle hand pressed his arm, and caused him to miss the periphery of a rounded curb by an eighth of an inch instead of the customary quarter as they skirted the somnolent Public Gardens.

"I love you and Mr. Evans," she said.

"You don't say," exclaimed Finke. "Well. Wallace Beery once divvied an Oscar with Frederic March. Neither one turned it down."

He spun the wheel into a smooth U turn.

"I wonder what Mr. Evans is doing," she said.

3
Late Curfew by the River Charles

HOMER, AS SOON AS HE had watched Finke drive off the parking lot, walked over to Ferguson's '41 Dodge and tried the doors. They were locked. He had assumed that they would be. To a man of the Scot's cautious temperament, the exposure to close inspection of any interior, material or spiritual, would seem loose, in the sense of *los*, or *louche*. He would exercise his virtuous policies as a Sandow his calves and biceps. Homer glanced in, and was happy to note that the stern wool man did not make a practice of checking his own wraps in his car, free of charge.

It was to Daisy's cloakroom that Homer next repaired, but he preferred not to traverse the hotel's tortuous corridors, and thus miss enjoyment of the starlight and mild salt air. So he strolled to the corner shack, saluted Clothhead and Wallyo amiably, and walked along the Newbury Street sidewalk, on the parking-lot rim, and as he was glancing without special interest at the fronts of the brick and brownstone apartment buildings across the street, as he passed them in turn, two men in tuxedos, without topcoats or hats, cut over from a rear exit of the Dorsetshire and entered a brownstone building. From force of habit so long established that it operated without volition, Homer registered the house number, 14, and that the men, who evidently lived there, entered without unlocking the front door.

"Two schools," he murmured. "One locks empty parked cars, the other lives in apartment buildings unlocked at 2 A.M. Ah, democracy."

At the southeastern corner of the Dorsetshire, the rear one nearest the Fenway, Newbury Street took a sharp right-angled bend, to avoid plunging into the creek, and fed itself into Commonwealth Avenue as the Fenway flows into the Charles River a few blocks beyond, to the westward. The abbreviated bend in Newbury Street, forming the southern boundary of the Dorsetshire property, affords space for an ideal around-the-corner taxi stand which, in busy hours, accommodates eight cabs. At 2 A.M. there were three. The driver of the front one, who had been a Checker driver since the First World War, was known to Homer and recognized him.

"Been here long?" Homer asked.

"All evening," replied the cabman. That meant since 6 o'clock P.M., a matter of eight hours. Of course, he meant "off and on" and Homer understood it that way. The taxi drivers who habitually waited for fares at that stand were kept fairly busy by the Dorsetshire patrons and knew the regulars by name and destination.

"Has any of you gentlemen driven Mr. Ferguson home since midnight?" asked Homer.

"Not likely," the cab man said, and grinned. "He drives and shaves himself."

Homer thanked his informant, said *au revoir* but not good night, and the response was out of World War I.

"Three beans in the messkit," the taxi driver said.

At the cloakroom, Daisy was preparing to leave. She ordinarily went home about two-thirty, and if any hats or coats remained on the hooks and hangers, Bozo carried on, between elevator trips, and attended to the formal closing. The midget was back on his own elevator, just right of the registration desk. When Homer started questioning Daisy, Bozo eased himself within range.

"Has Mr. Ferguson left yet?" Homer asked Daisy.

Bozo pointed in his lordly way to a certain felt hat and topcoat. Daisy, coincidentally, turned her pretty head and saw them. "No, Mr. Evans," she said.

With a smile, Homer suggested, "He finds reasons for lingering behind his cronies, for a bachelor's prayer at cockcrow to St. Valentine, one might say?"

"One might say the darnedest things, especially you," Daisy said, and added piquantly, "after all, he's better off getting his kicks across the counter from girls like me than making some good woman a husband. Mr. Ferguson's no sap, at that."

Without changing his tone or expression Homer continued, "That stagnant pool just outside the hotel, on our left. Have any bodies been dredged out of it, since you've been concessionaire?" he asked.

Daisy reacted with superstitious dread.

"Please, Mr. Evans. Don't talk like that. Not even in fun. I walk home from here almost every night," the girl said.

"Believe it or not," agreed Bozo. He, too, was uneasy, even shaken. "You're not suggestin'—anyone we just mentioned?"

"Perish the thought," Evans said. "Forget that I inquired."

As he walked away, Bozo hopped back into his elevator and reached way up to draw the door closed. Daisy made up her mind to stick around awhile, until Mr. Ferguson showed up, so she would not have bad dreams. She was not reassured when she saw Homer go up to the night bell captain and ask a few more questions. Hastily, somewhat ashamed of her panic, she slipped through the rear door of her snug concession, leaving the few articles temporarily unguarded, made a restrained dash for the Lantern Room, and glanced in through the Judas window of a service door.

There were about ten people inside, counting the waiters and Jellyroll. Ferguson was not among them, but her heart pounded a little when she saw the long-nosed man in a double-breasted suit at one table, staring into space, quite impatiently but covertly being watched by Mr. Bengay, Mr. Mirakian, and Jellyroll, who seemed fed up with playing. Daisy rushed back to her cloakroom. To get the most out of single life, she knew that a girl had better be conscientious, up to a certain point. Before many moments had passed, she realized that the sight of Pointed Face, who had stirred up so much conjecture in the hotel that night, had disturbed her more than Evans' reference to the Fenway pool and corpses.

She saw that Homer was telephoning, over an instrument that had been plugged in at a writing-room desk. Beckoning the night clerk's assistant, she learned from him that Mr. Evans had asked about a telephone message that Mr. Ferguson received about one o'clock.

"Who was this call from?" Daisy asked.

"Some dame. I was the one who took it, and sent a bellhop to ask Mr. Ferguson to come to the booth, that one (he pointed across the lobby) first in line over there."

"She didn't leave her number for him to call back?"

"I've just got through telling you that she insisted on holding the line, although she knew Mr. Ferguson would be in some whiskey-serving public room, so full of Haig and Haig his back teeth would be floating."

"Was that what the dame said? She had her nerve," Daisy said, an edge on her voice. "I wonder who she was? He hasn't any family."

"Maybe she works for him, and something vital came up. A man who drinks Scotch at present-day prices night after night must have to do plenty of business in the daytime, just to break even."

"Did Mr. Evans think it might be some girl who works for Mr. Ferguson?"

"So what?"

"So you didn't know, I suppose. So nobody around here knows who works for Mr. Ferguson. And Mr. Evans is calling every girl in the telephone book, alphabetically, no doubt?"

"If so, he's found one he likes. And got her first shot out of the box," the assistant said. "Mr. Evans has brains and luck."

Daisy, her eyes on Homer's eloquent back, was fairly sure his luck was letting him down, this one time. She saw him hang up the phone. A slight frown creased his high forehead. Then, seeming to sense that he was under scrutiny, he confirmed the fact and came over to where Daisy and the assistant night clerk were standing.

"Ronnie," he said. "I overheard Mr. Ferguson refer earlier this evening to a certain Miss Appleby, his secretary. The night chief operator of the Metropolitan district has just informed me that no female Applebys have unlisted numbers, or have subscribed since the last directory was printed. So our Miss Appleby may be one of the thirty-two Applebys in the book." Pausing to give the clerk,

Ronnie, a ten-dollar bill, he added, "Will you please do the need-ful? I'll check with you in about half an hour."

"Thanks, Mr. Evans," the clerk said. "What shall I tell her, in case I get her on the phone?"

"Ask her pardon, for awakening her at this unseemly hour. Say 'Sorry, there's been some mistake.' Report how she reacts. And, of course, make note of her number and street address."

"But—the phone call . . . The message," Daisy said, incredu-lously. "Shouldn't she be asked about that?"

"Not just yet. Ronnie, I'm sure, will follow directions explicitly."

"I don't get it," Daisy said, but again she had left her cloak-room vacant, although she was not ten yards away from the front counter. She hurried back, with nervous haste, and suppressed a little scream. Not a piercing cry of horror. She was merely unstrung.

"Why, Miss Daisy," Homer said, kindly, taking her arm and patting gently her hand. "I've been inconsiderate, with my talk about pearls that were eyes. What startles you now?"

"Mr. Bengay's hat and coat. They've been taken, while I've been standing right here, talking to you. Oh, dear," she exclaimed.

"You're not going to cry," Homer said, quite tenderly. "Let's go together, by the back way, to the Lantern Room. We'll find, unless I'm mistaken, that the gentleman who, without his knowledge, I hope, is acting as our mock-up, has quite normally departed. So Bengay, who knows the hotel byways as well as we do, has slipped into your cloakroom from behind and taken the liberty of remov-ing his homburg, drape and dagger. What?"

"Don't say things like 'dagger' any more," she begged, but did as he suggested and found the Lantern Room empty, except for Mirakian, who was finishing an Alka-Seltzer with Jellyroll, who was moodily consuming another glass of cold milk. Both looked exhausted, if not dejected.

Daisy, relieved, began to cry. "I won't sleep a wink tonight," she said.

Evans, touched, and anxious to undo the mischief to her peace of mind, suggested that she turn over her keys to Bozo and accom-pany him on a restful walk, indoors and out.

"We'll find trace of Mr. Ferguson, never fear," he promised.

"I don't want to find trace. Please find him. You know as well as I do that he must be around here, somewhere," she said. "And don't jump at conclusions, just because I'm in tears. I'm not in love with him, or anyone else. There's something in the air tonight that makes everybody act crazy."

"I've noticed strange portents, myself," Homer agreed.

He had the idea of taking Daisy out one of the numerous back exits, across the parking lot, and around the huge block. His mind reverted to Pointed Face, and Bengay's self-appointed task. Daisy's clinging presence reminded him that the quarry's hat and coat had never reposed in her two-bit sanctuary. Somehow the recollection of the two men in dinner dress who had left the hotel, hatless and coatless, to cross Newbury Street and enter the building in which, presumably, they lived, combined with other items in Homer's mind. He was convinced by now, since none of the employees knew Pointed Face's name or significance in the scheme of things, that the man was not stopping at the Dorsetshire. Neither had he a car on the lot, or been seen by Clothhead or Wallyo. There remained the taxi drivers as a possibility. Perhaps the enigmatic stranger had ridden in a cab. If he were Bengay, Homer concluded, he would check at the taxi stand, and consider as well the row of brick and brownstone apartment buildings so accessible from all the back exits. Also he would find out which bank Solange de Lassigny patronized in Boston, and scan the roster of its employees. Luckily, he mused, aware of Daisy keeping step with him and growing less tremulous by the minute, Bengay is Bengay. So that's that. Tomorrow, he promised himself, I shall hie me, while the dew still quivers on the thorn, and revel in skunk cabbages and stinkweeds, whose vulgar designations belie their beauty of form, line and color. And Finke . . . Where was Finke, by the way? Most likely, by the way.

"Are you always as happy as you seem?" Daisy asked.

"When you say that, smile!" Homer said, evasively. "The gayest chap I know is nicknamed Foolish Phil. He's like Rabelais' fool who decided that a man can pay for the smell of roast goose with the sound of his money."

"I'm nuts about the way you sound," she said. "You and your Mr. Finke."

"We like the way you smell," Evans said.

They walked through silent corridors awhile, turning right, then left, then zigzagging somewhat.

"You know, intelligent men like you do something for me. I felt rotten back there in my pen. Now I'm on Cloud Nine."

Mr. Evans never could be rude, but she was abruptly aware that his attention had strayed. He was looking at an open door, and within, a large, brightly lighted and absolutely untenanted banquet room.

"Do you mind?" Homer led her into the great hall where, as far as they could see, not a creature was stirring, nor had stirred for a matter of days. The chairs were stacked in pairs, like vertical sixty-nines, locked together, and the tables, sideboards and cupboards were bare.

"He isn't here," Daisy said, revealing that Ferguson's whereabouts and safety were still in her mind.

Homer unstacked two of the gilded banquet chairs and offered one to Daisy. "Would you excuse me a moment?" he asked, then headed for the adjacent men's toilet, but not without an extenuating word. "I'm puzzled by the lights ablaze in there," he said. She nodded. This particular banquet room, of major proportions, was situated behind the huge but relatively private entrance from Commonwealth Avenue, the one that matched the main entrance in shape and size, but was usually as blank as the southern portals were busy. That whole section of the ground floor of the Dorsetshire was earmarked, it seemed, for infrequent use. It was kept dustless, as city rooms go, and unostentatiously clean. Why, Homer wondered, were great batteries of electric lights left burning on a summer night, sans servitors, surveillance, ghosts of absent roisterers, sans everything?

At the door of the men's room, Homer turned to smile, reassuringly, at Daisy, so solitary in her golden chair with vacant spaciousness above and around her, and kilowatts enough to have staged the Miracle of the Loaves and Fishes by night. Homer opened the door a few inches and looked inside.

"Anybody in there?" Daisy asked.

"I think not," Homer said. As he stepped in, Daisy rose from her chair and took station at the men's room doorway. Homer, unaware that she was watching him, took no pains to cover his startled reaction. And that frightened Daisy to such a degree that she threw amenities to the winds and ran to his side.

"Nothing too alarming," he said. There were half a dozen wash-stands, and one of them had been used not too long before. It was not untidy, exactly. But there was a soap contour at medium level. A single rumpled towel was in a catch basket nearby. The brush and comb were on the glass shelf, but placed haphazardly, whereas all others along the line were in symmetrical order. What had caught Homer's eye, and also Daisy's, was the glitter of a resplen-dent double-decked spittoon, bepolished, utterly empty, but stand-ing, in contrast to its mates placed strategically around the wash-room, at an angle like the Tower of Pisa's. Homer picked it up. The bottom had been dented.

The privy cabinets numbered twelve, and their doors were all closed. Ten had coin devices, which promised precautionary facilities for the ultra-fastidious. Two could be used by clients with-out nickels to spare.

The door of the pay cabinet adjacent to a free one—the only pair of closets so placed—was ajar, as if whoever had made use of it had wished to avoid the exertion, or noise, of closing the door firmly enough so that the patent lock would relatch itself. This meant that no attendant had been present, as, indeed, was prob-able and logical. Just in front of the free toilet booth, whose swing-ing doors had closed of their own accord, because of the spring hinges, Homer saw a pink card on the floor. He stooped, picked it up, read its text at a glance, and took Daisy's arm as he handed it to her to examine for herself.

It was a numbered courtesy card for Leon and Eddie's, New York City, made out to Angus J. Ferguson of Boston, Mass.

"He was here," Homer said. "As was said of Kilroy by our fore-most dramatist."

"Someone hit him—with that," she gasped, indicating the slanting spittoon.

"Don't take on," Homer said. "No criminal in his right senses would turn on no less than a thousand lights to dispose of a body by way of an enormous banquet room. Especially when he could leave it where it lay, with little risk of its being found for hours, if not days. And unless he came in equipped with a mop and bucket, no traces of blood have been washed from the floor."

"You mean, Mr. Ferguson's alive?" she asked.

Homer, although disposed to spare her anxiety, spoke, as always, with accuracy. "I believe we can assume that Mr. Ferguson, whether or not he was felled by yon blunt instrument, quit this refuge under his own steam. Most likely his assailant, if there was an assailant and Ferguson was the victim, left him lying unconscious on the floor, walked out unobserved, without turning off the lights which Ferguson, preceding him, had turned on as he entered. When Ferguson regained consciousness, he found his pockets had been rifled. It looks to me as if his assailant, having use for Ferguson's identification documents as well as his cash, took everything our friend was carrying and left behind the Leon and Eddie card either on purpose or by accident."

"What are you going to do?" Daisy asked.

"Let's keep this between ourselves and Bengay. We ought to tell him what we stumbled on, if he still is around, and I think it likely that he is. Let's go now, back to the lobby, and see if Ronnie has contacted Miss Appleby."

"You'll tell Miss Appleby?" Daisy asked. "Mr. Ferguson might not like that. She's probably a shrew."

"From what Mr. Ferguson said at the table tonight, she's zealous about his interests, which conform with her own," Evans said.

"And the house detectives? They like to be notified if anything goes wrong, so they can be the ones to call the police," said Daisy.

"Miss Daisy," Evans said, firmly. "If a man is struck on the head and afterward is able not only to walk out of two large rooms but to leave without trace, unobserved, a hotel as competently staffed and well patronized as this one, he can also decide who to inform about occurrences."

In the lobby, Homer found things quite to his satisfaction, or so it seemed. Bengay was in the writing room, poring over a typewritten list. Both Finke and Solange had gone to their respective bedrooms, on the best of terms. Ronnie had secured *the* Miss Appleby's phone number and address, at the cost of harsh words. There was no news, from any inside or outside source, about Ferguson, except that which Homer and Daisy passed on, in private, to Bengay.

Bengay would have liked to report his lamentable lack of progress informally to Evans, but Homer demurred. "Save it for this evening," he said. "I won't hedge on my bet."

"But," Bengay said, in distress, "I don't know his name. Before I could get my hat and coat, he got away again. Nobody saw him leave the hotel, and if he went upstairs, he used shanks' mare. The elevators were all covered. The house detectives swear there're no card games going on."

"Just for luck," Homer said, "try the brownstone on Newbury Street, No. 14, across from the center of the parking lot. The front door's probably unlocked. You may not find card games, but there might be cards on the apartment doors, since there seems to be no place for mailboxes downstairs."

Bengay was so grateful for the suggestion that Homer was almost ashamed of himself for getting Lever all worked up with so little to build on, such a long, slim chance. But the hours were running short, so he sent Daisy home, in care of his trusted Checker driver, left a call for 5 A.M. so he would not miss the best hours at the verdant Arboretum, mounted to the commodious suite he shared with Finke, on the top floor, front, and soon was fast asleep.

4

Not Bad, Not Good—But Not Bad

ALONE IN THE WRITING ROOM, at 3 A.M., Bengay, reviewing the events of the evening, was not his usual carefree self. He was beginning to wonder how he had got mixed up in such an undertaking, and why what had seemed, at first glance, to be easy, was turning out contrariwise. Ferguson's stuffy attitude had irked him, then Solange had appeared.

"You are not Mr. Finke, or Mr. Evans," she had said. And, in effect, he was not. Bengay was not vain, but he had received flattering attention from women, as a rule. Surely, he thought, this vision in black, with verve, charm and allure, would not persist in sidetracking him in favor of a private eye. She was giving them all an incentive to show off, and he had responded like a dancing bear.

Bengay had learned that Pointed Face had ridden in Bozo's elevator to the sixth floor. Then, within the half-hour, he had materialized again at his solitary table in the Lantern Room. Two hours after that, meanwhile drinking four ginger-ale highballs, the maddening chap had done another disappearing act while Bengay was making a quick dash for his homburg and topcoat.

In contrast, Bengay reviewed the behavior of his friend, the *bona fide* criminologist, Homer Evans. It had been Homer who proposed the bet. He had encouraged Bengay and maneuvered the others. Concerning Pointed Face, he had suggested that he was from the South, and might work in a bank. The master mind had stumbled into disconcerting indications about Ferguson, and observed that a brownstone on Newbury Street was left unlocked at night. Had Homer followed either of those leads? Not he. He had passed them on, debonairly, to his friend, Bengay, and wafted off to bed. Bengay, the dupe, the fall guy, must work while Evans slept. And Solange had laughed, and insisted on betting against him. Bengay could bumble in the stag line while she danced with Finke Maguire. He would see about that.

Out in the starlight, Bengay relaxed a little, but on his way to No. 14 Newbury Street he was noticed by Fritz, the doorman, three taxi drivers on the Fenway side, and he knew not who else. One pair of windows, draped and shaded, were alight on the sixth floor of the Dorsetshire, and Bengay had an uncomfortable feeling that someone was peeping out at him through a vertical slit that showed alongside the high window frame. He abandoned the notion as ridiculous. It irked him vaguely, nevertheless. How was it that Ferguson, hatless, coatless, carless, with a bump on his obstinate head, could barge out of the Dorsetshire and vicinity unobserved? It was annoying enough for Bengay to feel self-conscious, without also acting like a chump. Having kept in the shadow of the buildings, as best he could, he mounted the stone steps of No. 14 Newbury. The knob turned in his grasp. Of course. Whatever Evans predicted would eventualize. This much was accomplished. He was inside, with the front door closed behind him. For the moment, he seemed safe. The brownstone and its occupants were still.

Because it seemed logical that the janitor—there would have to be a janitor—would be sleeping in the basement, among the heaters, meters, mops and pails, Bengay walked softly up the carpeted stairs, all the way to the fourth floor, the top. He had no flashlight. The corridor lamps were so dim that he could not read the name plates on the doors of the apartments. He had to strike a paper match and cup the flame with his hand. That could be seen, he had heard, at least fourteen miles at sea. Damn and blast. If he were caught, what of it? He would claim that he was looking for a friend.

He made the rounds of the four top-floor apartments, and filed a mental note of the names. None of them was promising. The match flame died, and he descended to the third. Same tour. No success. On the second floor, he felt a rising excitement. At the rear, on the northeast corner of the building, the tenant's card read: "Blaise Laneer." His floor neighbors were self-listed as Etchegaray (most certainly a Basque), and in front, north and south, respectively: Sanson Gutierrez (a common Spanish name) and across the hall a pair of medicos, Dr. Oviedo and Dr. Hoff, presumably another Spaniard and a Hun.

The man with more nose than chin, who wore blue, might be Blaise Laneer. Laneer, a variation of Lanier, was prevalent among good families from the Gulf to the Mason-Dixon line. The *prénom*, Blaise, was most un-Yankeefied. A Blaise Laneer, whose kith and kin had seen better days, could be working in a Boston bank.

A quick inspection of the ground floor, and then, safely away. That was in the cards. But when he was halfway down the roomy flight of stairs, he was startled silly by a voice from below, somewhat to the rear. It issued from the dimness.

"Looking for somethin'?" it asked. It came from a man with a trace of Cockney accent. Bengay saw the figure shuffle forward toward the front door. The janitor, most likely, for the fellow was in carpet slippers, pants and an old-fashioned flannel nightshirt, some of which had been tucked in, the remaining yardage flapping free.

"Just popped in to say hello to a friend of mine," Bengay answered, with what aplomb he could muster. He made a wild stab for a name and came up with Etchegaray. "Mr. Etchegaray," he added.

"Second floor back, east by south," the janitor said, not much concerned.

"Exactly. He isn't awake. I'll come back another time," continued Bengay, trying not to talk too fast. He looked around the entrance hall. There were no mailboxes, and no wall directory.

"Suit yourself," the janitor said. He was outstandingly unexcitable. Still, he did not leave Bengay any longer to his own devices. He casually showed him out the door, and stood behind him in the doorway. Lew Sullivan, the night patrolman on the beat, was standing near the parking attendants' shack, talking with Clothhead and Wallyo beneath the thinning stars.

"Know this man? He all right?" asked the janitor.

Officer Sullivan brightened and saluted Bengay. "That I do," he replied. And to Bengay, "Good evening, sir."

That was good enough for the janitor, who went back in and closed the door. The night patrolman strolled away toward the nearest call box, to ring in. So Bengay found himself alone with Clothhead and Wallyo.

"Find your bloke?" the latter asked. "We piped him going in, maybe an hour ago. But we couldn't locate you."

"Just after he went in, the windows lighted up on the second floor back, this side," Clothhead chimed in. "He's been living there, it seems to me, at least three, four months. I never had paid him any mind till you described him."

"Keep all this under your hats," Bengay urged, giving each man a five-dollar bill.

"We'll find out more from the Limey," Clothhead promised. The Limey meant the janitor, it seemed.

"I'll appreciate that," said Bengay. He wanted to get back inside the hotel. How many witnesses had seen him, on his first simple errand? He counted to a total of eight, without including the questionable sixth-floor window peeper. Nice work, he didn't think. If any one of them caused Blaise Laneer, thank God the duffer had a name at last, to get the wind up, up the flue would go Bengay's chances of a neat follow-through.

The same pair of windows on the sixth, still dimly alight, went dark. Bengay was midway across the broad parking lot, a foot or two from Ferguson's abandoned car. He stopped short, to gape at the high windows, so nearly opposite the brownstone he had just awkwardly cased. Wallyo's voice, behind him, caused gooseflesh to stipple the back of his neck.

"Should we move Mr. Ferguson's car? Where it stands, it might get nicked," the Italian said.

"It's locked," said Bengay. "He surely didn't leave his key with you."

Clothhead had come up in time to hear the question and comment. The parking-lot pair exchanged a glance that would have graced the *Beggars' Opera*. It conveyed a disdain of car locks and keys that was practically poetic.

Eyes still tilted upward, Bengay advised them to let the Dodge stay where it was. The pair of windows on the sixth which had blacked out lighted up again. They were still draped and shaded, but a faint glimmer showed through. He thought he saw the shadow of someone peering down at him. The shadow moved away. A vertical slit was promptly obstructed. Bengay counted windows, carefully, then checked and rechecked. The room, according to his calculations, was third from the central back stairway. He must sketch a sixth-floor plan, and check on that room. If he were conjuring up spooks, he must dispel them. He had seldom felt so much like an ass, or more determined somehow to transcend his limitations.

As he entered the hotel, intending to find his way to the middle block of elevators, he encountered Bozo Shafter. Bozo, who had been so cagey when Bengay had first set out, now stuck close, with ears wide open. There was no plausible way for Bengay to shake him, so Lever had to ride up to the sixth in Bozo's elevator. He was careful not to take from his pocket either his fountain pen or the list of sixth-floor tenants the assistant night clerk had prepared. Let Bozo figure out for himself, if he could, what brought Bengay aloft again. Before doing any sketching, Lever found the room for which he was looking and was reading the number, 607, when the house phone buzzed inside. A woman's voice, barely audible, answered "Who's calling?" The tone was fearful, and, after the initial question, less anxious but more subdued. Bengay, ears straining, thought he heard another voice, which could be a man's. This was promptly hushed.

Bengay was aware that both his ears were hot. That phone call to Room 607 from elsewhere in the Dorsetshire had been too pat. Could it have been a warning? If so, from whom, if not Bozo? That fresh midget was somehow playing fast and loose with him. He would see about that. He must cool off at once, and think. He resorted to a childhood trick and counted to one hundred, the expeditious way: *ten* ten *double*-ten *forty*-five *fif*teen.

Now. Supposing the woman in 607 had been tipped off by Bozo that an amateur dick was prowling the floor. Grant that someone might be with her, in her room. A man. Who cared? What would they do? The woman, if the sound of her voice had been indicative, would cower. The man, if he were worthy of that designation, would cautiously investigate.

Acting on that hypothesis, Bengay decided to stage an act that would give them a chance to betray their curiosity. He stepped to the other side of the corridor, and began noting on the back of his tenancy list the room numbers on each successive door, proceeding very slowly. Should anyone in Room 607 venture to open the door a crack, a quick glance over his shoulder would cause the peeper to reclose the door. Bengay halted in front of Room 612, imagined he was on television so his postures would be eloquent, hunched his shoulders, cocked his head slightly and peered at the number on the door. A bass voice just behind him whispered "Boo!" and in his panic his list and pen slipped from his hands. Worse still, his homburg toppled, then followed. He felt sure, in spite of his spasm of nerves, that he had seen or heard a door close. He hopped off the floor, wheeling around like a cat, and was facing a grinning house detective.

"I shouldn't 'a gave you such a start," the house dick said, apologetically.

The detective handed him back his pen and list. The homburg he brushed gently with one enormous hand, and sighed, "Now there's a proper Kelly."

Bengay, restraining his chagrin, took the hat from the other's huge hand which was holding it like a chalice. He realized he was being ungracious, not saying a word, but what was there to say? He beckoned the big man to follow him around the corner, toward Bozo's elevator, many yards distant. When they were safely out of sight and away from Room 607, Bengay, having recovered his poise, said, "I want to ask you just one question. You've heard about that damned bet?"

"I have," the house dick said.

"You're betting on the side?"

The house dick nodded. "Most everybody is," he admitted. "But don't ask me what odds or which way."

"Thanks, for everything," said Bengay. The elevator door opened, Bozo invited him in, his face an impudent, impenetrable mask. On the way down, Bengay pretended to ignore the midget. Without dissembling he consulted his list and murmured: "Señorita Erica Strella, 38 Pardal Street, San Diego, Calif., Student. Registered July 1." Not clear about what he should do next, he crossed the corner of the lobby to the writing room and resumed his place at the desk. He had not long to wait. Within five minutes he saw Bozo close his elevator door, evidently in answer to a summons from above. When the same cage door reopened, two men stepped out. One was the upstairs house detective. The other, clad in his working tux and wearing a woebegone expression, was Jellyroll.

Jellyroll went through the act of discovering Bengay at the writing-room desk, and then approached and sank into a nearby chair.

"I'm pooped," the Missourian said.

"As you see, I'm fresh as paint," responded Bengay.

"I can't go to sleep, right after working. Never could," Jellyroll volunteered, uneasily.

"No need to explain," said Bengay. Even to himself, his voice sounded mean, and he had not felt that way, exactly. Piqued, perhaps, but not resentful.

"You haven't found that fathead?" Jellyroll asked.

"I'm not supposed to report before evening. Not finally until tomorrow evening," Bengay reminded him. "I trust you're wishing me luck. You picked out the man! Remember?"

"He looked to me like a natural," Jellyroll said.

"You didn't have a go at tailing him, yourself?" suggested Bengay.

"I got curious, when I thought you'd let him get away," said Jellyroll. "I asked some of the boys that work around the hotel, and none of them knew him."

"He rode up with Bozo to the sixth, and turned to the right," said Bengay.

"Look, Mr. Bengay. If that party should get caught in any kind of monkey business, and finds out it was I who'd sicked you on him, he'd get sore. Not at you. At me. I showed you that letter in the magazine. I should have kept my big mouth shut. But how could I figure that, before you could give me your opinion, Mr. Evans would sashay in. And with him, his leg man."

"You can't be held responsible for the vagaries of Mr. Evans," Bengay said, lightly. When he saw how troubled Jellyroll really was, he added, "I'll ease your mind this much. The victim you tagged is not presently engaged in crime. To use your jazz language, he's on the righteous pad collaring himself a nod."

"That's more than you or I can say," muttered Jellyroll, and shuffled out the front exit, where he was met at the curb by the first taxi from the line.

The night bell captain passed by, and remarked, "He sure has changed."

Unquestionably, within the past several weeks, Jellyroll had undergone a transformation. Formerly, like others of his exigent profession who were obliged to turn night into day, and *vice versa*, Jellyroll, of an evening, had kept himself pleasantly mulled. The top of his reliable old upright had been garnished with glasses containing ginger-ale highballs, sent up by festive customers. He had eaten like an ogre, without gaining a pound. He had seldom looked worried, and even less frequently had shown signs of other than jazz exultation, in common with fellow enthusiasts known collectively as "cats."

Of late, the Missourian had confined his diet mostly to cold milk and the white meat of chicken. He had seemed jumpy, sometimes blackly depressed. To all solicitous acquaintances who had inquired, he had replied by touching what he called "the old gut." To Bengay, in his exhausted state, there seemed to be something screwy about the whole setup. Beginning with Jellyroll's precious "gut." It had thrived for years on rich food and steady alcohol. He had said nothing about undergoing treatment, or consulting a doctor. Before his recent reform he had not acted like the type who cares about living forever. And why, just because Bengay had learned that he had ventured upstairs, had Bozo been so scrupulous about covering for him? And Bozo had telephoned to warn that woman in Room 607. Did that suggest a connection between Erica Strella, student, who would be about twenty-two, and the Missouri musician who was shading forty-five?

What would tie the whole affair into a neat package would be an established connection between Señorita Strella and Blaise Laneer. Or the eternal triangle, with two masculine sides. The conception was amorphous, like a rock from which a statue has yet to be carved.

Bengay knew that he should go to his club and have two hours of sleep. Some strange inertia seemed to hold him back. He was aroused from drowsiness by the voice of the bell captain who was on the house telephone, memorandum in hand.

"Good morning, Mr. Evans. It's five o'clock. . . . Where? The writing room? As you say, Mr. Evans. *Tout de suite.*"

Beckoning the bell captain to him, Bengay demanded, incredulously, "You mean—he's rising at this hour?"

"For some research work in the Arboretum, so I hear. You know. Everything has a way of getting around this hotel. Information, I mean."

"Does he usually breakfast down here?" Bengay asked, with some asperity.

"He's sharing a suite with a Mr. Maguire and doesn't want to risk waking him."

Bengay narrowed his eyes. "That companion of his, the private eye, must be a light sleeper, indeed," was his comment.

"Oh, it isn't the noise, Mr. Bengay. The odor of coffee. That's what penetrates the subconscious, in a traumatic state. Mr. Evans' words, not mine. I know beans about psychology, myself."

"Beans suffice," grumbled Bengay. "But bring me, too, whatever Mr. Evans ordered, and the stronger the odor the better."

When Homer descended for his light breakfast, he spied Leverett at the desk where he had been when they had said good night. If Homer found that odd, he gave no perceptible sign.

"A lovely morning," he remarked. "Ah! You're breakfasting, too. That's fine! I can give you an idea of how luxuriant the *Arisaemae* will be, in the Arboretum swamps. Director Holz wrote me that they are just approaching the height of their growth and beauty. A neglected decorative plant, picaresquely named in English. Jacks-in-the-pulpit, indeed! Jack must have been used, by those rascally old Angles and Saxons, in the sense of knave. But *pulpit!* What delicate sacrilege! If the Jack, or *spadix*, is suggestive of what Rabelais refers to as the 'trapstick' or 'cod,' the spathe, or pulpit . . . Need I be explicit?"

Bengay, baffled by this unexpected botanical assault, was frowning at the pair of crisp brown crescent rolls and pot of very black French coffee, with hot milk and cream on the side, that was being spread before him. He was more inclined to the traditional English breakfast, with tea and at least a dozen hearty edibles to choose from.

Evans smiled. "I shall breakfast again, about nine, with Dr. Holz, in his official bungalow. What a man! And what a destiny! I could almost envy him the perpetual company of trees and wood creatures. The great wars he witnesses are in miniature, and beyond human savagery in ruthlessness. Man looks to Nature in vain for a merciful example. Or illogical morality."

Thus Homer discoursed and apostrophized, and Bengay got more and more disgruntled. He expected at least that Homer would ask him how he was doing with Pointed Face, or if there were news about Ferguson. What had he discovered, if anything, at No. 14 Newbury Street, etc., etc.

Homer finished his Continental *petit déjeuner* and was most courteous, if detached, in his farewells as he started for the realm of trees and predatorials. Only at the threshold of the lobby did he remark, with his maddening casualness, "If you have occasion to consult the State Department, in the course of your investigation, phone directly my old colleague, Louis Atlas. A most accommodating man."

"Thanks," Bengay replied. "And no doubt you've a bosom pal in official San Diego, who has all local knowledge at his fingertips."

"By Jove, I have. Try Detective Lieutenant Stevenson, the genius of the West Coast homicide departments. Don't hesitate to mention my name."

Again Bengay could think of nothing to say but "thanks" and this time his tone was more humble than resentful. He could use a source of information in San Diego, and no mistake. How was the time out there? Now that it was 5:15 in Boston, it would be 2:15 A.M. in California. Not the hour to call a detective lieutenant out of bed, if he had yet got to bed. How peacefully, as far as indications went, had watched and slept the Boston police force the night through! How well nearly everyone had slept, compared with Detective Bengay!

He had not, like the village blacksmith, "earned a night's repose." For him, a brief two hours. Then on with the case.

5
The Forenoon of a Faun

PROMPTLY AT 7 A.M., Moncriff, Bengay's valet at the Mayflower Club, over on Beacon Street not six blocks from the Dorsetshire on Commonwealth, tapped circumspectly on the door, entered, set a pot of tea on the bed table, stepped over to the windows, soundlessly, and drew the drapes. The August morning sunshine flooded in and from the sea a light invigorating breeze. Bengay awakened, feeling fine. As a part of his routine, the valet paused in the doorway and asked, "Is there anything more, sir?"

"Since you mention it, the homburg," Bengay responded.

"The homburg, sir?"

"If it fits you, please accept it. In any event, remove it. I shall not be needing it again," Leverett said.

"Very well, sir." The valet departed with the hat in his hand. Mr. Bengay, as Moncriff well knew, was moody, but never unpleasant. When he was in good spirits, he was likely to give articles away.

In his tub, Bengay sang. "If I had the wings of a turtle-dove, from these prison walls I would fly." He was thinking, not so much of the case, although its various odds and ends were in the back of his mind. It was that wonderful woman, Solange de Lassigny. From Department Store, province of Quebec. He had been silly to sit back last evening and let the others get ahead of him. He should telephone her at the earliest plausible hour. Perhaps Miss Canada would enjoy making the rounds with him, to clear up doubts as to her "partner," Angus Ferguson. The lively interest she had shown toward detectives might be kindled to a flame by detection itself.

If she laughed at him some more, she might later have more to retract.

Well-dressed and adequately fed, he drove briskly to the Dorsetshire parking lot. Leaving his coupe, he walked to No. 14 Newbury Street, entered without cavil, and found the janitor in the basement.

"Good mornin'," the janitor said. Bengay took out a twenty-dollar bill. The Limey's eyes did not pop, but neither did he look unreceptive.

"I want some information," Bengay said. "And not about Etchegaray."

"I don't know much about any of those people," said the janitor with a gesture upward.

"You know who's in, and who's gone out, perhaps," Bengay suggested.

"Mr. Lancer, you mean? He's still up there, asleep," the janitor said.

"He wouldn't know that anyone had inquired about him?" asked Bengay, uneasily.

"Not bloody likely," the janitor said. "You could a come straight to me in the first place."

"My mistake," admitted Bengay. "You understand, don't you, that I'm not intending . . ."

The exact words did not present themselves, so the janitor nodded. "Just a sporting proposition," he agreed. "I understand sport and money. So what people do or don't do, I let pass."

"A chance and change philosopher," said Bengay. "Now if the tenant we mentioned works in a bank, or some place that opens around nine, wouldn't he ordinarily be stirring before this?"

"It could be his day off, in which case he'd not be leaving before noon," said the janitor.

"Shall we make it twenty a day, until this bet is settled?" Bengay asked. "If that suits you, then I might get in touch with you from time to time by telephone."

"If you won't miss it, I sure can use it," the janitor said, with more earnestness in his voice than he had heretofore displayed.

As he walked back to his coupe, Bengay was elated. Driving neatly around to the main front entrance of the Dorsetshire, he asked the doorman to let his car stay at the curb a moment and tripped nonchalantly into the lobby. Without attempting to be inconspicuous, he braced the day bell captain, took him aside to the writing room, and said, man to man, "This has nothing to do with a bet, so you can help me without disloyalty to anyone else. You'll know if Miss de Lassigny calls for service on the house telephone. When she does, I wish you to give her a message from me."

"But certainly, Mr. Bengay," the bell captain said. "And the message, sir?"

"I'd be pleased if she'd ride with me this morning, in my motor, that is, so we can set her mind at ease about her partner, the one who disappeared."

"I won't mention his name?" the bell captain asked.

"You haven't any news of Mr. Ferguson?" Bengay inquired.

"Not a word," the bell captain assured him.

Bengay made his way to the hotel telephone switchboard. The day operator, buxom and surcharged with good will, received the same request, in case Miss de Lassigny made use of the general exchange. "Yes, indeedy, Mr. Bengay," she promised.

It was 8 o'clock. High time he was calling on Ferguson's landlady in West Cedar Street, where the denizens of the right side of Beacon Hill rose betimes on principle. Mrs. Townsend had finished breakfast in her roomy old-fashioned kitchen. She proved to be just the way radio females impersonating New England housewives would like to be, and can not. She made it clear that the first move was his.

"I hoped to catch Mr. Ferguson before he started for his office," Bengay said.

Mrs. Townsend eyed him rather sternly. "Are you from United Fruit?" she asked.

His mind was clicking this morning. Unaccustomed telephone call relayed, not by Miss Appleby, his secretary, to Ferguson in his favorite drinking room last night. United Fruit. But directness is the watchword, he recalled, just in time.

"I'm not with that company," he said, frankly. "I'm only a friend. I was with Mr. Ferguson just after he received some kind of message last night, and wanted to tell him that after he left the hotel . . ."

The landlady looked puzzled. "So he left the hotel," she said. Her tone alarmed Bengay, or the implications of what she said.

"He didn't come home?"

The landlady shrugged. "I'm not narrow-minded," she said. "And this doesn't happen very often. Only last night, of all nights, when this United Fruit concern was after him, and kept calling me out o' bed."

"Was there another message, then, that Angus didn't get? A later one?"

"That must have been it," she said.

Nothing was clearer than that Mrs. Townsend, the liberal-minded licensed lodging-house keeper and proprietress, knew nothing more about Ferguson than Bengay did, now that he had the sender of the night messages. The United Fruit Company, the world banana empire with far-flung transportation lines by sea, and branches in principal ports of several continents. If only he could share this with Solange. She would be thrilled.

A fast talk with his sources at the Dorsetshire left him where he was before, as far as Solange was concerned. Unless she was equipped with a walkie-talkie, she was still incommunicado.

With regard to Ephraim Poole, the mountainous, myopic accountant, Lever had no scruples. Knowing that Poole, other things being equal, habitually slept until noon, Bengay rang him up. The fat man who liked to meditate on the properties of numbers was not effusive, neither was he ungracious. Warily, Bengay withheld any reference to United Fruit or Angus Ferguson. He asked about banks. In the course of his work, Poole was called into close consultation with banks which were in trouble. Now if Pointed Face were, in fact, a bank employee, as Evans had conjectured, and had no car of his own, would he not, like any other lazy Southern gentleman, choose lodging within easy walking distance of his place of employment, or *vice versa?*

"Why not try the Pequot National, Kenmore Branch? The quaint little duck who drank with us last evening, Edgy Gerry, is a messenger there. He gets around the banks in town, especially in that neighborhood. I seem to remember that he beat it before Pointed Face was made our candidate. Gerry might even know the guy's name." With that Poole said, "Good night."

Another lead. Bengay, ordinarily reserved, was getting unusually keen. He wanted to be with Solange. Did he not now have a reason for phoning her, at 8:30 in the morning? She was betting against him. Well and good. She could not, as a good sport, refuse a small item of information which he could surely obtain in a tiresome roundabout way. He would ask her from which bank she had drawn crisp new money the preceding afternoon. And urge her to join him.

Both the day switchboard operator and the bell captain assured him that Miss de Lassigny had not used a telephone. She had, however, passed through the lobby and been driven away in her own smart roadster by Mr. Maguire. No one had been informed where they were going, or when they might be back.

Grimly now Bengay set to work. He was going to have a straight look at Señorita Erica Strella. He would beard that terrible Miss Appleby in Ferguson's wool den. He would corner that milquetoastified young Gerry against the marble walls of the Pequot National Bank. In that order, one, two, three, because of the clock.

Thoughts of Señorita Strella associated themselves in his mind with drapes. Either she peeped around them, or harbored males who stooped to that. There was no reason to believe that the Strella woman knew what he looked like in the daytime, even if Bozo or some other counter-agent had made free with his name. He would get some samples and pass himself off as the drape man under contract with the Dorsetshire, obliged to inspect window hangings periodically and replace them on occasion. There was a luxury store just off Charles Street, were he practically had to overpower the Syrian who wanted to show him Baluchistan rugs, but Bengay came out of the place with a line of drape samples in his pocket. He drove rather recklessly to the Dorsetshire, went in by a rear entrance and took a back elevator to the sixth. The first chambermaid he encountered did not know him, and showed no outward antagonism. He plied her with a five-dollar bill.

"I want to talk with the lady in No. 607. She doesn't know me. I don't know her. I'd like to have you go in with me, while I look over the window drapes and compare them with these samples. Any objections?"

"My good deed for the day," the maid said. "For all I care, you both can be very happy. No. 607's some kind of a Latin, but she's not stuck up. She's nice."

"Sure she's not still sleeping?" Bengay asked.

"No. She's up, and had breakfast. By the back window. Not in bed."

"A nice view, from that back window. Tops of buildings, railroad yards."

"'Twould make a lousy postal card," the maid agreed. "I'm Elsa," she said.

"Congratulations," said Bengay. "Is 607 alone?"

"Poor girl," was Elsa's comment, along with an affirmative nod. They approached the door and the maid tapped. No response. "It's the maid."

"Ai," was the soft exclamation from within. It had a Spanish flavor, as distinct from Oh, Ah, Uh, Eh, or Oi.

"Can I come in?" Elsa asked. "I got the drape inspector with me."

The voice inside showed confusion, if not consternation.

"Please. No. I am brushing my hair."

The maid, using her passkey, opened the door and stepped in, regardless, saying, "This is only routine." Seeing through the opening that Señorita Strella was adequately covered by a robe, Bengay entered apologetically, smiling, felt hat in hand.

"I won't trouble you a moment, madam," he said.

She tried to be gracious, although it seemed to Lever that she was trembling. He was conscious, mostly, of her dark tragic eyes and her wealth of long hair, bleached to a fine wheat color. Her complexion was light olive.

"Please, sir. I like the drapes I have," the girl said.

Her tremulous attitude was getting on his nerves, none too tranquil before he came in. "They tell me you're from San Diego," he said.

Had he known the shock he was inflicting, he would have spared her. She was suffering, and no mistake. Those pleading eyes were fixed on his, and the chambermaid's allegiance was shifting to her side. Bengay steeled himself, and drove the barb deeper. "Is there something wrong with what I said?"

"I can't wait here much longer," Elsa said. "Let's get on with what you got to do."

"Do nothing, please," urged Señorita Strella.

"Just a minute," Bengay stalled, and pretended to glance at a notebook. "My next call. On Newbury Street. Could you tell me, madam (addressing the señorita most pointedly), what numbers are across from you here? I've made a sale to a Mr. Blaise Laneer. With a nose like this."

He started from his own well-modeled nose and brought his fingers to an imaginary point, several inches in front.

It looked for a split second as if Erica Strella was going to faint, but she regained control of herself and stared at Bengay with a desperate resignation.

"I'm sorry," Lever said. But the dirty look he got from the maid, Elsa, goaded him to more cruelty. "You are from San Diego? What part? I lived on Pardal Street, myself. As a boy."

"Please to go," Miss Strella said, with dignity.

"You heard her, mister," said Elsa, stepping between them to confront Bengay. "Outside."

As Lever made his inglorious exit, he heard the maid say reassuringly to the señorita tenant, "If I'd a knew that drip would upset you, he'd a never got in." The door closed behind Elsa as she emerged. Coming toward them was the house detective who had boohed a few hours past.

"Ah, still at it," the house dick said, grinning.

That was all Elsa needed. "You mean you know this jerk?"

The house dick watched her with a puzzled frown as she flounced hurriedly away. He was not happy when he turned his eyes back to Bengay. Another association of ideas flashed between low cloud banks in Bengay's brain.

"You know what I think?" began Lever. "Our friend Jellyroll hasn't got ulcers. He's in love."

"Don't tell him I told you, but maybe you're right," the house dick said, with a glance over his shoulder at the door of Room 607.

Both men nodded, as if a fog had lifted and the motto was "Full speed ahead." To Bengay that meant a skirmish with Miss Appleby. How wistfully he wished he could take Solange de Lassigny along, and bring her up to date. She had everything other women lacked, as well as whatever they had. So firm was his inner conviction that Solange should share the adventure that Bengay revised his schedule. Instead of getting in touch with Miss Appleby and the United Fruit Company, which meant a drive into the gnarled and congested business district, he made straight for the Pequot National Bank.

The Kenmore Branch of this New England institution opened its front door, on Beacon Street just above the square, at 9 A.M., for its personnel. An armed messenger, who chanced to be a direct descendant of Edward Everett Hale, stood guard and a clerk held a list at his elbow and marked each name with a brisk check as its possessor entered. The vice president in charge of depositor relationships was Quin Cabot, an acquaintance of Bengay's since boyhood. Lever stepped up to the door, confident that he would be admitted ahead of the customers' deadline. The clerk turned out to be Elbridge Gerry, who beamed and was comradishly respectful.

"Mr. Cabot's at his desk," Gerry said.

Indeed, Vice President Cabot was glad to see Bengay. Because Cabot's father had made a point of being at work by 9 o'clock, Quin Cabot kept up the tradition, and experienced much loneliness, since customer relationships between bankers and other members of Boston's financial community seldom get going before the midday cocktail hour, just after clocks have struck eleven. They exchanged pleasantries while the last of the employees trailed in, each saying "Good morning, Mr. Cabot" in passing. When Bengay saw that they would not be likely to be further interrupted, he asked, "Have you a chap working here named Blaise Lancer?"

"I believe so," the vice president said. The question puzzled him somewhat but, of course, he gave no sign. Instead he pressed one of a neat set of buttons. And, responding with just the right degree of promptness and deference, Elbridge Gerry appeared at the rail of the vice president's enclosure. Again, with naïve, somewhat nervous satisfaction, he said, for the second time, "Good morning, Mr. Bengay."

"Bengay's asking about one of our men called Laneer." Then, to Lever, "What was it, exactly, about Laneer, old man?"

It seemed simpler to address Gerry directly. "Whatever you have, Mr. Gerry."

The clerk beamed again at the use of his name. "We have only our records, Mr. Bengay. Confidential," he said.

"Just what I'm curious about," Bengay said. "I've always wanted to know what kind of stuff a bank found out about a man before hiring him."

Gerry looked to Vice President Cabot for instructions. Rules could only be suspended by executives. Cabot gave the all-clear signal.

"All the records?" asked Gerry.

"All," Bengay said.

It was a matter of minutes before Gerry returned with a sizable portfolio.

"Thanks. If you don't mind, I'll mull the lot over," Bengay said.

"Mmmmmm. Quite a linguist," he remarked, after a moment of perusal. "Comrade Blaise speaks French, Spanish, Italian, Portuguese and German. Besides English, that is to say."

"I daresay that's why we hired him," said Cabot. "There's been such an influx of South Americans toward Boston lately. For some reason or other, they seem to settle in this Back Bay area."

"Then they can't be peons," commented Bengay. "No. Nor salesmen, either. Mostly research Johnnies and professional men. On special grants."

It was not difficult for Bengay to establish that Laneer had produced a certified copy of his birth certificate stating that he had been born in New Orleans, Louisiana, in December, 1910. That would make him slightly over forty years of age. In full face, head erect, he photographed fairly well. Only in profile or when he bent his head to reflect did he leave that pointed, birdlike impression.

At the Pequot National, Blaise Laneer was rated as temporary cashier. When Bengay asked Cabot why the man was "temporary" the vice president explained that it was the custom to so designate employees who had served less than two years with the organization. Laneer had been there about six months.

Bengay noticed that, of the ten men Laneer had listed as references, there were no previous employers among those who had replied. Faced with a query about that, Cabot pressed one of his desk buttons again. Again, Gerry appeared.

"Mr. Cabot let that pass," Gerry explained. "Laneer had just spent eight years in Buenos Aires on some project of his own. And we needed cashiers who could speak the South American languages."

After Gerry had gone, Bengay, before taking his leave, was struck by a disconcerting thought. He shuffled through the memos, forms, affidavits and documents. That the chap had come from the South, and worked as a bank cashier, Evans had plucked out of the ether, as a theramin intercepts melodies. Everything else Bengay had learned had been submitted by whom?—by Laneer, himself. He said something to this effect and the vice president, admitting that most of the stuff was unverified, shrugged and smiled.

"What are bonding companies for, if not to do our worrying?" Lever could see the vice president's eyes straying toward the entrance, and turning, he saw, to his delight, that Solange was entering, alone. He was about to rise and exclaim, when something quite perverse deterred him. She had had no way of knowing he was here. Why not get a line on why she was making this visit?

"Excuse me a moment," Vice President Cabot said. He walked out to meet and greet Solange, who, in her gay summer print dress with picture hat and furled parasol was quite as striking and mysterious as she had been by lamplight in black lace. She exchanged a few pleasant words with Cabot, and then seemed to wave him back to his enclosure.

It was natural for a man of taste to look at another with a touch of pardonable pride after having spoken with such a lovely woman. Cabot carried this off rather well.

"We handle her dollar transactions, American dollars, you know," the vice president said. He saw that Bengay's eyes were following his ravishing depositor's progress. The lobby of the bank was oblong, with proportions like a shoe box. The short side in front bordered the street, and consisted of the marble entrance and spacious windows. The cashier's cages were ranged side by side along the other short side, far from the entrance. As Bengay, in common with practically everybody else in that part of the bank, watched Solange, he marveled at her self-possession. She was so accustomed to being admired, he concluded, that she could some-how project her acknowledgement of mass tributes without seem-ing either indifferent or vain.

Bengay smiled. She was, as he had hoped, actively curious about the case. For, taking from her handbag a brand new C, she started at the teller's window on the left of the row, glanced at each caged man in turn, all the way to the extreme right, where she replaced the banknote in her purse again. She had been looking for Pointed Face. Lever could not resist evening the score with Cabot. He ex-cused himself, stepped up toward Solange, who, when she recog-nized him, looked a little dismayed that he had caught her in the act. She had intended to steal a march on them all, perhaps.

"It's his day off."

She looked quite serious, and said, "Mr. Evans was right, then. Mr. Pointed Face knew who I was."

"Mr. Evans is invariably right," said Bengay, in such a tone that she laughed again, a silver jet among the devotees of gold. She said, "I was out this morning, early. So I didn't get your invitation until I returned to the hotel. What have you found out about Mr. Ferguson?"

He passed the question. "Ah. You must have changed costume, after breakfast, before coming to the bank. Shall you dress again, for lunch? I was hoping you might join me."

"As I am, *until* lunch, if we can find out about Mr. Ferguson."

"His hat and coat are still in the cloakroom," Bengay told her. "A preference card of a very gay New York night club, in his name, was found on a washroom floor."

"I met Mr. Ferguson for the first time last evening," Solange said. "Unless I am badly mistaken, it would not be like him to leave a group of friends without a word, abandon his automobile, his coat, and, above all, his hat."

Bengay considered telling his lovely companion about the dented spittoon. But he understood sharply for the first time that the inferences Homer Evans had drawn from a few bare facts might prove unsound. All right, he said to himself. I'll let her have only the facts. So he told Solange about his call on Mrs. Townsend, and the messages from the United Fruit Company.

"Did they not reach Miss Appleby, the secretary of whom Mr. Ferguson spoke with such awe?" she asked.

"Why don't you call her?" Bengay suggested. "She wouldn't know your voice, but it ought to make her jealous. Just ask for Mr. Ferguson. . . . Better make it Angus. Then, if he's out of communication, follow with the natural questions."

"I'll try," she said. They moved over to Vice President Cabot's office. There were two phones on his desk. "Can those be hooked up, so Miss de Lassigny can phone someone, and I can listen in?" Bengay asked.

This was the morning, Cabot thought, when friends and clients acted strangely. He pressed another button. Again Gerry responded. That reminded Bengay of another pressing mission.

"Excuse me," he said. He handed Gerry the sixth-floor tenant list with the name and address of Señorita Erica Strella checked. "Would you mind calling Detective Lieutenant Stevenson at San Diego, California, and asking him, to oblige Mr. Homer Evans, to call back and give the bank any information he can dig up about Miss Strella of Pardal Street?"

The clerk showed eager animation. "Yes, *sir*," he promised.

Then deftly he hooked up Cabot's desk phones. Bengay handed one to Solange, and took the other. Gerry whisked himself away and Cabot politely withdrew as far as a front window, where he looked out aimlessly on upper Beacon Street. The dialogue, heard jointly by Solange and Bengay, follows:

"Ferguson, Incorporated, Miss Appleby speaking."

"Good morning. May I speak with Angus—Mr. Ferguson—please?"

"Who's calling?"

"Miss de Lassigny."

"I'm sorry. Mr. Ferguson's not here."

"Could you tell me where I might reach him?"

"Sorry. I've no idea."

"Alas. When do you expect him back?"

"I couldn't even guess."

Solange became rather haughty. "How long since Angus left his office, if you please, mademoiselle?"

There was a grim pause, faint scratching of a pencil on paper, then Miss Appleby said, "Sixteen hours and twenty-two minutes, *mademoizelle*."

That was too much for Bengay. He let an involuntary guffaw escape. Miss Appleby heard it, and slammed her instrument down on its crotch. It was then 10:22. The Scot had been out of touch with his wasp, it seemed, since the closing hour of 6 last evening.

Across Vice President Cabot's desk Bengay and the Mademoiselle from Montreal looked at each other. Gerry came back from the rear echelon.

"Detective Lieutenant Stevenson sends his compliments to Mr. Evans, sir, and says there's no Pardal Street, and never has been, in San Diego. As to the young woman in question, the lieutenant will investigate and call the bank later, it being, now, out there, only half-past 7 o'clock," the clerk said.

"Carry on, Gerry," urged Bengay.

A quick check with Mrs. Townsend revealed that Miss Appleby had phoned to ask when Mr. Ferguson had left his lodgings that morning.

"I told Miss Appleby that I had not seen Mr. Ferguson leave, and that he was not in his rooms," Mrs. Townsend informed Bengay.

There was one more chance: The United Fruit Company. Both were agreed that they should visit the company's main office in person. It was on Atlantic Avenue, across from the fruit pier. Solange's sleek roadster and Bengay's nifty coupe were both parked outside the bank. Solange urged Bengay to ride with her, and pick up his own car later, since she had an engagement at 1 o'clock, downtown. The traffic on the Boston waterfront and around the South Station was so dense and intricate that it might well take a couple of hours to get to the fruit wharf and back. He dared not ask whom she was meeting, but a sickly inner feeling made him sure it was Finke.

"At least, you might let me drive, in traffic," Bengay said. But Solange, smiling, pressed the gadget that let the top down.

"Let me exercise my feminine wiles," she begged.

Indeed, she drove expertly in traffic, and the men, especially the truck drivers, gave her all the best of it. Furthermore, most of the waterfront employees of United Fruit proved to be men, and so, in the office waiting room they were received with deference and piped through to the Boston manager in jig time. His name was Cleaves. He was glad to be of service to such a good looker, so Bengay was relegated to the background.

Cleaves called in his clerk, and told him to find out who called a Mr. Ferguson, Angus Ferguson, a wholesale wool dealer the night before.

After the clerk had been gone a few minutes, and Solange had talked very intelligently with Jed Cleaves about the banana trade in Montreal, Cleaves' desk phone rang. He held it close to his off ear and half-closed his shrewd eyes. The expression on his face changed. That is, there seemed to be less of it.

"Maybe you'd like to see the shipping news. I got to leave you, but I'll be right back," Cleaves suggested. He handed a copy of the morning *Herald* to Solange, open at the shipping and financial page. To Bengay he tossed over a back number of the *The Open Road*. As Cleaves quit the office, Bengay chucked the out-of-date magazine aside and read over Solange's shoulder. An item caught his eye. The United Fruit Liner *Cecilie*, bound for South American

ports, would leave Boston a day ahead of schedule. Instead of sailing Friday afternoon, August 17, she would go out at 5:30 P.M. on
Thursday.

"You don't suppose Ferguson's been planning one of his clever
business trips?" Bengay asked Solange, when she had shared the
item. Before she had a chance to comment, Cleaves came back.

"Some darn fool might have called, but there isn't any record.
Or maybe a smart-aleck used our name in vain."

"Did you ask in the shipping department?" Bengay asked.

"Yep. They couldn't tell me a thing."

"The *Cecilie* takes passengers?" Bengay persisted.

"A few," the manager said. "But we don't print any list."

By now Bengay was convinced that Cleaves was withholding
something. "Your line complies with passport regulations, I assume?"

"To the letter," Cleaves assured him. "No one can buy a ticket
without one. There's a lot of red tape."

"Who sells your tickets?" Bengay asked, somewhat as if Cleaves
was under cross-examination.

"We do," Cleaves came back.

Solange took over, all fragrance and smiles. Cleaves did not
even try to resist.

"Your purser *could* tell us who has tickets, for the sailing set
for Friday, now moved back twenty-four hours," she suggested.

"I'll have him bring in the typewritten list, miss," Cleaves said,
and promptly the purser came in. Twenty passengers were listed,
fourteen male and six female. All had submitted their passports
and all passages were paid, except that there were reservations for
a family of four, in one double and two single cabins. These were
tentative and were being held in the name of J. Cleaves. It did not
take a detective or psychologist to see Cleaves' resigned disgust
that those reservations were tagged on the bottom of that list.

"So *you're* planning a nice ocean voyage," Solange said, approvingly. "I wish I could join you."

Cleaves, who had been eyeing the purser as if he were going
to transfer him to the pursership of a rowboat, up some creek,

without oars, responded, drily, "If I can hold you to that, I'll gladly chuck my missus overboard, and bung both kids back into their summer camps."

She laughed in that musical and irresistible way.

"You tempt me," she said. "It wouldn't be that, to provide for your last-minute friends, you keep those reservations as a matter of precaution, and relinquish them when and if you please?"

He squared off, and looked her in the eye with admiration. "You thought that out for yourself?"

"After all, I run a large department store," she said.

Cleaves grinned. "Wish I could help you about this Ferguson man," he said, but no more. By the time she and Bengay had got back as far as the exit from the waiting room, both looked grave.

"Should we try the hospitals? Or the bureau of missing persons?" she asked.

"Not yet. If he were safe and sound, he'd never forgive us," Bengay said. "His connection with this investigation is like yours, after all. Forty-eight hours after the bet was made, at midnight tomorrow evening, Thursday, you'll each have to fork over eight hundred dollars."

"Then why, my dear investigator, have you spent so much time and effort probing into Mr. Ferguson's affairs?" she asked. "Is there something about me which prevents men being frank?"

Her tone and hurt expression put him squarely on the spot. Before sending her on her way to lunch with Finke he had to tell her about the dented spittoon. And what rankled even more, of how Homer Evans, on *his* way to his botanical debauch, had flung a hint over his shoulder that perhaps the State Department might prove helpful.

6

Some Place to Go

FINKE, SITTING ACROSS from Solange, in her flower-print creation, was wondering what had gone wrong. He had secured a window table in the superb second-floor dining room at Locke-Ober's, from which there was a snug view across a six-foot-wide tiled alley. The food was good, the wine better, the service best of all. The lunch had been her own idea. She had wanted a date, so that she would be free not to make any other engagements. Now she was not doing justice to the fare, or her share of the talking.

"Sister," Finke said, as the cheese was laid before them. "You've got something on your mind that wasn't there last night, or early this morning."

"You see so deeply into a woman's heart," she said.

"Let's skip the *chinoiserie*," he suggested. "What gives?"

She told him all she could about Ferguson, and her concern for the Scot. "Please help me," she asked.

He shrugged. "I've got nothing to do but wait for those lawyers to wind up the estate and tell me where I stand. I've signed all the papers," he said.

They said no more about Ferguson until the lunch was over and the liqueurs drained. If she was really worried, the play was to be casual, he decided.

"I look at it this way, Mr. Finke," she said, at last. "Should I have been called to a telephone, as my betting partner was, and then vanished into thin air, leaving flimsy traces behind, I'm sure someone would have tried to make sure I was unharmed and well."

"You can say that again," agreed Finke.

"Mr. Bengay thinks Mr. Ferguson wouldn't like it if we called the police and they found there'd been no foul play."

"I think so too. Where's Bengay now?"

"At his club, most likely. You see, the terms of the bet authorize him to turn over Pointed Face to Mr. Mirakian between the hours of noon and 6 P.M."

"He didn't have to call in Mirakian. The opposition agreed that he could, if he got tired," Finke said.

"Mr. Bengay was afraid Mr. Mirakian would feel hurt if he was left out of it, after he'd made himself available," explained Solange.

"Bengay's got quite a line, at that," commented Finke. "Let me get this straight," Finke continued, after thinking a while. "You want to make sure Ferguson isn't hurt. You don't care where he keeps himself, if he's feeling O.K."

She nodded. He shrugged. "In that case, we've got to try the hospitals." He sighed. "One by one."

"You mean, by telephone?"

Finke shook his head. "Unless he had papers on him, he'd give a phony name. And you can believe me, sister, if he was rolled his passport would be gone. We'll check on the recent head cases."

"Can we be sure he was struck on the head?"

"Where else can you knock a man out with a high brass cuspidor? And leave a dent in the bottom?"

"Be patient with me," she said, and they rose.

As soon as Solange had left him, with six blank hours on his hands, Bengay checked with the janitor of the brownstone at 14 Newbury Street. Laneer's window curtains were up and the drapes drawn back, but he was still in his room. So Lever telephoned Mirakian and asked him to take over, informing Mirak that their quarry was named Blaise Laneer, and worked as temporary cashier in the Kenmore branch of the Pequot National Bank, but only four days a week.

Mirak roomed a few blocks from the Dorsetshire. He passed the taxi stand on the Fenway side of the hotel and just as he rounded the bend in Newbury Street, half a block from No. 14, he saw his man, now wearing a seersucker suit and a Panama hat, walking with apparent unconcern toward Commonwealth Avenue. Luck was with him, he thought, as he followed.

When the unsuspecting chap called Blaise Laneer reached Commonwealth Avenue, Mirakian saw him raise his arm and signal the Dorsetshire doorman, who was at his post nearly a block away, for a cab.

So Mirakian had to face about, dash around the Fenway corner of the hotel to the taxi stand, take the one that had been second in the row and urge the driver to follow the cab that had just pulled out.

"You're not kidding?" the taxi driver asked. He could not see his passenger blush a little, self-consciously, as he drew out a *Herald* pass.

"The press," Mirakian said. His feature articles were printed about once in two months, mostly on Sunday in the supplement, but that was neither here nor there.

Both Mirak and his driver had their eyes to the front as they made the turn into the Avenue.

"I'll be jiggered," grunted the taxi man. The cab he was tailing was behaving queerly. Its chauffeur, a reliable old-timer, was making a forbidden U turn, heading back toward them a few yards on the wrong side of the street, then ducking over to the right side of the divided highway and proceeding toward Kenmore Square.

By taking advantage of a legitimate maneuver through a transverse passageway, Mirak's driver was able to pull up two cars behind.

"Not too close," counseled Mirakian.

"Say, what *is* this?" demanded Mirak's driver, as the lead cab made a sudden left turn, doubled back into Kenmore Square through which they had just passed, and brought up at the curb exactly in front of the Kenmore Cafeteria. Seeing that Pointed Face had entered the busy restaurant, Mirak dismissed his cab, gave the bewildered driver a dollar, waved away the suggestion of change, and went into the cafeteria himself. He could not guess what his quarry's bizarre course could have meant, unless he was indolent, as Southerners are, and given to minor extravagance on free days when he might have skipped breakfast and was hungry for lunch. Mirak slept late every day, and felt quite as hungry as anyone.

His man was at the counter, so Mirak got a tray of his own, filled a glass with cool water, took up a folded paper napkin with enwrapped utensils, and after a long look at the menu on the wall, secured minced lamb on toast with beef gravy, avocado salad with grapefruit, and a piece of lemon pie. Then he drew a cup of coffee, and was in the act of sitting down at a vacant place behind Laneer when he saw, with disgust, that Pointed Face, who had contented himself with one cup of coffee and part of a twisted sweet roll, was already headed for the exit.

"Damn," Mirakian muttered, but there seemed nothing to do but abandon his feast. His guts were rumbling, if not roaring. His check was punched for a dollar and a half. And once out in Kenmore Square again, the capricious man he was trailing, and who would not walk a quarter of a mile before breakfast, set out for what looked like a stroll, the pace of which increased until it was brisk. Mirak, faint from hunger, bumbled along in pursuit, ready to duck into a doorway if the man glanced behind him. The man did not. He walked along the hot sidewalk, untroubled by the August sun, as if all were right with the world. Of that Mirakian was convinced. The quarry showed no signs of worrying about anything, and Mirak doubted if he ever had.

Then the seersucker and Panama veered into the entrance of a large white building which proved to be the Lehigh Clinic. In attempting to follow, Mirakian brushed past an outbound citizen. The outgoing party had averted his face, and did not stop to apologize. Mirak's mind had been so intent on Blaise Laneer that it was not until he saw the hatless passerby whom he had awkwardly jostled, or *vice versa*, entering a taxi that he realized the man was Angus Ferguson. This did not seem important to Mirakian, who knew only that the Scot had been called from the gathering in the Lantern Room to the telephone, and had not returned. Mirak turned back and found that he had lost track of Laneer. He dashed into an elevator of which the door was sliding shut and could not get his breath to say "Up" until after the car had started down. There was a basement through which ambulance patients were admitted. No sign of his man down there. The elevator man advised Mirak to inquire at the "office" on the second floor.

There were four nurses in uniform, one at a desk more or less in the open, two behind wicker windows, and another leaning on a counter that was split like a half door. All were middle-aged, looked hard-boiled, and in first-class physical condition. To his relief, Mirak saw, near the main stairway, an approachable Negro in a blue porter's uniform.

"Did you notice a tall man in a seersucker suit, a Panama hat, and a nose like a top on its side?" Mirak asked.

"That was a fine-woven hat, expensive and clean," the porter replied.

"Where did it go?" asked Mirak. "With the guy?"

The Negro pointed aloft. "Way up to the seventh. That's the top," he said, and tapped his head with two fingers. "The head ward."

"He's been here before? Is he an out-patient? He can't be a doctor, part time," Mirakian said.

"He comes here often, to see South Americans, some of them doctors, some patients, some interns or students, and their relatives and friends. He speaks their lingoes," said the porter.

Relieved that his quarry was safely upstairs, Mirak slipped the messenger a five, and asked him if he could locate Mr. Blaise Laneer, find out, if possible, without attracting too much attention, whom Laneer had seen and where he had been since he entered the clinic, and report to Mirak while Laneer was still aloft.

Mirak took from the table a back number of the American Medical Association *Journal*, and found a seat on one of the marble benches provided for that purpose. He ducked his face behind the open periodical when he saw Solange de Lassigny, too beautiful for words, and Finke Maguire advancing, side by side, from the main stairway. His assumed detective instinct prompted him to observe this pair before intruding. It seemed to Mirak that every man in the place was gazing at Solange, and the women looked at both of them.

Finke went straight to the hardest-looking nurse, behind the open desk. He showed her what must have been his California detective license. Mirak heard him say, "Have you got a Mr. Ferguson, who got hit over the head with a metal instrument, Lieutenant?"

What gave the nurse an unexpected jolt was the "lieutenant." She could not help glancing at her white-clad shoulder, and echoing Finke's grin.

"You held your breath when you first heard that plane that just passed over," Finke explained.

"What outfit were you in?" she asked.

"G-6. Don't rub it in."

"Are you a close relative of the Mr. Ferguson you're asking about?"

"How close should I be? A brother-in-law, for instance?"

The nurse nodded. "That'll do," she said, and thumbed through some cards in a neat wooden filing box. After the first time through she tried it again. "No Ferguson," she said.

"Could you show me the file?"

He thumbed a few, then picked one out. "Maybe his name is Townsend," Finke ventured.

The nurse glanced at the card he had extended. "That one's just been discharged—and he hasn't paid his bill."

Finke nodded. "So he could have been conked and rolled," he said. "Thanks. Be seeing you in World War III."

Solange had been watching and listening with mingled bewilderment and admiration. Both she and Finke were surprised to see and hear Mirakian, who had not missed a word.

"I could have told you Ferguson had been here. I passed him on the way out, as I came in, and he either didn't see me, or put on an act."

"What brings you here?" asked Finke.

"I'm on duty. Remember? From noon till 6." And he told them how he had caught up with Laneer's trail in the nick of time, and what had befallen since.

Finke said generously that Mirak was doing fine, and was about to escort Solange back toward the exit stairway. She restrained him, rebelliously.

"Can't we stay here a while, please?" she begged. "You surely must be curious about what Pointed Face can be doing in the head ward," she insisted. "That's where Mr. Ferguson must have been treated."

The Negro messenger emerged from an elevator at that moment and advanced. Mirak indicated that he might speak freely in front of the others.

"He's in the head ward, making the rounds with a new doctor and Dr. Deyo."

"Dr. Abel Deyo?" interrupted Mirakian. To Solange and Finke he added that Dr. Deyo could be one of the tenants of the brownstone where Pointed Face lived. The name was one Bengay had noted, and passed on to Mirakian.

"Let's all go up," Solange said, her excitement rising.

They took an elevator to the seventh floor, and as they emerged they saw Pointed Face and the man the messenger had described as "a new doctor" step out on the pleasant roof garden enclosed in special glass so that convalescents could either bask in sun or lounge in shade. As several nurses, patients and visitors were moving about, or had gathered into groups, Solange, Mirakian and Finke were able to take a position fairly near the quarry and his Latinesque companion. They saw the Latin reach into an inside pocket—he was not in white—and take out a sheaf of small oblong-shaped papers which looked like ordinary bank checks. The checks were not of uniform size or color, but seemed to be assorted, and not too smooth. Laneer had a small black-covered notebook in his hand, and was evidently making note of the separate amounts. A man writing figures makes motions quite different from those he uses writing script. There is no flourish or flow.

When the first batch of checks, if they were checks, had been separately noted, the "new doctor" reached into a side pocket and produced a second lot, and then a third. Each found its way from the Latin doctor's pockets to Laneer's inside jacket pocket. Laneer then scribbled something, tearing a back page from his little note-book to serve the purpose. This he signed or initialed perfuncto-rily and it was accepted and pocketed by the young foreign doctor.

Finke strolled over to a nurse enjoying the view. "Who's the new doc with Mr. Laneer?" he asked. The nurse looked in the direction indicated by Finke. "The one who made the rounds to-day with Dr. Deyo?" continued Finke.

It required a slight effort for the nurse to recall the newcomer's name. "I think he's Dr. Gonzalez," she said. "Another Argentine."

Young Dr. Gonzalez looked rather gay as he walked near them, with Laneer, on their way back. They were speaking in normal tones, and, indeed, had at no time since Finke had seen them showed inclination toward concealment.

"Before you go," Dr. Gonzalez was saying to Pointed Face, "I'd like to have you meet one of my compatriots connected with *La Prensa*."

Laneer acquiesced with a kind of languid politeness.

"Had enough?" asked Finke of Solange, when the pair had gone out of sight and earshot.

She sighed reluctantly, but saw the wisdom of letting well enough alone. Mirak, who had throughout the incident shown ner-vousness about the risk of putting Laneer on his guard, decided to ride down to the office floor with Solange and Finke, and send the colored porter upstairs again to cover the meeting between Laneer and the *La Prensa* chap, who was Dr. Gonzalez' compatriot.

There were synchronized electric clocks in all the main corri-dors. All noticed, and Mirak observed aloud just before they left him on his own again, that the hour was half-past two. It was a hot, sleepy afternoon and an hour that seemed to be on dead cen-ter, to the point that Finke, when he got into the roadster with Solange, was stuck for a plausible destination. They sat there, like a couple of book ends. She was so full of life and eagerness that he felt he was letting her down. Hell, he thought to himself. Are men put on earth expressly to keep high-strung women on the non-stop *qui vive?*

Then things started happening fast.

Firstly, Pointed Face came barging out of the clinic, in a rush. There was only one taxi on that side of the street, and he grabbed it and started the driver down Beacon Street, headed back north whence he had come.

"Oh, Finke. He's getting away," Solange said, coaxingly.

"That gives you an edge," he said, but she had stepped on the starter. Occupied with watching Laneer's cab and starting the roadster she missed what caused Finke to say "Hold everything!"

Out of the clinic came an elegant, dark-complexioned stranger, a most Argentine type, who looked after Laneer's receding cab with dismay, risked his life crossing the street, and plumped into another taxi across from the Lehigh.

Solange's motor was running and again Finke held her back. The harassed Mirakian had emerged just in time to see Cab No. 2 light out after Cab No. 1. There were no other cabs anywhere to be seen. In his forlorn situation, Mirak did not see the roadster with the Canadian license plate and his two friends nearby. But another private car came alongside very slowly, and Finke, also Solange, heard its driver ask Mirak something in a language so strange that it at once suggested the Armenian. Mirak, relieved, hopped in, pointed to the cabs ahead.

Solange did not ask Finke's approval in bringing up the rear.

7

Some Place to Spend All Evening

THE LEAD TAXI carrying Pointed Face went straight ahead. Upper Beacon Street led into Kenmore Square, and Laneer's cabman veered right, and rolled down Commonwealth Avenue. When, after having passed the Fenway and the Dorsetshire, the quarry took a right turn toward the brownstone on Newbury Street, Finke, feeling not at all brilliant, said to Solange, "Hell. He's going back to his apartment again."

"With all those checks," she breathed.

Finke grunted. "Sailors on shore leave go rowing in the park. So what do bank tellers do? Collect pocketfuls of checks. We may as well stop at the hotel and start getting a skinful."

She was paying no attention to his discouraging words. She saw that Cab No. 2, with the Argentine type aboard, had been suddenly braked, and was standing innocently at the curb, some distance back, when Pointed Face paid his driver and went into No. 14. The jalopy in which Mirakian was riding had taken the same side street leading off Commonwealth toward Newbury Street, but when it became clear that Laneer was homeward bound Mirak asked his Armenian friend to turn left on Newbury and circle the block.

Solange, at her wheel, caught up with Mirakian. That was easy, because Mirak's Armenian acquaintance simply drove back to Commonwealth Avenue and, by the rather complicated process prescribed by traffic rules, brought up in front of the Dorsetshire.

A few feet behind him, Solange attracted his attention by a restrained toot of her horn. Mirak, signaling that he had heard and would be with her promptly, stepped out of the jalopy and hurried along the sidewalk until he could see the brownstone. Returning, he reported that the face of No. 14 was blank, and the cab that had brought the Argentine to the vicinity had gone.

"Bengay says I can phone the janitor to make sure Laneer's in," Mirakian said.

"From the Lantern Room," said Finke. "I'm dry." Mirakian introduced the other Armenian as Aran Kevorkian. The foursome crossed the lobby and as they were walking down the plush corridor, they heard the sound of Jellyroll's Hammond organ. "What Is This Thing Called Love" was being played by someone who jabbed the keys quite viciously. The player made a slip, leaned on the notes with both palms, producing an atrocious squealing discord. Then there was silence. By the time Finke parted the entrance drapes the platform was empty, and only a day waiter coming in from the pantry, saved the room from being deserted.

"I haven't eaten yet, today," Mirakian said. "I'm starved."

"Better make your phone call to that janitor," said Finke.

A telephone was plugged in. Eating brittle cheese sticks as fast as he could, Mirak found his notation of the janitor's number and asked for the connection through the switchboard.

"I'm talking for Mr. Bengay," he said, into the phone.

The others heard some vocal crackling.

"I know he went out and came back," Mirak continued. "Is he up there now?"

"Yup"

"Good. In case he starts to leave again, before 6 o'clock, could you give me a buzz . . . ?"

"Spare no expense," whispered Solange.

"I'll see that you get twenty extra," said Mirakian. The crackling in reply was terse and appreciative. "In case he phones you Pointed Puss is leaving, what then?" asked Finke.

"I'd have time to get to a back door where I could see him," Mirakian said.

"All right by me. It's your funeral," Finke said.

Before long he rose, restlessly, and left the others to have a look at the layout, himself. Taking the first corridor leading to the Newbury Street side of the hotel, he found a screened doorway from which No. 14 was within plain sight. And, emerging from the brownstone was Jellyroll. The Missouri piano player was making a bee line for the very door behind the screen of which Finke was standing. As he drew near, it seemed to Finke that he was acting as if doped. His eyes looked glassy, his arms were not swinging, his hands drooped. What made Finke most annoyed with himself was that, in order not to be caught, he had to step lively and duck around a corner. He got lost in the maze, and had to flag a bellhop to guide him back to the Lantern Room. If any Armenian wanted to spy on a displaced Southern gentleman, let him do it in his own sloppy way. And if any woman had to have an extra thrill, let her chute the chutes, or sit on a sunflower. Whatever any of them did, he, Finke Maguire, was going to sit in that barren drinking room and get slowly and peacefully intoxicated.

If his trio of pals had not formulated a similar idea, at least, subconsciously, they were feeling no pain. Solange, with her impeccable taste, was enjoying mint smashes, while Mirak and his fellow near-Easterner had reverted to anisette spiked with gin. The blending of two civilizations. Finke asked for another bourbon old fashioned, without fruit or bitters, and only a single hard cube of ice. Solange, so soft and eager in the dimness, pressed close to him and turned up her petal-like face.

"Ça va?" She whispered.

"Sure," he said.

They all were happy and content. It turns out that way, sometimes, when folks least expect it. They meet by accident, go through a few futile motions, then blunder into a snug cove where cares and indecisions pass them by for a while. Ah, blessed alcohol. To Solange, it was like a bridge from one garden to another. Mirak drew from it a kind of Olympian reassurance. Kevorkian derived an extra kick from the guilty knowledge that he should be elsewhere, and otherwise occupied. Finke was grinning to himself, because the wisest man he knew was culling weeds from mud, exposed to ants, mosquitoes and the danger of learning too much.

Time had passed in easy stages, none of them cared how much, when the dwarf, Bozo Shafter, peered in. Finke reached over and drew him through the drapes, by the collar.

"Have a drink," Finke said.

"If Mademoiselle does not object."

"Will you do me a favor," Mirakian asked. "Take a look at No. 14 Newbury, and let me know if everything's all right."

"You mean it?" Bozo seemed to think Mirakian was kidding.

"You heard what the man said," said Finke, making a pass at Bozo that missed his face by an inch. Bozo, pretending to ignore the indignity, turned his shrewd little face up to Solange.

"If Mademoiselle wishes," he said.

She nodded, smiling.

When Bozo came back, a few minutes later, there was a strained look on his face.

"Well. What about it? Is the house still there?" Finke demanded.

"Yes, sir," replied Bozo.

"Nothing strange or unusual about it?" Finke persisted.

"A couple of men are standing outside."

"Who are they? You know them?"

"Not their names," Bozo said.

"Are they together?"

The midget had to think a while. "In a way."

"What do you mean, in a way? You seen them before? Are they friends?"

"Guys like them don't have any friends, not even each other."

"Cops!" said Finke.

"Look," Bozo protested. "I'm not having any part of this. You folks sent me out to look. I looked. And two flatfeet were stationed outside. There's something fishy about this whole business."

The midget made himself scarce. Kevorkian, blissfully unconcerned, admired some rainbow tints in his moist empty glass. The waiter, who had seen and heard everything, tried to pretend he had not. The other customers, who formed the vanguard of the early cocktail crowd, were paying no attention. Mirakian, reluctant to stir up more activity, tried to find reasons for passivity. Solange was vibrant and chilled. The air conditioning. Policemen, a pair.

"Better call that janitor," suggested Finke.

Mirakian agreed, and tried. "He doesn't answer."

"Go over and have a talk with him. We don't have to blow our tops about a brace of uniforms. They work for the city. That's all," Finke said.

"It's almost 6 o'clock. Shouldn't I tip off Bengay?" Mirakian suggested, hopefully.

Finke advised Mirak to make sure Laneer was still in his apartment, and find out what he could about the cops. As Mirak complied, Finke beckoned Primitivo, who had waited on them the night before and was just coming on shift.

"Don't you have music for the cocktail bunch?" Finke asked.

"Ordinarily, beginning at 5. Señor Jellyroll's late," Primitivo said. He paid his respects to Solange. There was just that shade of gallantry and true sophistication in his manner that conveyed a considerate meaning. She caught its overtones, and gasped. Here she was, in a public cocktail room, at almost 6 o'clock, in a summer print dress she had chosen for lunch! What promised to be a banner evening of her life lay just ahead. She took both of Finke's hands, appealingly, as if Kevorkian were not there, as indeed he mostly was not.

"I must go to my room and dress for evening," she said. "You won't desert me?"

"I ought to bat you in the jaw," he said.

"I won't be long. If only I can be sure I'm not missing anything important," she promised.

She was having such a good time that he could not be a killjoy. As a matter of fact, the setup was not so bad, however he looked at it. He did not give a tinker's damn what happened to Pointed Face, or who won the bet, or who would be to blame for winning or losing it. Ferguson had been examined at the clinic, and turned loose. He would have to show up and join the crowd tonight.

"O.K. Doll yourself up to the gills. If anything breaks loose I'll ring you up. Don't worry," Finke said, and she withdrew.

"Who's the lady?" Kevorkian asked.

"She goes by the name de Lassigny. Espionage."

"So what?" Kevorkian shrugged. "Don't we do the same thing, abroad? No way to solve it short of disarmament. On both sides."

There was movement on the platform and a man sat down at the Hammond. It was not Jellyroll, but a coffee-colored Negro who wore a couple of war decorations on the lapel of his tux.

"What time does it get dark—outside?" Finke asked his dreamy table-mate.

"Oh, half-past 8, 9, 9:15, 9:30," Kevorkian replied.

"Daylight saving?"

"Probably," Kevorkian ventured.

An elegant figure stepped through the drapes just as the substitute piano player started fooling around with "Buttons and Bows." It was Bengay. His jacket and vest were blue, his trousers neutral gray. His felt hat, which he had not deposited with Daisy, he held in one hand.

"Miss de Lassigny told me you were down here," he said.

Finke introduced Kevorkian. Bengay, while still shaking hands, asked "Where's Mirakian?"

"He's checking on your pigeon," said Finke.

"Ah! Capital!" Bengay said, and continued to Primitivo, who had materialized at his elbow, "*Una para todos.*"

"*Si, señor.*"

"Across the way?" Bengay asked of Finke, with a gesture over one shoulder, in the general direction of Newbury Street, No. 14.

"That's where he started for. Did you pass there?"

"I came in the front way," Bengay said, shaking his head negatively.

"It's quite a while after 6," Finke suggested.

"I'll take a quick one, and spell him. First I'll try the telephone," Bengay said, picking it up.

"Is this the janitor? This is Bengay."

The answering voice was audible. "He just stepped out. Any message?"

"I was hoping he could put me in touch with Mr. Mirakian," Bengay ventured.

"Oh, yes. The party who was inquiring about Mr. Laneer. He was here, and left."

"Mr. Mirakian?"

"And Mr. Laneer."

"They left, together?" asked Bengay, bewildered.

"No. Separate."

"Which one went first?"

"Mr. Mirakian."

"And Mr. Laneer was in his apartment then?"

"He sure was."

"You couldn't tell me where he went?"

"Why, sure. I have the address. He's over at 784 Massachusetts Avenue. He'll be there all evening."

"Thanks," Bengay said, and hung up.

"What number, Massachusetts Avenue?" Finke inquired.

"He said 784. This is a bit confusing, the way Mirakian's acting. He probably knows where Laneer is, too, and will be waiting over there on Massachusetts Avenue, with no chance to warn me."

"You'd better make sure," Finke advised.

At that moment Solange made her re-entrance, not in a dazzling *décolletage*, but a simple tailored suit with snug hat and accessories to match. Her coloration was such that, at twilight or in half-darkness, she would be inconspicuous if not invisible. Finke realized what an adaptable face she had. All purpose. Finke figured that she had, after a talk with Bengay, switched to the outfit that would pass in the shadows. One thing stuck way out. Bengay was principally concerned with enjoying her company, *à deux*. The detective stunt was now a means to an end. Well. She wanted adventure. What was the harm? So Finke offered neither objections nor encouragement when Bengay urged her to accompany him to the address on Massachusetts Avenue.

As soon as Solange had departed, with Bengay, and left the two men alone, Finke looked at Kevorkian.

"Live in Boston?" he began.

"Always. Since I was three."

"What street?"

"Massachusetts Avenue," Kevorkian said.

"Whereabouts on Massachusetts Avenue?" persisted Finke.

"The 700 block."

"Anywhere near No. 784?"

It was then that another smile crossed the permanent pleased expression on Kevorkian's face. "Across the street," he said.

"And who lives at 784?"

"Old Doc Ford."

"A regular doctor?"

"He's pretty busy with his county job, but he takes a few patients on the side."

"On the side o' what?"

"He's medical examiner," Kevorkian said, and beamed.

8

The Quick and the Dead

JUST AFTER KEVORKIAN had dropped his gentle little depth-bomb, making it all too clear that Blaise Laneer must be dead, he took his leave, and Finke was alone at the table. Pointed Face must have met death in a way that required a police checkup. There were hundreds of similar routine investigations for every case of homicide. But he preferred not to think about murder; his conjectures centered around the wager. It would be null and void, since the quarry seemed to have lasted less than the prescribed forty-eight hours.

Dimly, Finke wondered why Mirak Mirakian had faded from the sequence, after having set out on a simple errand of inquiry. Also he was hoping that Angus Ferguson would show up for the 10 o'clock rendezvous that evening, either to explain himself or dodge some very embarrassing questions.

Being in a mellow mood, Finke did not take the tangled situation too much to heart. What bothered him most was having seen Jellyroll Morton emerge from No. 14 Newbury Street, sometime between 3 and half-past. It was conceivable that Finke was the only witness who had noticed Jellyroll, and had observed his stunned, confused manner.

What the hell? Finke asked himself. He had been urged by Solange to find Ferguson, or make sure the Scot was safe. That he had done for her, with dispatch. The rest of the muddle was for Bengay, and the Boston police. He had never been in it. So he was out.

The only decision Finke had to make just then was whether to sit where he was, or move to a stool in the bar. He chose the latter alternative. So it was there that Homer Evans, returning from his long exciting day with swamp plants in the Arboretum, found him.

Having ordered his drink, and another for Finke, Homer chatted pleasantly about the *simploarbi*, the erudite Dr. Holz who presided over the finest tree park in the world, and the prospects for completing, in the near future, the unfinished work of the murdered naturalist (see *The Black Gardenia*) whose life Homer still felt that he should, somehow, have saved. Since Evans made no mention of the wager, or anyone involved in its developments, Finke swore to himself that he, also, would pretend that the *affaire* Laneer had slipped his mind.

"How did you pass your first day in Boston, after all these intervening years?" Homer inquired.

Briefly Finke replied that he had spent the morning at the lawyer's office, signing documents; that he "had had lunch" downtown; and that he had loafed around the hotel most of the afternoon. But while he was talking, he paused to sigh and grit his teeth. For the handsome Dr. Gonzalez from Buenos Aires, accompanied by the Argentine character who had shown such avidity in following Pointed Face, entered and took places next to Evans, at the bar. The South Americans had not exchanged many words before it became apparent that Dr. Gonzalez' companion was "the *La Prensa* man." Of course, Evans knew the Spanish language, thoroughly. Finke had about one hundred key words.

The Argentine doctor and newspaperman seemed to be on easy friendly terms, not as if they had been bosom pals, but more as well-bred countrymen behave toward each other in a foreign land.

"I was so deeply interested in what I saw at the clinic today that I overlooked supplying myself with ready cash," said Dr. Gonzalez.

"Permit me," the *La Prensa* man said, drawing forth a wallet. As Dr. Gonzalez selected fifty dollars, in tens, he murmured "*Gracias, señor.*" The other shrugged reassuringly.

The newspaper man remarked that Dr. Gonzalez had spent most of his day "with the head cases" and asked if Dr. Gonzalez intended to specialize. Gonzalez nodded.

"Concussion," he said. "I observed, right away, that when North Americans with means sustain head injuries, however mild, they make it a practice to submit to what is called a 'check-up.' Can you imagine a hardheaded Argentine making his way, at considerable inconvenience, to a clinic, just because someone had bumped him on the cranium with a metal vase or jar?"

"That tears it," grunted Finke, to himself. For Evans was listening, eyes alight with amused satisfaction. The way Homer joined the conversation caused Finke to squirm. The master mind, Finke thought, would find out more in a few casual moments than the rest of them had unraveled all day.

"Your specialty, Doctor," Homer said to Gonzalez, "is one in which sensational progress is now in the making. I'm familiar with the works of Von Preitzelbonck and Wodsz, dealing with head injuries from blows inflicted by instruments harder and more rigid than the human skull. And, of course, with Pouffin and Lelangier on the softer weapons."

"Indeed," said Dr. Gonzalez, enthusiastically. "Dr. Abel Deyo, at the Lehigh Clinic where I am privileged to study, is a high authority, but, alas, so constantly in demand for emergency work that he has little time to write."

"He had time enough to talk with each patient about whatever business the patient chanced to be in," the *La Prensa* man remarked.

"Naturally," Dr. Gonzalez said. "Dr. Deyo, in examining a head case, would draw the patient out, on subjects most familiar, and a few that were totally unfamiliar. Bone structure, if damaged, can be mended. If pressure on the brain occurs, the utmost precautions must be taken to safeguard the patient's future. Any man who has sustained too severe a shock must be protected from the possible aftereffects."

"In other words—complete rest?" Evans suggested.

"Complete rest, like infinity or absolute zero, is only a philosophical ideal. We had one chap today, in fact, who was so afraid that his injury would become public gossip, that not even Dr. Deyo could get anything definite out of him, about his habits, occupation, or the mishap he had incurred," Dr. Gonzalez said.

"A tall man, middle-aged, rather thin, who entered hatless and coatless? Whose pockets had been emptied? A manner of speaking, perhaps, that you found a bit thick, or unusual?" Homer asked, with that gleam of amusement in his eyes.

With an equally affable smile Dr. Gonzalez said, "We cannot disclose the affairs of our patients," but his manner was such as to leave no doubt that Evans was on the beam.

"Could you assure me that the man in question was not gravely injured?" Homer asked.

"With pleasure," Dr. Gonzalez replied. "In the case of our incommunicative patient, we relieved his headache with a very common remedy, somewhat disguised for psychological effect."

Homer smiled understandingly. "What should we do without aspirin?" he asked. For answer Dr. Gonzalez took from his own vest pocket a small bottle of white tablets.

"I'm subject to headaches, myself," he confessed.

About that time, two more customers approached the bar and, to make room for them, the *La Prensa* man considerately stepped closer to Dr. Gonzalez, who was so intent on his talk with Evans that he adjusted his position quite subconsciously.

Suddenly the *La Prensa* man seemed to remember a previous engagement. Without pausing to look at his wrist watch, he excused himself, hastily, and left the bar with a perfunctory "*Hasta la vista.*" Dr. Gonzalez turned aside just long enough to say to his departing countryman, "See you later, at the house" and continued his conversation with Homer.

"At the house?" repeated Finke, silently to himself, and aloud he asked Dr. Gonzalez if he had found satisfactory lodgings already.

"By the best of luck," Dr. Gonzalez said. "And only across the back street from this hotel. A German doctor named Hoff, who was sharing an apartment with a countryman of mine, is moving out.

So I am moving in. This neighborhood seems to be the choice of visiting Argentines, and the house, No. 14 Newbury Street, is within convenient walking distance of the clinic. Dr. Abel Deyo, himself, rooms there. Don Julio Etchegaray . . ." Gonzalez made a gesture to indicate that other acquaintances and compatriots were numerous throughout the apartment house. "Quite a South American colony," he said. He sighed and added, "In the home of the free."

Quite casually Evans asked if Argentines who wished to travel were not limited as to the amount of money they could take out of their country, under Peron's decrees. That gave Finke quite a start. Homer Evans, he knew, had concerned himself since the late 1930's, on behalf of the government's most confidential bureau, G-6, with foreign counterfeiting, debasement and black-market operations involving U.S. currency and international monetary exchange. The master mind might talk himself blue in the face about concussion of the brain, with stiff or limp instruments. Could Homer's real interest in this whole affair revolve around the Yankee dollars obtained by foreign visitors, in various ways? Dr. Gonzalez' reply did nothing to switch Finke's mind from that new line of thought. The gay young doctor smiled, shrugged and said, "One finds a way to relieve the pressure of almost any kind of restrictions. Unhappily we Argentines are getting to be adept at evasion of what passes for law—as you North Americans did, so I've heard, in Prohibition days."

"I'll say," volunteered Finke. From then on, both Evans and Dr. Gonzalez were careful to include him directly in the conversation. Finke found himself increasingly anxious to break up the meeting. So, with a sardonic eye on Evans, he told Dr. Gonzalez that a group of friends, including his erstwhile patient, planned to gather at the big round table in the Lantern Room between 9:30 and 10 o'clock and invited the doctor to be present. Gonzalez, apparently pleased, thanked him and promised to be on hand.

The moment Dr. Gonzalez had taken his leave, Finke guided Homer by the elbow to the writing room, where they could talk in privacy.

"I don't know what this is all about, or whether you're in it, or not. Speaking for myself, I see no sense in our playing games any longer," Finke began. He saw that Evans was listening gravely, so he went on, and told Homer everything he had learned from Solange, Mirakian, and, second-handedly, through Solange concerning Bengay's investigations, touching upon the Pequot National Bank, Mrs. Townsend's establishment, Erica Strella, and the unfortunate Blaise Laneer. He decided not to hold back the coincidence by which he, himself, seemed to have placed Jellyroll Morton in a highly suspicious place at the most unfortunate time.

Concluding, Finke said, firmly, "Now you have the works."

Homer sighed. When finally he spoke, his tone was almost fervent. "It has been said that the Deity exercises an especial protective care over good-hearted men in their cups," he mused. "In the case of reformed devotees of alcohol, the heavenly solicitude seems to be automatically suspended. When a man's habits become temperate, all nature's sorrows fall upon him. And a few others, contrived by his fellows."

Somehow Finke felt immense relief. "So we're in Jellyroll's corner, I take it," he ventured.

Nodding assent, Homer added, "We have been, from the beginning."

Finke shook his head resignedly. "I might have known," he said. "You sized up this whole gag, from the first, as real and earnest."

"The poet adds 'And the grave is not the goal.' It's too late to save Pointed Face, but let's limit the carnage, as best we can," Homer said. "Of the innocent, above all."

"Gripes. You assume Laneer was murdered? Have a heart! He was picked by Jellyroll."

Wincing, Homer said, "Please don't express it just that way."

"And why not?"

"On my way from the hotel parking lot to the bar, not long ago, I was informed by Clothhead and Wallyo, in strict confidence, that poor Laneer was picked again this afternoon. In fact, he was icepicked. The cause of death, it seems," Homer said.

"What else did you find out? Just by chance?" asked Finke.

"Our bottle and betting companion, Mirakian, was intercepted on the sidewalk in front of No. 14, where, at your suggestion, he evidently had presented himself to make inquiries. Mirak was placed in a police car by a Sergeant Ryan, of the homicide detail, and the vehicle started due north, most likely headed for police headquarters at Pemberton Square," Homer said.

He reached for the phone, and to Finke's surprise, called St. Clair Endicott, senior member of the same firm of renowned lawyers to which Homer had steered Finke. This is all screwy, Finke said to himself. None of the Endicotts, Walpoles or Winthrops, most probably, had ever handled a criminal matter, except the nonviolent type that involves great sums of money. Homer, as usual, seemed to sense what Finke was thinking. When he got the blue-blood barrister on the line he smiled and prefaced his request with the words, "I know, St. Clair, that you are a babe in the legal woods except on fiduciary affairs, but, as a favor to me, accept this little chore as an adventure. An acquaintance of mine, a Mr. Mirak Mirakian, has been most arbitrarily bundled into the wagon and, I think, is being held at Police Headquarters on orders of one Sergeant Ryan of the homicide squad. When civil rights are trampled, we all must rally round. Get Mirakian out, I beg of you. Don't even wait till after dinner. You may have heard or noticed, in the course of a lifetime of practice, that the police headquarters in Boston are situated in Pemberton Square. Within sight of the Historical Society. You'll find the place without difficulty. And— don't hesitate to throw your dignity around."

"Wait a minute! Wait a minute," protested Finke, but Homer already had hung up.

"My old friend, Endicott, should make quite an impression with the heads of the local force," Homer said, with a perverse gleam in his eye. "Now, shouldn't we make a call in Room 607?"

They took Bozo's elevator. The near-midget seemed too nervous to retain his mastery of the cage's mechanism. He started down instead of up, reversed, and missed floor six by several inches. Homer deliberately kept the car out of contact by holding the safety door open as he stood, half in, half out.

"Bozo," he said. "I want you to get this straight, and pass it on to the working staff of this hotel. I am Jellyroll's friend."

The dwarf's teeth were shimmering. "I haven't heard or seen nothing, and I'm saying nothing."

"Has Sergeant Ryan been snooping around?"

"I can't remember nothing," insisted Bozo, visibly terrified.

Homer sighed and relaxed. "If he threatens you again, call on me. . . , You haven't given out any leads, as yet?" He answered himself. "Of course not. But whatever you do, keep mum about Jellyroll. Give Daisy, Primitivo, all the folks of good will, the same advice. Talk, if you must, on any other subject."

"Nobody can make us talk on any subject. But someone must have squealed about Mr. Ferguson," Bozo volunteered. "Those fathead cops think they've got something on everybody who failed to report the assault with a dangerous weapon and robbery that was pulled off here last night."

Somehow Bozo eased Homer out of the cage, pulled the door shut, and caused the elevator to plummet downward.

"Can Ryan nab Ferguson for concealing crime?" asked Finke. "Can't a citizen be conked and frisked, and keep mum, if he wants it that way?"

"I'm more concerned as to whether our Scot has notified Washington about a lost passport," Homer said.

"Look," Finke objected. "You can't tell me that a conservative businessman, established and prosperous, and more cagey than a cockle, is mixed up in the death of a temporary bank teller."

"The only possible connection, it would appear to me, is the staple commodity, wool. There is a surprisingly large amount of it in Peron's Argentina. Señor Peron has a distressingly small store of dollars, or gold. We must, indeed, approach Ferguson's irreproachable secretary, Miss Appleby, or some amenable person with access to his records and his bank accounts. We ought to know about his habits of foreign travel, if any, and how he wangles imports most economically," Evans said. "Bear in mind that Pointed Face spent years in Buenos Aires. And here in Boston he worked in a bank."

It was hard for Finke to believe his ears. "You want to get something on Ferguson? Expose his business affairs?"

"When the schemes of men are so desperate that they include murder, the most innocent of bystanders is drawn into the vortex of intrigue and violence. A few short hours ago, we had no profound interest in the late Blaise Laneer. Now, until we find out who icepicked the chap, we can't even be sure who, among our friends and acquaintances, is safe. First let's talk with Señorita Strella."

The house detective hove into sight, and Homer detained him with an affable gesture, and showed him his most impressive credentials, featuring the letters "U.S."

"I'm Evans," Homer said.

"I know, Mr. Evans," said the dick.

"I want to convey a message to Señorita Strella in Room 607," Homer said. "Do you know her?"

"I know what she looks like."

"Does *she* know you?" ventured Finke.

"She knows I work here," the house dick replied.

"The point is, does she consider you a friend of Jellyroll?" Homer asked.

"She's a jittery dame. Especially today."

Homer nodded. "You mean because of Mr. Bengay, in the role of the drape man?"

"You know about that?" the house dick asked, warily.

"More or less," Homer said. He got right down to business. "Here's what I'd like to arrange. I want you to give Miss Strella a message for Jellyroll Morton, by word of mouth. Urge Miss Strella to ask him, the sooner the better, to communicate, through Daisy in the cloak-room—everyone trusts Daisy—where I could meet him, right away. Tell him not to worry about my being followed. In Boston's little Harlem, or elsewhere."

"O.K., Mr. Evans," said the house dick. "I'll try."

In a little while he came back, looking like the groom who had locked the stable door too late.

"She's gone!"

"You mean she's not there?" asked Evans.

"I didn't see any of her stuff. But she couldn't have checked out. I would have been notified."

"May I look at the room?" Evans asked. The house dick nodded and led the way. The door of Room 607 was ajar. They pushed it open and entered. At first glance nothing except the bare hotel furnishings met Homer's eye, neither in the combination living-and bedroom nor the adjacent bathroom. The waste baskets were empty. So were the drawers.

"A swell job of cleaning, for amateurs," the house dick commented.

Just then Homer opened a clothes closet. A small trunk, stripped of monogram and labels, stood empty in one corner. On the top shelf was an unlocked pigskin suitcase, from which stickers and initials had been removed with scant regard for the excellent hide. On a lone hanger was a dress, also without identifying marks. It was factory made. When Homer tapped his hands together and smiled with evident satisfaction, Finke and the house dick looked at each other, bewildered.

"Could you bring me the maid named Elsa?" Homer asked. "I need another witness. Nothing here should be touched."

"Excuse me, Chief," the house dick said. "No murder was pulled off here. It was a guy across the street who got killed. I got the low down from Lew Sullivan, the night cop on the beat."

Homer nodded. "Bring me Elsa, please. We may have to work fast."

The house dick absented himself and in a few moments returned with Elsa. The maid was in her street clothes, and had been on the point of leaving for the evening.

"Elsa," the house dick said. "Meet the famous criminologist, Mr. Homer Evans, and his assistant, Finke Maguire."

"Do I have to?" Elsa said.

"Please don't touch anything in this room, Miss Elsa," Evans said. "I want you to observe the articles which have been left here, so you can testify later, if we need you."

"If you or anybody else tries to drag me into court, I'll make you good and sorry," Elsa promised.

"Were you on duty when Señorita Strella moved out?" Homer asked.

"I was, but I didn't know she'd moved out," the maid replied.

"That's odd. She must have had quite a load of possessions besides these," Homer said, indicating the trunk, suitcase and cheap dress. "Any idea why she left these behind?"

"No ideas about anything," said Elsa. "Now can I go? I'm late."

"Have you ever seen Miss Strella wearing this dress?" continued Homer. As he spoke he walked over to the window, held aside the drapes, and gazed across the parking lot toward No. 14 Newbury Street. The maid had not answered his question about the dress. A little more sharply than he had spoken before, Homer said to her, "Come here!"

Elsa did not budge.

Homer showed her a badge on which she caught the letters: "U.S." Finke gave her a playful shove. She brought up before the window.

"Thanks," said Evans. "Do you know anybody in that brownstone house, No. 14?"

"Who's in there?" Elsa asked. "A bunch of Latins!"

"Thank you," Homer said, with ominous restraint. "You may go."

The maid strode from the room and down the corridor, as mad as a hornet. Finke saw that Homer seemed pleased.

"Were you on duty when Miss Strella moved out her things?" Homer asked the house dick.

"I was in a rummy game, most of the afternoon," he admitted.

"Did Jellyroll know that?"

"Maybe," the house dick said.

"Did the chap who got killed know you'd be playing?" persisted Homer. The house dick's wide face showed plainly that he was shocked and pained by the mere suggestion of such a circumstance.

"On the level. Not a chance. Unless somebody told him. There's no connection between him and me. Never has been. I never saw him before last night, or early this morning," the house dick said.

"Then he did call on Miss Strella last night or early this morning," Homer said.

"All right. Since you know all about it," the house dick said. "Look, Mr. Evans. Should you and me misunderstand each other?"

"Not at all," Homer said. "We're all friends of Jellyroll—you, Finke, Bengay, Bozo, Elsa. The whole gang. Especially me. Why can't that confused musician see things that way?"

"That Thing Called Love," the house dick said. "It's been going on for weeks."

"About six weeks. No?" suggested Evans.

"That's right. The poor guy is nuts about this Strella number. He's out of his head."

"But you didn't see them make a getaway?" Finke interposed. "Neither you, nor the maid, nor that runt, Bozo. How much baggage did she have? When she checked in six weeks ago?"

"Plenty," the house dick said. "A lot."

"Many thanks," Homer said, relieved.

As they rode to the street floor with Bozo, Homer pointedly ignored the dwarf.

"Quite an organization in this hotel," Evans remarked. "A tenant can remove any quantity of baggage without attracting the notice of anybody in the lobby. Not any of the clerks, not Daisy, or the elevator men, or the bell captain and bell hops, the doormen . . ."

Finke caught on. "What about the rear doors?"

"It would seem that the chef or his crew, the parking-lot attendants, or someone might be on the job," said Evans.

They left Bozo in a state bordering collapse.

9

A Routine Stroll for Two

WHILE HOMER AND FINKE were talking with Gonzalez, phoning St. Clair Endicott in the interest of Mirakian, and inspecting Señorita Strella's now vacant room on floor six of the Dorsetshire, Solange and Bengay were on their way to No. 784 Massachusetts Avenue, having been assured that Pointed Face "would be there all evening." Bengay had suggested that they walk. Even casual passers-by could not help noticing how lovely she was, and that the attractive gentleman with her was off the deep end on her account. He acknowledged the predicament himself. He had never felt quite that way before.

"We'll have to be careful approaching this place," Bengay cautioned. "It wouldn't do to be conspicuous, or overanxious."

"In other words, we first must case the joint." The phrase, when she pronounced it musically and self-consciously, had a charming effect. Bengay squeezed her arm, gently, and she responded. As a result, he led her off a curb ahead of a traffic light and they were nearly run down by a truck.

"Nice work, Algernon!" yelled the truck driver, without rancor.

They passed south of the Christian Scientists' Mother Church and north of Symphony Hall. Then they entered a few darker blocks, with warehouses and residences where anything might be stored or any kind of saint, sinner or screwball might be living.

The 700 block reminded Bengay of the claim of a former head of Rotary that he was "the most average man in the country." The term fitted that stretch of Massachusetts Avenue. No. 784, viewed from a safe distance, seemed to be a brick residence of two and one-half stories which formerly had been a two-family house and had been converted into one. There were still two entrance doors, side by side, with corresponding porches. On the half that bore the doctor's shingle reading "Thaddeus U. Ford, M.D." the lower windows were alight. The rest was dark.

"A doctor," gasped Solange, and tightened her grip on Bengay's arm. Then she screamed. They had been standing on a pair of metal sidewalk flaps or doors which had started inexorably to rise and part, spilling each of them off in opposite directions. A platform bearing loaded ash cans came slowly upward, inch by inch.

"Forgive me. I'm nervous," she said.

"*La méchanceté des objets*," murmured Lever. It is a perfect French phrase for comment on situations in which material objects take on devilish aptitude for creating mischief. They both laughed, but both had been startled. "I'm not one of those chaps of iron, I guess," Bengay admitted.

"It was I who cried out," she insisted. "I'm just a damned mid-Victorian. No use pretending."

Resolutely she took his arm again and propelled him across the avenue. "We're going in," she said.

"But won't our man get the wind up?" objected Bengay.

"Doctors may be consulted. If Pointed Face sees me, he's seen me before. Same bank. Same physician. Nothing wrong with that," she insisted.

"What could a fellow be doing at a doctor's all evening?" inquired Bengay.

"He might be under an anesthetic, or playing pinochle. We should be able to find out, if we're detectives."

"Quite so. You mean, an expert like Maguire would pull it off?"

She had meant to be kind and complimentary, but what came out was, "Yes."

Bengay squared his shoulders. "In we go," he said. "Which one of us is ailing, and in what respect?"

"I'll be the patient. With a headache. A doctor can't examine one below the neck for that, first visit."

"I don't see how they stand it, prodding and staring at beauties unclothed," said Bengay. "It must dull their finer feelings. I'd hate to be a doctor's husband."

When Solange and her escort were admitted by a nurse who was told that "Mademoiselle" wished to see the doctor, the nurse got out of the way and Doc Ford ambled into the reception room. He turned out to be a slight, weary, amiable man in shirtsleeves and spectacles which slipped to the end of his nose.

"Come this way," he said, beckoning with a long tired finger. Bengay hesitated, so the doctor added, "Come along, both of you."

He led them through a consulting office, an anteroom, and into a back chamber. The center was occupied by a table or slab on which some figure had been draped with a sheet. The instant her initial terror passed, a wave of anger swept over Solange. Her fists clenched. Her eyes blazed. "Doc" Ford recoiled in astonishment.

"Is that Blaise Laneer?" Solange hissed, pointing straight at the thing on the slab.

"I'd consider it a favor if you'd identify him, miss," the doctor said. "You, too, mister."

They stood transfixed, Solange and Bengay, unable to protest or take their eyes away as Dr. Ford turned back the sheet, not stopping when the icy pointed features were revealed but only when the naked chest was also exposed. Pointing with his long index finger at what looked like a nail hole just left of center and under the lower rib, the doctor said, "That's it. He got it there."

"He got what there?" stammered Bengay.

Reaching into a small box the doctor tossed out an ice pick, the metal stained brown. Then he started forward and said "Catch her, you dope, so she won't bump her head."

The next thing Solange heard was Bengay murmuring, "You *are* somewhat mid-Victorian, you know." She was on a couch in the doctor's consultation office. Bengay continued talking to the doctor. "You see, Doctor. She didn't know the chap was dead." That brought her around, and she sat up, asking hotly, "Did you?" She was aware of the doctor looking speculatively at Bengay.

"You can't think I'd put you through an experience like that, for a laugh," Bengay said.

She had never been angrier in her life. "There's someone who would, and did," she said, grimly. "If I don't pay him back . . . !"

Bengay most surely had no objection to that, but he was jolted when it became clear what was expected of him.

"If we don't solve this before Mr. Maguire does, I'll never speak to you again," Solange was saying.

"I say. He's a professional, you know. And keen!" Bengay said, dismayed and determined at the same time.

"He's a brute!" she snapped.

"Who's this?" the doctor asked, innocently.

"Someone you never met," said Solange.

"Got all this down, Nurse?" Dr. Ford asked patiently, and "Nurse" stepped in from somewhere with a stenographic notebook and stylo in her hand.

"I got what they said," the nurse replied.

"They couldn't have done it," the doctor said, regretfully, "not a shipshape job like that. . . . Still, you never can tell."

That set off Solange again. "We can do anything anybody can!" she said. They were about to take their leave when a police car slid to the curb in front of No. 784 and out stepped a tall, impressive man who, had it not been for his trim police uniform, might have been an Irish envoy ready to discuss his country's grievances on an intellectual plane.

There was a flicker of something in Doc Ford's urbane manner as he urged his guests to "hold on a minute and meet the captain," which led Bengay to believe that the shorthand-writing nurse had phoned headquarters as soon as they had arrived.

"Miss . . ." the doctor started.

"De Lassigny," supplied Bengay. "And I'm Leverett Bengay," he added.

"Captain Moriarty," Doc Ford said.

The captain bowed gallantly, cap in hand, to Solange. To Bengay he said, somewhat to the doctor's surprise, "I've read about you, of course, on the society page. Now what could bring you to a place like this, on such an occasion?"

"I was told that Mr. Laneer—the fellow who seems to be dead—would be here all evening," Bengay said.

"That he will," the captain agreed.

"We didn't know Mr. Laneer was dead," Solange explained.

"Then what, miss, would he be doing here, all evening?" Moriarty asked.

"We didn't know what sort of place this was," Solange said. Seeing that the captain looked more baffled than ever, she added, "We were given only the address."

Captain Moriarty took that so easily that Solange was not satisfied. "Mr. Bengay was told, over the telephone, simply that Mr. Laneer had left his apartment and would be at 784 Massachusetts Avenue . . ."

". . . all evening," the captain said, resignedly. He turned to Bengay.

"You understand, Mr. Bengay, that when somebody gets murdered . . ."

"Murdered!" gasped Solange. She confronted Doctor Ford. "You didn't tell us he'd been murdered. I thought he'd stabbed himself."

"A natural mistake," agreed Captain Moriarty. "You thought he took his own life, too, I suppose, Mr. Bengay?"

Lever was caught unprepared. "To be frank, that never entered my mind—the suicide possibility," he said.

Sighing with relief, the captain faced one, then the other.

"I'm glad you're being straightforward and helpful. You haven't got together and made up any story," he said.

"Why should we?" Solange asked, indignantly. "And why are you so sure the poor man didn't stab himself?" She went through a descriptive motion. "I could have done it to myself, with an ice pick. If I'd known where to find the right spot."

"Could you have turned on a gas fire, afterward, so *rigor mortis* would be delayed?" the captain inquired. Then, seeing that Solange was acutely distressed, he begged her pardon. "The saints above forbid you'd ever have such thoughts in your head, miss."

Bengay was not quite satisfied. "You're sure, Captain, that the gas fire was turned on afterward, not before the stabbing?" he asked.

It was the captain's turn to look nonplussed. "Wurra, wurra. An old hand like me. And I never thought of that, so help me." He seemed to reflect a while, then relaxed. "Come to think of it, this unlucky man could have driven that ice pick into his heart. But there are a few things he couldn't have done, after he was dead."

"For instance?" Bengay asked.

"He couldn't have removed from the apartment all his keys and papers. Nothing else. No other articles or objects. Just keys and papers. He must have had a key to let himself in."

"Not necessarily," Bengay objected.

"All right. He left his door unlatched, in case his pockets were picked. But there's no case on record of a man who does clerical work and has lived in a place a number of months without a paper in his room, not a card, not a notebook, pad, or memorandum. No bills, receipts, checks, canceled or blank."

"No checks?" slipped from Solange.

The captain did not seem to notice. "The apartment had been cleaned of documents and keys. I haven't got an expert on the force who could do a better job of its kind. So if this unlucky gentleman killed himself, somebody else got in, and made off with the keys and papers."

"No fingerprints?" asked Bengay.

The captain looked a trifle pained. "No fingerprints that are useful. Mr. Bengay, I understand, was talking on the phone, and was told that Mr. Laneer would be at this address *all evening.* You didn't mention the name of the party who told you."

Lever said, after embarrassed hesitation, "Sorry. I don't know. I'd never heard the voice before."

"There are so many voices. Woman or man?"

Solange was determined she was not going to flutter and stammer when telling the truth. "A man," she said, for Bengay.

"A friend of the janitor of the house in which Laneer stayed," supplemented Bengay. "The janitor had just stepped out."

"He'd just happened in, this man who steered you here?" asked the captain.

"It sounds ludicrous, but those are the facts," Bengay said.

The captain shrugged. "Am I to understand that the lady and yourself were acquainted with the deceased?"

They looked at each other, Solange and Bengay. Neither derived from the other any flash of guidance or inspiration. Don't lie. Stick to the truth. And give out as little as possible, thought Solange. "Mr. Laneer was a cashier in my bank," she said. "That is, a local bank where I have an account."

"I see!" the captain exclaimed, as if that cleared up everything. "Now let's simplify everything, so you young folks can go along and have a fine, happy evening. As a matter of form, just tell me where you were this afternoon. We know Laneer was killed between noon, when he got up, and 6 P.M., when Doc, here, had the body removed." He turned first to Bengay. "Ladies last, in a sad affair like this."

"About noon I left Miss de Lassigny on Winter Place, at the mouth of the passage to Locke-Ober's. We were in her car, which I parked, and I made arrangements for an attendant to drive it back when she had finished lunch. I then returned to my club, had a bowl of crackers and milk, and turned in. I slept until about 5 o'clock, tubbed, dressed, phoned Miss de Lassigny at the Dorsetshire, where she has a suite, joined her in the Lantern Room, tried to phone the janitor of No. 14 Newbury . . ."

The captain nodded his thanks. "The rest I know. You seem to be in the clear." He faced Solange.

"I had lunch at Locke-Ober's. The man I had lunch with drove me around to show me the various hospitals. I was curious about seeing an interior of one, so we chanced to pick the Lehigh Clinic. That must have been about 2 o'clock."

The captain nodded encouragingly. "I know."

"You do?" asked Solange. "Who told you?"

The captain had a reassuring smile. "It just happens that Mr. Laneer was there, about that time. He must have got in before you did, and left shortly afterward. You didn't see him there, by any chance?"

Seeing that Solange was confused, the captain made haste to calm her. "There's nothing mysterious about this. We questioned the other tenants at No. 14 Newbury Street. A few of them were doctors who were familiar with the Lehigh Clinic. Now when anybody's murdered, we keep tabs on outgoing trains, planes, boats and do what we can about automobiles. So if I know you and Mr. Bengay were calling at the United Fruit this morning, asking about a certain acquaintance of yours, and that you and a Mr. Maguire inquired about the same party at the Lehigh Clinic this afternoon, and didn't find him, don't be astonished. Those coincidences don't mean a thing. The hardest part of one of our investigations is sorting the wheat from the chaff, and, believe me, miss, with every grain of wheat comes tons of chaff. We even know that you talked at the clinic with a Mr. Mirakian, and drank with him and others a few hours, and that he was curious about the deceased and one of my sergeants, not bothering to find out Mr. Mirakian was a newspaper man, took him to headquarters. I released him, with apologies, and I hope he won't hold the blunder against me."

"You know everything," Solange exclaimed, her eyes wide.

The captain shook his head. "In a city the size of metropolitan Boston," he said, reflectively, "two violent deaths occur in every ten thousand, and one of those is a murder. Of the murders, we fail to solve, on the average, only one each year. We could double our convictions if the public would help us."

"I'll help you," Bengay said with unmistakable determination.

"So will I," promised Solange.

The captain became quite paternal. "I'll tell you what," he said. "You're both nice people, who don't mean any harm. You ought to have a chance to get together, compare notes, talk things over. And then, if you've anything you'd like to tell me, I'll be seeing you later in the evening. Why should I try to run a bluff with you? I don't think it's likely you murdered Mr. Laneer, or anybody else. The only trouble is, you may not understand about withholding information, or telling half-truths which may operate to obstruct the enforcement of law. I'd hate to have to hold you as material witnesses."

"I shall call the Canadian consul if you try to hold me for anything whatsoever," Solange said, eyes flashing.

"I know," agreed the captain with a winning Irish smile. "And Mr. Leverett Bengay will retain the Hon. Mr. St. Clair Endicott, of Endicott, Endicott, Walpole, Winthrop and Swig. More power to both of you."

"We're willing to answer your questions right now," Solange said, linking her arm impulsively with Bengay's. "You want us to consult each other, so you can trap us."

"Take it easy, miss," the captain urged. His eyes twinkled indulgently. "Now run along. You surely won't think hard of me and my boys for clearing up a murder, if I can."

Out in the fresh air, Solange, still clinging to Bengay's arm, looked up at him, ready to burst with indignation.

"You'll help me show up that insufferable . . ." She groped for words.

". . . Shall we say, practical joker?" Lever suggested. "To do him justice," he added, knowing it would infuriate Solange further, "Maguire's hardened to scenes of death and violence. All in his day's work, as it were. Perhaps he didn't mean any harm."

"I'll make him grin on the other side of his mouth," she promised. "He deliberately made a fool of me. With you as a dupe, in the bargain."

"My face is red," said Bengay.

"Just wait!" exclaimed Solange. "Him and his phenomenal Mr. Evans."

10

A Loan from a Bank, and Other Developments

NEITHER FINKE'S NOR HOMER'S EARS seemed to be smarting while Solange, not two miles distant, was speaking of them so tartly. Bengay, almost too content to contain himself, took Solange to dinner at the Union Oyster House.

As Finke and Homer set out to carry on their inquiry, Mirakian complacently joined them.

"So Endicott found a way to spring you," said Homer, drily.

"Did they explain what had happened in that house you tried to crash?" Finke demanded.

"Oh, one of the tenants had died, and a routine checkup was being made."

"Suspicious circumstances?" inquired Homer, casually.

"They must have thought so at first. But it all blew over," said Mirakian. "They were just about to turn me loose when in came Mr. Endicott. God. It must take generations of privilege to breed a guy who can snoot other guys like that. He made all of them feel like 30 cents, in plugged nickels. Moriarty, the captain, had to swallow it and like it. I felt sorry for Ryan, the sergeant, so help me. I walked out of headquarters, with Mr. Endicott, and he took me around to the Parker House and bought me a drink. I invited him to join us at 10, in the Lantern Room tonight."

"Capital," said Evans. They were approaching the Lantern Room and suddenly Homer halted, cocking his ear. Someone was playing the Hammond and the piano, one with each hand. The tune was "Ai Barbariba" and the instrumentalist was not Jellyroll.

Homer escorted Mirakian and Finke into the room, they ordered drinks, and at the end of a chorus Evans beckoned the piano player to join them.

The piano player was named Wilson, no relation to the famous Teddy Wilson, but with a meaner left hand. Wilson had been asked, between 4 and 5 that afternoon, to take Jellyroll's place "until he showed up later in the evening." Evidently he and Jellyroll were on good terms, and Wilson had acted as relief pianist on other occasions.

As Homer thanked Wilson, tipped him graciously, complimented his jive, and sent him back to the platform, Finke looked at the master mind reproachfully.

"You didn't ask him a thing," Finke said. "Here our tongues are hanging out, to know where Jellyroll was between 4 and 5, or any time after Laneer was icepicked . . ."

"Lancer! Icepicked? Was he the party who died in No. 14?" Mirakian asked, incredulously. "No wonder I was pinched."

"I wonder who else is still in the dark. Mind if I phone Vice President Cabot, of the Pequot bank?" Homer asked. "Most likely he hasn't been informed that he's—short of help."

"May I interrupt on a question of information?" Finke asked. "When a bank teller's bumped off, what about his accounts?"

"Exactly," said Evans, approvingly. "The bank, in this instance, will call in our friend, Poole, if I'm not mistaken, for a quick audit. The police, who are playing this very close to the vest, will try to get their accountants in there first."

"So?" asked Finke.

"So we must secure for Poole, our ally, the inside track. He knows the ins and outs of the Pequot National. The police accountant will have to go in there cold. From what Bengay told Mademoiselle de Lassigny, and she told you, Finke, who in the Pequot National, would you say is the fountainhead of pertinent facts?"

"That cautious little guy who was with us a while last night. Elbridge Gerry," replied Finke, and Mirakian nodded in agreement.

Homer asked Primitivo to plug in a phone at their table. Then he called Ephraim Poole. The huge accountant moaned and groaned

at the prospect of rush work, but he was obliged to admit its ne-
cessity under the circumstances. Because it meant exertion for him,
Poole took the news of Laneer's death as a personal misfortune.

"Go straight to the Pequot National, gather up everything you
consider pertinent, and put it somewhere inaccessible to others,"
Homer urged. "I'll make the arrangements with Cabot."

Replacing the instrument just long enough to break the connection and hear the dial tone, Homer got Cabot on the line.

"Quin?" he asked.

"Who's this?"

"Homer Evans."

"Fine. How are you?" Cabot asked.

"Well," Homer said. "Have you heard anything disconcerting
lately?"

"Nothing of first importance, since the 1932 election," Cabot
said. "What's up?"

He was properly shocked to hear of the death of his temporary
cashier, and deeply disturbed when Homer made it clear that
Laneer had been murdered.

"Damn and blast!" Cabot said. "That means all sorts of red tape
and fiddle-dee-dee. I'll have to yell for Poole without delay."

Evans told him about his conversation with Poole.

"There's just one thing more," Homer said. "I'd like to borrow
Elbridge Gerry for a few days, to help me with some tabulation
and clerical work at the Arboretum. Can you spare him, now
Laneer's gone?"

"You know I'd do anything I could for you," Cabot said. "But—
Gerry. We all depend on him so much. . . ."

"Wouldn't you rather he'd be giving me a lift, than have him
badgered night and day by the cops and their accountants?" asked
Homer.

"I get your point," Cabot agreed. "And believe me, Poole can
take care of himself, and all of us, where records and figures are
concerned. I can't thank you enough for getting him promptly on
the job. As for myself, all the police in the land, with rubber hose,

racks or Iron Maidens couldn't get anything from me, since I know practically nothing but customer relationships—almost exclusively in clubs or bars. Occasionally at the desk where my father sat before me. Even there, details do not reach me from the inner offices."

Both Finke and Mirakian had been able to overhear both ends of the dialogue. Homer led them to the parking lot where he borrowed a car from Clothhead.

"Could I get one thing straight?" Finke asked. "Why is it you proclaim one minute that you are Jellyroll's friend, and all the rest of the time you seem to be fixing things so that the cops will make him their No. 1 suspect? Or have I misinterpreted your strategy and tactics?"

As Evans continued driving them toward Elbridge Gerry's address in Hemingway Street, he said, "What is more useful than a ripe red herring?"

The lower door of Gerry's apartment building was unlatched at that hour, and the odors of cooking experienced as Homer and his seconds mounted the stairs were no worse than the average, and not much better, either. Only as they approached the Gerry flat did Evans stop and sniff.

"By Jove," he said.

When, in response to the bell, the hall door was thrown open, the aroma which had caused Homer to comment was intensified. The pleasant little woman, who could not have been much over twenty, seemed confused at the sight of three strange men.

"Who is it, Bunny?" called a voice they recognized as Gerry's.

"There must be some mistake," she said. Gerry, relieving her at the door, recognized Mirak, then Evans, and lastly Finke, as his wife set out for the kitchen.

"Why, good evening," Gerry said. He was quite as much at a loss as his wife had been.

Without waiting for a formal invitation, Evans stepped in, bypassed the fussy bank clerk, and stood by the gas range, at Mrs. Gerry's shoulder. He pointed reverently toward a *paella* gaily bubbling its last ounces of liquid away, and an open casserole in which squid simmered in a sauce that was as black as India ink, and as redolent as a sorcerer's ambrosia.

"*Por Dios!* Like your mother used to make?" he asked.

"Edgy's mother," she explained. "She was a Basque."

After more appreciative words, but no more questions, Homer rejoined the men in the living room. "I fixed it up with Mr. Cabot to borrow you from the bank for a while," Evans said.

Gerry blinked. It looked as if he thought the idea was preposterous. Homer made haste to reassure him.

"It's only for a few days, and you'll get a good bonus."

Bunny, who had crept to the doorway said, "A bonus! That's fine."

"Where shall I have to go?" Gerry asked.

"Not far. I'm doing some research at the Arnold Arboretum," said Homer, and to resolve Gerry's further bewilderment he added, "Within the city limits, out Jamaica Way. You know. Between Routes 1 and 138. A park with all kinds of trees."

Homer turned back to Bunny. "You must forgive your husband for staying out last night. It was our fault. Did you wait up for him, with a rolling pin?"

She shook her head. "I dropped off, in the chair, after the clocks had struck two," she said.

"Lucky he could make up his sleep this afternoon," Evans said. "I tried to get him at the bank, but he didn't come back after lunch."

"You're wrong, Mr. Evans," Gerry said. "I did go back, after lunch. And then I had to go out again, and was busy doing errands till after quitting time. Plenty of times, my work keeps me outside."

This little eager beaver hasn't heard about his Comrade Cashier, either, Finke said to himself. And look at how the chief butters up the little wife. He couldn't be crass enough to take them away from such a delectable dinner, which money couldn't buy. But since Edgy had *his* night out the evening before, why can't *she* have an outing tonight? They both must join the party at 10 o'clock. He can't take "no" for an answer. Free Fundador.

"Oh, *could* we, Edgy?" Bunny implored.

11

The Beauty of Co-operation

THERE WERE A FEW ODDS AND ENDS to gather up before Homer would be ready for the evening conclave. He was obliged to split his forces.

"Finke," he said, "we have already ascertained that Miss Appleby, from whom we could otherwise get much useful information, is a cool customer with an ingrown distaste for life and humanity. But, Mrs. Townsend, Ferguson's worthy landlady, said that la Appleby has to share a single room with another working girl. Any young woman who can room with Miss Appleby very long must be co-operative, to a fault. Need I say more?"

As Finke shrugged, Evans gave him Miss Appleby's street address. He descended the broad stone steps of the Dorsetshire's live entrance, flagged the first taxi in line, and set forth.

Standing patiently at Homer's side, Mirakian waited for his assignment. His dark forehead was creased with a frown of apprehension, but it was no deeper than the frowns he customarily wore when exertion of any kind loomed in prospect.

"I always get into some kind of a jam," Mirak ventured.

"Precisely," agreed Evans. "Don't we all? But the few simple errands I shall ask you to perform involve no embarrassment or danger. You can help us by calling at the Lehigh Clinic, and finding out, discreetly, which members or agents of the police have called there, inquiring about any of our principals, including Angus Ferguson. Get what you can about our *La Prensa* man. Find out from your friend, the colored porter, what trustworthy sources of information might be open to us in the little Harlem around

117

Lafayette Square. Get in touch with someone on the *Herald*, and without giving any of our show away, try to learn whether or not the newspapermen and editors have any inkling of a murder on Newbury Street today."

Reluctantly, Mirak scribbled the following items on the back of an envelope from his pocket:

Cops
Prensa
Little Harlem
Herald desk.

With that, he shook hands gravely, and ambled away.

The first move for Homer was to check with Daisy, at the cloak-room counter. She had no message for him from Jellyroll, and was almost in tears. She was exasperated with the piano player who, having a chance to benefit by the co-operation of the world's top criminologist, chose to take it on the lam. In fact, Daisy had said harsh words to Bozo, to the point that the near-midget avoided her eyes and would not speak to her.

"Don't feel badly, Miss Daisy," Homer said, taking her hand and smiling into her eyes. "We'll save this impulsive pair of lovers, in spite of themselves."

"Whenever you say 'we,' I get gooseflesh all over," Daisy sighed. "You don't know what it means to a girl in my position to meet a man who's not weighed down with his own troubles, and cares about what happens to somebody else."

"We all should care what happens to everybody else," suggested Homer.

"Damn it. I suppose so," said Daisy, with a kind of volcanic regret.

When Bozo opened the door of his cage, Homer collared him. "Call for a substitute. We need you over here," he said. He motioned Daisy to come out. "We're going on a little tour of inspection. You bring me luck." Then, as he and Daisy stood just outside the counter, he said, so the outraged Bozo could hear, "I want to have a look at the chef's storerooms and imported goods."

Whatever Bozo had been feeling before mounted to real consternation, but he could only stand there, shaking and helpless, as the others turned their backs and sauntered away.

Somewhat to Daisy's surprise, Homer did lead her to the provision rooms, and it did not take him long to expose, stacked cleverly in a corner and completely shielded by cases of Japanese shrimps, French snails, Italian macaroni, Chinese white water chestnuts, German rollmops, and other cosmopolitan delicacies, a quantity of baggage easily identified as belonging to Erica Strella. Some of the articles had been packed in cardboard cartons.

"So that's what Bozo's been trying to hide," Daisy said. "He helped Jellyroll with this Operation Scram."

"Obviously, such a lot of stuff could not have been spirited out of the hotel through the lobby, or by way of the parking lot. Ergo: Miss Strella's personal belongings and containers had to be somewhere in the building. Bozo has been most assiduous in trying to keep secret Jellyroll's connection with Miss Strella, Laneer's call on Miss Strella last evening or early this morning, and whatever else Jellyroll himself would not want made pubic. The little runt is too loyal to his friends to let them down, and too fearful of his own skin to contemplate the consequences of his extralegal cooperation."

"But the police. They're coming back. That awful Sergeant Ryan. Our boss, the owner, and all the staff are scared witless," said Daisy.

"Exactly," Homer said. He led her to the office of the chef, and was greeted by Maestro Piccini most warmly. Linking his free arm with that of Chef Piccini, Homer conducted the culinary artist back to the storeroom in question.

"It doesn't matter whether or not you knew about this concealed baggage," began Homer.

With a cunning, ingratiating smile, Piccini interrupted. "Naturally, I know nothing of any irregularities. You, Monsieur Evans, a U.S. agent in the confidence of the few who sway the world, have but to suggest—and command me. You may well imagine that my heart is torn with sympathy for our musician and his lovely foreign lady, even though Monsieur Jellyroll—a disgusting cheap

pastry fit only for diverting flies from more delectable desserts—
neglects Monteverdi, Palestrina, Corelli, Paganini, Scarlatti,
Provenzale, Verdi, Puccini, Rossini, Galuppi, Giuseppe and Anna
Lorenzo, Gabrieli, Pergolesi, even Cimarosa, Tagliavanti, Roxi, and
Elbo, for (the chef spat and begged Daisy's pardon) Olivero,
Satchmo, Dizzo Gillespi, Basie, Hot Lippo—jazzo, swingo, bip and
boppo, be-boppo, reboppo, hatta caldo. . . . Bah! I love him just
the same. What shall we do?"

"I think the lovely lady's luggage is well hidden. Should Sergeant Ryan be more perspicacious than we expect, claim ignorance.
By the way, Maestro, where were you this afternoon? From 2:30
until 4, let us say?"

A dark, frustrated look passed over the chef's round face.

"The laws of chance do not operate fairly. They tip the percentage against those who bring skill and brains to any sort of contest.
Particularly cards." The chef made card-playing motions.

"Gin?" asked Homer.

"I made no idiotic mistakes. Therefore I lost, to inferiors," the
maestro declared. "Ask Jellyroll, who looked on for a while."

"Ah, thanks," said Evans, and Daisy realized that he had heard
exactly what he wanted to know. "A rivederci!"

He and Daisy walked around the crook of Newbury Street to
the taxi stand, took the first cab in line, and rode to the Kenmore
Branch of the Pequot National Bank.

It would be hard to imagine a man more indolent by nature
than Ephraim Poole, nor one who, when he was obliged to use all
the swells and stops, could get more out of work's full organ, in
volume, quality and velocity. Already he had sorted stacks of
papers with a bearing on the late Pointed Face's temporary
tellership. The banal or routine accounts he had left intact, for
others to examine.

"What shall I do with these? Where can I stow them, and go
over them, without police breathing down my neck?" Poole asked.

For answer, Homer turned to Daisy, "Would you commit a
merciful crime, for my sake?" he asked.

"Would I?" she answered, quite ecstatically.

"We'll take all these records and documents to Miss Daisy's lodgings. She's brave enough to take the risk, for Jellyroll's benefit."

"How does Jellyroll figure in this?" Poole asked, and Homer put him up to date.

As Evans was about to help Poole and Daisy away with the significant papers, he asked the accountant if he had noticed anything strange or out of order, at first glance.

"There's something fishy," Poole said. "Laneer, I'll bet my boots, has not stolen one penny from the bank, in any ordinary way. But he has made use of his position here, and the bank's inner facilities, to carry on some kind of hanky-panky I won't pretend, as yet, to understand."

"Involving South America or South Americans?" Homer asked. "More specifically, Argentines?"

"Quite possibly," Poole said. "I can only say that the number of personal checks for small amounts which passed over his window shelf seems disproportionately large. Huge, one might say, in comparison to the other tellers lined up beside him, equally accessible, and with longer terms of service in which to attract a personal clientele or following."

"Indeed," Homer remarked, gleefully. "That fits."

"That fits with what, for Pete's sake?" demanded Poole, and Homer told him about Laneer's taking bundles of what looked like personal checks from Dr. Gonzalez. In fact, with his amazing talent for oral recapitulation, Evans gave Poole all he knew about the day's developments.

"There's another lead that looks queer," Poole said, after he had received and digested Homer's summary of the case thus far. "Far too many of the personal checks for small amounts are dated several months back, too far back for any ordinary teller to cash them without formalities."

"That doesn't surprise me. Particularly if they had been written in Buenos Aires, or had been taken down there, accepted for payment, exchanged and brought back here," said Evans.

"Another hitch," continued Poole. "None of the checks dated far back seems to have been written in January or February, and twice as many as the average were dated in November and December."

"Even my poor head for figures can account for that," Homer said. "Checks too far out of date, if dated with the figure 1 to indicate January, need simply the insertion of another simple pen stroke to read '11', meaning November. February checks, if the month is indicated by the figure 2, can be jumped ten months ahead, to 12, or December."

"One more item," continued Poole. "Mr. Laneer kept a key and combination tab in code in a box of paper clips in his file drawer marked 'Private.' I've been able to open a safe-deposit vault he was using either officially or informally, and it contains, among other things I haven't had time to look at, a number of personal checks written by various persons months ago, and an account involving 180,000 Argentine pesos—roughly $5,000 U.S. at present-day exchange—in which the name of the party with the pesos is indicated by crudely formed stars."

"God, what imagination!" Homer groaned. "Star in Latin is Stella, in Spanish Estrella."

"Strella!" exclaimed Poole. "Naturally, until you told me what you did just now, I was at sea. Now it's too damned clear. Suspiciously infantile."

"Remember Laneer was a linguist among colleagues who are tongue-tied, except in their own language. Superficial men, under similar circumstances, form a low estimate of their associates' intelligence. An inverted form of vanity bred by bizarre accomplishments, you know."

"Such as accountancy?" Poole suggested, grinning.

"Even the Negroes we like so well are inordinately proud of their jive talk, and look down on Ofays who can't understand it," Homer added. "And you know how doctors love to write unintelligible Latin prescriptions, how conjurers gloat because the hand is quicker than the eye, how competent housewives despise girls whose gifts lie in other directions. . . ."

"I can keep house, too," insisted Daisy.

All three quit the bank, enjoined the night watchman to absolute silence concerning their visit, hailed a taxi at a safe distance from the Pequot National, and directed the chauffeur to an address on another street, a block from Daisy's small apartment. Poole was installed there with their loot, and agreed to be on hand in the Lantern Room at 10, or thereabouts. Daisy was deposited at her cloakroom counter, and Homer went unhurriedly to the bar, to await Finke and Mirak.

The hotel staff still was agog, in anticipation of an onslaught by the police. None had occurred, not even a phone call. That was ominous.

The first emissary to report back was Mirakian. He pulled out the envelope on which was his terse memorandum. "Cops," he said. "They've been all over the place, at the clinic, since 5 P.M. None of the doctors or nurses, interns or employees are on the police payroll, as stoolies, as far as anybody knows. Sergeant Ryan talked with several taxi drivers. They all hate his guts. Laneer had been calling at the clinic, a few evenings a week, on week-ends, and on his day off, Wednesday or Thursday. He liked to talk with South Americans, doctors, patients, callers. They all were cordial to him. Ferguson had checked in about 4 A.M. Nobody felt at liberty to discuss his case." Mirak had been able to find nobody who had given the police any significant information, principally because "nobody seemed to have any."

Nobody knew anything much about the *La Prensa* man, it seemed. His name was Julio Etchegaray, and he had been hanging around the clinic, to chat with compatriots, about a week. He seemed amiable, harmless and had much time on his hands.

In Boston's little Harlem, Mirak had been directed by the hospital porter to a certain cigar store from which for a fee of 25 cents anybody in the district could be located. Mirak had paid his quarter, and had got a fantastic runaround. Not a single man, woman or child anywhere had ever heard of Jellyroll Morton. Regarding Wilson, the substitute piano player, Mirak accidentally stumbled on his father, a preacher, who had not seen his son for a year, and knew not where he dwelt.

The Boston *Herald* crew had no inkling that a murder had been perpetrated anywhere in the city or state that day.

With a deep sigh, Mirak put his memo envelope back in his pocket. His eyes opened wide when Homer congratulated him.

"Don't rub it in. I got nothing at all," Mirak protested. "We middle-Easterners are good at intrigue that spreads out over centuries and generations. This flash stuff rattles us."

"Nevertheless, thanks to you, I am forewarned in many respects. The police may know anything a taxi driver could know. Our Boston Harlem has clammed up so tightly that Jellyroll must be there, somewhere, and X-rays could not likely penetrate his hideout. We now have the name of our *La Prensa* chap, and the fact that he, like Dr. Gonzalez, is a newcomer to the city. He frequents the clinic, the Pequot National, and resides at No. 14 Newbury Street. The press has been kept in the dark all these hours, so reporters and editors will be madder than wasps at Sergeant Ryan when we take it upon ourselves to spill the beans and earn press co-operation."

"We?" repeated Mirakian in horror. "Ryan would beat my brains out."

"Over St. Clair Endicott's dead body, to say nothing of the corpses of Endicott, junior, Walpole, Winthrop and Sol Swig," added Homer. "Also mine and Finke's. I'll make a suggestion. Go at once to the *Herald* office, take my old friend, Bill Gavin, aside, and give him the lowdown on everything. Let him get his best men to work, and his photographers, too. Only impose these conditions. That the story may be set up, proofed and ready to go into an extra, with an up-to-the-minute lead, when I phone in the word. Naturally, if any of his men find out anything, on their own, or the police release any bulletins, the *Herald* would be at liberty to print their own discoveries or official handouts, on a par with the other papers. If all of us are lucky, it will mean an exclusive the news world will not soon forget, if ever. Be sure to tell Gavin that I assert flatly that Jellyroll Morton is not guilty. Let him make it clear that the police are barking up the wrong totem and that ye *Herald* is not falling for the official line of least resistance."

Mirakian saluted limply and started toward the *Herald*, by taxi. "My old man should have stood in Turkey," he groaned.

What has, meanwhile, been happening to Finke merits a play by play announcement.

First, he taxied to within a few doors of the address on the wrong slope of Hancock Street (named for John, that is, on Beacon Hill) where Priscilla Appleby and "another working girl" roomed together, according to Finke's best information. He was confronted, on the lower landing of the stairs, by the landlady-housekeeper named Enid O'Toole.

"Where do you think you're going?" demanded the widow O'Toole.

"Who wants to know?" retorted Finke.

"No women in this house receive callers in their rooms," the widow said, glaring.

Finke pulled out a five-dollar bill.

"I'll leave the door wide open all the time," he said.

"See that you do," the widow said, snatching the five. "Who is it you're wanting to compromise?"

"Miss Appleby," Finke said.

The widow, suddenly switching all the way to mirth, held her ample slats to keep from laughing too loud. "Dear saints above," she gasped. Finke held out another greenback, this time a two.

"I forget the name of her roommate," he said.

"You mean Flossie? Flossie Bunter? Now she's more my idea of what a girl should be. How she puts up with that picklepuss is a mystery to me, but they get on. And lucky for them. If they made any noise yelling at each other, I'd put 'em out in the street."

"Which room?" Finke asked, to cut off the comment.

"Second floor, left, front," the widow told him.

"Are they in?"

"I heard one of 'em go out, but I don't know which one. I was—tied up at the time."

"Try natures backwards," said Finke.

"Try your grandfather likewise," replied the widow, getting purple in the face again.

Finke gave her a crisp raspberry, mounted to the second floor, and proceeded to the door, left, front.

"Who is it, please?" a pleasant voice responded.

"Miss Bunter?" he asked.

She opened the door, tentatively, holding her moon-colored housegown around her slender body, protectively but not at all fearfully. He saw that her eyes were blue, her hair the color of honey, and her hands long and reposeful. She had a nice neck. Her shoulders were appealing, her legs, though unexposed, gave the effect of being long.

"Holy cats!" Finke exclaimed, spontaneously. "You're twice as good as the expert deduced, and his rating was high."

"You have the advantage of me," she said.

"What a break," Finke agreed. "Believe me. I'll try to hang on to it. May I come in a moment? I promised the harridan downstairs that I'd leave the door open. Am I right in assuming it is Florence?"

"Everybody calls me 'Flossie'," she said.

"You'll always be Florence, then, to me," Finke said, firmly. "I am not deceived by your pretty exterior, or that silvery robe. You have a mind."

"Say! Who *are* you?" she asked, letting him in and waving toward the best easy chair. There were two, just alike, but one faced the cold fireplace. Finke looked at the sleeping arrangements, camouflaged for the day.

"Mmmmmm. Twin beds," he murmured.

"I'll say," Flossie asserted, with a gasp. "But I still don't know who you are. Should I?"

"I'm Finke Maguire. A private eye," he told her, and showed her his California license, his driving license, and half of a torn Chinese laundry ticket.

Flossie Bunter let out a little scream of astonishment. Her face became serious, if not stern.

"There must be some mistake, Mr. Maguire. I'm so innocent, it's embarrassing."

"Don't I know *that!*" Finke said. "I want you to answer a few questions about your roommate."

As she started to protest Finke held up his hand to stem her torrent of words. "Look," he said. "She'll be coming back soon, maybe. Why don't I look out the window while you slip on a dress. Then we'll go to some nice cocktail lounge where we can talk. This is important, on the level. All I can say off-hand, not to be repeated, mind you, is that Miss Appleby may be in danger. You know a shamus like me wouldn't come all the way to Boston from sunny California just for a gag."

"Gee! Jeepers Crow!" Flossie gasped. The robe was half off before Finke started his about face.

In a couple of minutes Flossie said, "Turn around, J. Edgar. I'm ready."

"Ciel!" Finke was not kidding. She looked like a cover girl.

"Don't expect me to do this consistently," she said. "I was washed, made up, and had on my foundation before you came in. That's practically 99 per cent of the battle."

"The battle hasn't started yet," Finke said.

"Well. Let's go before Priscilla shows up."

"O.K.," agreed Finke, offering his arm. "There ought to be a good drinking spot at the Bellevue. That's nearby."

They entered the Bellevue by the side entrance, bypassed the barroom where politicians congregate with stooges and dolls, and stepped into the cocktail lounge across from the Athenaeum. The place was so dark they both were blinded, at first. Flossie tightened her grip on Finke's arm. A soft-voiced colored waiter guided them to an intimate table near a corner. By that time, they could see that the denizens were paired, leaning close together and whispering. Some of the pairs were women, a few were men. Most were mixed, but nobody cared. The couples were in love, on the make, on the beam, self-hypnotized.

As soon as they were settled, knee to knee and shoulder to shoulder, in a cozy sort of way, and their drinks were before them— champagne cocktails he had ordered, with only one drop of bitters and a soupcon of orange peel—she said, "Gee! You speak French."

"I lived in Paris quite a while, before I hit California."

"Did you say you were born in Boston?"

"East Boston. But I didn't say it. You caught that on my credentials. Place of birth, etc. Nice work, Florence. Have you ever been in love?"

"Not all the way. I've tried."

"Ever been in danger?"

She shivered and leaned closer. "No," she said. "Nothing happens to girls like me."

"Come off it," Finke said, abruptly.

She brightened, squirmed with pleasure, and whispered, "How right you are. I'm having the time of my life. Usually I make out all right, but you're something special. You and your detective licenses, airplanes, cocktail spots where you can't see a hand unless it's right in front of you. Say, what is this?"

"You know what you like about me?" Finke demanded.

"No. What?"

"I seem not to give a damn about money or time."

"If you think that isn't wonderful, you're nuts," she said. "But pretty soon I want your story, and it had better be good."

Finke flagged the ghostlike waiter and ordered a drink brought whenever either of their glasses was empty.

"Yes, Mr. Maguire," the waiter said. "Certainly, Mr. Maguire."

That brought Finke up short, and caused Flossie Bunter to stiffen.

"He knows you! After giving me that stall about where is there a lounge, and maybe the Bellevue has one."

Then she saw that Finke was really taken aback.

"Lean toward us," Finke said to the waiter. He pulled out a ten-dollar bill, in such a way that the motion could not have been detected or interpreted four feet away in the darkness. "Now talk straight and fast," Finke said. "I'm a licensed detective. How did you find out my name? Or don't you want to make ten dollars? And keep out of trouble?"

The waiter, whose face was just a foot away, could not repress a grin.

"What's funny?" asked Finke, in his low ominous tone, and then he relaxed. "I get you. Someone else just paid you to confirm an idea of who I am. How much?"

The waiter was so disconcerted that he blurted out "Five."

"Somebody here in this blackout?"

"That's right," the waiter admitted.

"Who?"

"A lady and a gentleman, sir."

"What's his name?"

"A fine gentleman, sir. Mr. Leverett Bengay."

"Is her first name Solange?"

"Yes, sir. That's it. I couldn't be sure, because it's a strange name to me."

"French?" whispered Flossie, agog.

"Canadian," corrected Finke, from the side of his mouth. Flossie was utterly bewildered. "Where are they? Tell me. Don't point."

The waiter stole a backward glance then whispered, "Here they come."

And out of the dimness came Solange and Bengay. Ignoring Flossie Bunter, except for a quick once-over from the corner of her flashing eyes, Solange looked at Finke as if he were a cast-iron statue she loathed, then started to pass on.

"Believe me . . ." Finke began, earnestly. "I didn't intend to expose you to a shock."

"You succeeded admirably. All my felicitations."

"Don't be that way," said Finke. He turned on Bengay.

"I didn't mean to make a sucker out of you," he said.

"It's of no consequence," Bengay said, haughtily, although inwardly he was jubilant to see Finke in the doghouse.

Solange already had moved four steps toward the exit, her heels thumping hard on the carpet. Bengay followed.

"Now who were *they?*"

"Two people I met last night," Finke said.

"I never saw such a beautiful woman, or man—only I like your type better. And wasn't she fit to be tied!" Flossie quickly thought it over, and added, "Say! Just a passing acquaintance you met yesterday couldn't get that sore at you. Unless you *are* a heel. And I'm positive you're not. . . . Are you?"

"That remains to be seen," Finke said, laconically. "Are you free for the evening?"

"Not till you explain yourself."

"Forget this lady and gentleman, who are purely incidental," he said. "I really need your help to save Miss Appleby. Not from worse than death, but losing her boss."

"You mean her boss'll be killed?"

"I mean, he might get into a jam. For all I can say, it could lead to almost anything. I won't exaggerate. I can't. I haven't enough facts, as yet. And that's where you come in, besides being damn good company, with more sense than other beauties who are rich and spoiled, and jump at conclusions," he said.

"I haven't any conclusions to jump at," Flossie complained. "Can't you give me at least one, for Pete's sake, before I blow my top?"

"First, tell me about Miss Appleby. I understand she's sour on life because her boss is close-mouthed about his business affairs, and doesn't pay her enough so she can afford an apartment."

"You don't know women like Priscilla. She says this and that, but when you get right down to fundamentals, she's crazy to marry the damn fool, twice her age and three times as crotchety, so I hear."

"You've never met Mr. Ferguson?"

"No. And all she tells about the business is what she doesn't know, what he keeps from her, I mean. He's sly and secretive."

"As for instance?"

"He goes on trips. Foreign travel. God! You wouldn't believe it how that girl wants to go abroad, and see the churches and museums. To South America and the Andes. Africa, to smell cinnamon before the coast is sighted. And, to hear her tell it, he sneaks off just to spite her, saying he's got to make a trip to New York, and winding up somewhere to hell and gone, where he can't even speak the language, or fend off indigestion."

"He doesn't let her know, in advance, when or where he's going?"

"Too damned fearful his competitors might find out, and get there a step ahead of him. So he says. And that makes Priscilla really wild."

A tall dark young and handsome man materialized out of the scented gloom and peered, evidently thinking the table might be vacant.

"Hi! Dr. Gonzalez!" said Finke. "Won't you sit down?"

"Many thanks," said Gonzalez, remaining erect and bowing toward Flossie, awaiting an introduction. Finke did the needful and she made a dainty acknowledgement.

"How's the headache?" asked Finke.

The young doctor, frowning slightly, said apologetically, as if asking Flossie's permission, "It's still with me. May I?" He borrowed Finke's untouched glass of water, took a little bottle from his vest pocket, selected two tablets, and tossed them into his mouth.

"What should we do without aspirin, señorita?" he said.

"I could make some suggestions," she replied, brightly. "With or without. Are you Spanish, señor?"

"Argentine," he said. "We speak the Spanish language, more or less."

The waiter appeared and Dr. Gonzalez glanced at the other drinks. "*Lo mismo!*"

"*Rogerio!*" the waiter said, and turned.

As the waiter left, Flossie felt the handsome Argentine lean her way, and quite heavily. She supported his weight and straightened him up, more or less, instinctively. He slumped. He slid partly under the table.

"Oh, no!" protested Finke, and simultaneously was on his feet calling, "Is there a doctor in the house?"

Flossie screamed. Not softly. Loud, and hideously shrill. Somehow the table was moved out of the way, she and Finke and the waiter lifted the limp form of Dr. Gonzalez and placed it on the wide double seat. The house lights went up. Men and women milled and muttered. A doctor shoved his way to the corner, tried Gonzalez's pulse, then knelt swiftly and listened for a heartbeat. He held a pocket mirror to the Argentine's mouth and nose.

"He's dead."

A police officer bustled alongside, drew himself to an impos-
ing height, held up his hand. "Don't anybody leave, or move from
where you are sitting." To the bell captain who had presented himself, the cop barked an order to phone headquarters. Everyone was
silent, and awed. The faces of the drinkers and lovers and casuals
were pained and unbelieving. They had come in for a quiet good
time. And now this. A mess. There were two more policemen now.
Somehow the waiter to whom Finke had given ten dollars stationed
himself near enough so he could hear Finke whisper: "Get word
out to phone St. Clair Endicott. Lawyer."

The doctor and one of the cops edged over, but the waiter
passed the word along to another. It traveled all the way through
the confused mob to the kitchen, thence to the lobby and the alert
bell captain's more alert assistant. "Phone Lawyer St. Clair Endicott
for Mr. Maguire. P.D.Q."

It was only a three-minute drive from police headquarters to
the Bellevue, so that it took an astonishingly short time for Captain Moriarty to get there. As the harassed and elegant captain
passed into the Bellevue lobby, on his way to the cocktail lounge
he saw, sitting nervously together, Solange and Leverett Bengay.
The captain's eyes bulged and he said peremptorily, "You two,
again."

Pausing just long enough for a split-second decision, Moriarty
ordered them to follow him. Bengay tried to object. The captain
cut him off, while Solange, white and determined, drew him along.
After the encounter with Finke, Solange had seemed unstrung.
Unable to make up her mind about anything, she had plumped into
an upholstered chair in the austere lobby. The news that a foreign
doctor had dropped dead in the cocktail room had reached them,
but not until she found herself within sight of the corpse did she
sense any connection with the case.

A closer look at the dead man's face, and for the second time
that evening her legs almost buckled. "Gonzalez," she gasped.

The captain wheeled on her and Bengay. "So you know *this* one,
too!" He thumbed toward the body. Solange's eyes fixed themselves
on Finke, then, with Bengay's help, she sat weakly in a chair.

When a kind of order had been restored, Finke stepped up to the captain and showed him his California detective's license.

"What's your story?" the captain asked, gruffly.

The well-meaning head waiter interposed, "Sir. The deceased had just come in, not five minutes before he passed away. He was invited by this gentleman to sit at his table, with the young lady . . ."

"Hold your tongue!" barked the captain. "Proceed, Mr. Maguire!"

Before Finke could get started, the crowd parted, and St. Clair Endicott, trailing dignity like robes of deep purple, said, softly, "I represent Mr. Maguire, in this solemn emergency."

Again the captain's eyes bulged. "You! Again!"

"In person," admitted the advocate. He looked inquiringly at Finke and asked, "Well, old boy. Do we talk, or don't we? You know best."

"I'll tell the captain what I can, of course," said Finke. "It isn't much." Weakening, Flossie grasped his hand and his arm.

"I'll get to you next, miss," the captain assured her.

"Jeepers Crow!" was all she could say.

"Do I get a chance to speak my piece, or not?" demanded Finke. "We haven't got all night."

"That's where you may be wrong," the captain reminded him. "But proceed."

"Miss Bunter and I were seated at this table, side by side, drinking champagne cocktails with one cherry each, one drop of bitters, and a soupcon of orange peel."

"Keep it in American, if you please."

"A suspicion of orange rind, to you, sir."

"Omit irrelevant details. We'll test all the glasses," the captain admonished. A little more and his temper would burst all over the place.

"Dr. Gonzalez came in, alone. I invited him to sit down with Miss Bunter and me."

"Known him long?"

"I met him at the bar just off the Lantern Room in the Dorsetshire Hotel earlier this evening."

"As recently as that!" commented the captain, skeptically.

"He seemed glad to join us. Sat down. Ordered a drink, same as ours. I asked him if he still had a headache."

"Light conversation," grunted the captain. "Go ahead. Spin on."

"He said he had, took out a bottle from his vest pocket. I assumed it was aspirin. I think it was marked 'Bayer.'" Finke thumbed toward the corpse's vest. "See for yourself."

"In good time," the captain said.

"The doctor—the deceased is a doctor—took two of the tablets, borrowed my glass of water, swallowed them, and a few minutes later went limp, his eyes closed, he slid partway under the table . . ." Finke raised both hands in a pitying gesture of futility. "He died."

Wheeling on Flossie Bunter, the captain demanded, "Is that straight?"

"So help me," she said, faintly.

"So you see, that's that," St. Clair Endicott said. "Are we at liberty to go?" He took an engraved card from his case, scribbled an address, and continued, "At any moment, until further notice, we shall be there. Drinking."

"May I make a suggestion?" Finke asked. The exit was going so smoothly that it made him suspicious.

"We appreciate co-operation," the captain replied.

"Headquarters is only a few steps away. For our own protection, I'd like you to send a police witness with us, so we can stop in there and be searched, Miss Bunter and I. We were both sitting near enough the deceased to have poisoned him, sir," Finke said. "Naturally, neither of us did. But Mr. Endicott would like to establish that firmly, right at the start."

"A splendid precaution," the renowned corporation lawyer and leader of cotillions agreed.

"I've no objection," the captain said, in his best poker voice. He assigned one of the uniformed cops to accompany them and act as witness.

Bengay stepped forward. "One moment, St. Clair. If you don't mind. Miss de Lassigny and I would like to depart. We know nothing about this affair. I give you my word."

"Where can I reach you? No shenanigans, mind you!" the Captain said.

"We'll both be at the Dorsetshire, all evening."

"Birds of a feather!" the captain said, and sighed.

"Nothing of the kind," declared Solange.

"Dismissed!" the captain said, and busied himself with the technical arrangements, just as a flock of newsmen and press photographers barged in.

12

When Good Fellows Get Together

Two taxis, separate and distinct, set out from the Bellevue, inched their way down Beacon Street to the corner where formerly the King's Chapel, Houghton & Dutton, S.S. Pierce, and the Parker House ennobled the intersection. Thence they crawled along Tremont Street, past the Old South Burying Ground, Keith's Theatre, the *Herald* and the Common, and wheeled southward to the Dorsetshire, skirting other historical and recreational landmarks too numerous to mention.

In Taxi No. 1 rode Solange de Lassigny and Leverett Bengay. The latter sat erect in a corner, hopeful and dismayed. Two dead men in a single evening. A bit thick, and no mistake. He tried to decide whether to place his hand on hers. He tried it. She scarcely seemed to notice. But slowly, as they rode along, obstructed by traffic tangles that would make wild savages in treetops split their sides with laughter, the Mademoiselle from Montreal became her fascinating self again. She sighed, smiled, rubbed the back of her hand to stir the circulation, then gave it back to Bengay.

"I've been a bore," she confessed.

"You couldn't," he stammered.

"Shall I tell you why?"

"If it will relieve you."

"Thanks."

They rode two more blocks, consuming at least ten minutes, before she spoke again.

"That girl with Mr. Maguire," she began, simply.

"Rather attractive, by Jove," Bengay said, sympathetically.

"*Very* attractive!" Solange said, with emphasis. "I'm vain. I'm a cat."

"I've always rather liked cats, when they'd let me," he remarked.

"It was bad enough," she said, "when Mr. Maguire made me feel like a dunce. Then, when I realized he had ditched me to meet that—that attractive Miss Bunter. Oh, there I go again!"

"I've never met Miss Bunter. She's not in any set I know."

"Be nice to her," Solange said, with an effort. "I'll behave. You see if I don't."

They were held up in traffic again, after having gained another fifty yards.

"Mr. Endicott knew what he was doing, when he decided to walk," Solange said.

In Taxi No. 2, Flossie Bunter was clinging to Finke in a natural, girlish way, and he was trying to soothe her. He made no reference to Bengay or Solange, except that it seemed likely they would see them later.

"*That* woman?" gasped Flossie.

"Oh, she's O.K. Some things have happened to upset her."

Flossie shuddered. "A couple of dead men. Murders! But that isn't what's eating her. It's *you.*"

"She'll pull herself together," said Finke, as if nothing were less important.

"You have a way with women—of setting them off like Roman candles."

"Have a heart," Finke said, gruffly. "Do I stage these disasters? Did I drag you out of a comfortable negligee, just to show you the seamy side of life?"

"I'm sorry. Forgive me," she said. "I'm not used to unexpected events."

"So take it easy," admonished Finke.

"Must we really go where *she* is going?"

"Line of duty," Finke assured her.

"I'll do my best to have a good time," she promised.

"When that bunch of homicide cops gets to work on our mob, you'll have the time of your life. By the way, don't go out of your way to let Ferguson know who you are, or that you ever heard of him."

"Mr. Ferguson, tool Priscilla's boss!"

"I'll stop the cab if you want to walk home," said Finke.

"You're sure I look all right?" she asked, doubtfully.

When Finke's taxi pulled up as Solange and Bengay were descending from Taxi No. 1, Finke stalled a while, to let them get a start. Then he took Flossie into the deserted writing room and sent a bellhop to notify Evans, on the Q.T. A few moments later Homer, suave and elegant as usual, stepped into the alcove. Flossie, before Finke could introduce her, drew in her breath quickly.

"Miss Bunter," Homer said, after the presentation. "How kind of you to join us."

"Gonzalez is dead," Finke said, abruptly.

The announcement affected Homer to such a degree that he did not attempt to conceal his sorrow and resentment. He walked a few paces, back and forth, to collect himself, then urged Finke to give him the details. Finke did so, with such accuracy that Flossie was amazed. She felt chilled by the irradiations of Homer's concentrated cerebration. Such power of mind held her spellbound, and hurt her, all through and all over. When he relaxed, so did she, perforce. He smiled and said, "This is harrowing for you, my dear. We must make it up, somehow. . . . You won't desert us, on the side of the angels?"

"Angels," she gasped. "Will there be any more?"

"Not unless we continue to be careless. I should have suspected that Gonzalez was in danger."

"Then why would he take poison?"

"I'm afraid it's not as simple as that. He must have known something that made him an obstacle to somebody's plans," Homer said.

"I'll never dare take another aspirin," she said.

When the trio went into the Lantern Room, three large round tables had been placed together, like a clover pattern. Solange, like a reigning queen of beauty, was seated between Ferguson and

Bengay, with Mirakian and Poole on the fringe. St. Clair Endicott and Cleaves, of the United Fruit Company, had Bunny Gerry between them, and were seconded by Vice President Cabot, of the Pequot National, Edgy Gerry, and another clerk from the same bank, named Hector Deal. Hector's presence had been Poole's idea. Miss Bunter was introduced by Homer, who seated her between himself and Finke. On the platform was Wilson, the substitute jazz man. Primitivo, the Basque head waiter, and Jason Snor, the owner (51 per cent) of the Dorsetshire, collaborated in service.

Homer Evans did his best to create a companionable atmosphere. When all hands had drinks before them, he toasted the ladies, first Mrs. Gerry, as the only married woman present; next Solange, as the senior visiting lady; and with extra tact and grace, Miss Bunter, whom he made no attempt to explain. Of the women, Bunny Gerry was amiable and somewhat relieved that another girl had showed up. Solange was polite and gracious, like Greenland's icy mountains under the midnight sun. All the men were pleased with Flossie, according to their ages and temperaments, save two, who were notably distressed. The jittery minority was made up of Ferguson, who was present only because he dared not be absent; and Edgy Gerry, to whom any kind of unknown quantity was upsetting. After God had created arithmetic, the efficient little bank clerk believed, the Devil had brought forth algebra, with its x's and y's.

As gently as he could, Homer told them all (without regard to who might or might not already know) that Pointed Face had "died" that afternoon, therefore the bets were off.

"So eat, drink and be merry," Homer advised them.

"*Rather!*" agreed St. Clair Endicott. On the platform, the piano player, Wilson, struck up a King Cole masterpiece.

To the astonishment of all, the famous corporation lawyer, who had rescued three of the gathering already from the toils of the police, turned out to be a No. 1 jazz fanatic, all the way from Buddy Bolden and Dixieland through Ellington, Basie, Gillespie (bop) and Slim Gaillard, the exponent of Vout and O'Rooney. Such enthusiasm from a distinguished source set off Wilson until, as he expressed it, he was as groovy as a Chinese movie.

"And this, in the Athens of America," Mirakian sighed.

The party was on the verge of clicking, 100 per cent, when Jason Snor, the hotel owner, was called away. He returned, his face bleak and mauve. Finke sang softly under his breath: "Look out, here come the damn police, the damn police, the damn police . . ."

The head waiter ushered in Captain Moriarty, debonair and handsome in civilian clothes, and, also in mufti, a stocky, stone-faced man, twice as powerful and three times more grim, Sergeant Ryan.

"Aloysius, as I live," muttered Finke. "He hasn't changed, except for the worse." He wondered if his former enemy playmate from the alleys around Maverick Square would recognize him.

Homer rose, identified and introduced Captain Moriarty, and then, after a brief whispered consultation, Sergeant Ryan, of the homicide detail. "We've been expecting you gentlemen," Homer said. "We'll give you the utmost co-operation."

"Just answer questions plainly, and let it go at that," Ryan said. Looking from one to another, in turn, all around the cloverleaf tables, he let his eyes rest on Finke.

"Welcome back, just in time to stick your neck out."

Finke was not jarred from his complacency. "Hello, Laughing Boy," he rejoined. "Go home and get a handkerchief."

"Old friends," the captain remarked, drily, to St. Clair Endicott.

Ignoring those seated around the tables, the sergeant faced about, caught Wilson with such a baleful glance that the piano player stopped in the middle of a riff. Ryan said, "Come down here, you! You're first."

"Who? Me?" Wilson protested, hoarsely.

"You heard me."

Homer smiled at Wilson, reassuringly, and the jazz man seemed to take courage. St. Clair Endicott interrupted. "I represent Mr. Wilson, Sergeant. Should any of your questions seem improper, I'll advise him not to answer."

Captain Moriarty was calm and tactful. "This is merely routine," he assured them all. "A man has been killed. . . ."

"Two men!" This exclamation popped out from Flossie Bunter.

The captain beamed at her. "There's no connection, child. We're talking about a death you didn't witness."

"That poor young doctor died practically in my lap," Flossie said.

Quincy Cabot, frowning bewilderedly, asked, "What young doctor died?"

"Someone you don't know, sir," Edgy Gerry assured him. "He'd never been in the bank."

Homer looked at Ferguson and smiled, disarmingly. "You may remember him, possibly. A Dr. Gonzalez, from Buenos Aires. Here on a special scholarship or grant to study at the clinic."

"Never mind the clinic just now," growled Sergeant Ryan. "And all of you keep out of this, unless I ask you something. The next one who opens his or her trap, out of line . . ."

"There, there. It's all done with kindness," Captain Moriarty said. "Co-operation. That's the word."

The sergeant grunted and plunked Wilson down in an empty chair. "How come you're here, tonight?"

"I was asked to act as substitute," Wilson said. His manner was unruffled now, as if he were back in the South Pacific, and nothing could be worse than the trouble he'd seen.

"Who asked you?"

"My landlady."

"Nobody else?"

"No, sir."

"What time?"

"Between half-past 4 and 5. When she pulled aside the drapes, and served me my breakfast, in bed," said Wilson, calmly.

"At that time of the afternoon you have breakfast! In bed!"

"You had lunch at 9 in the evening yourself," Finke said. "And missed a chance to throw your weight around."

"Boys will be boys," admonished Captain Moriarty. "And those who start in East Boston keep it up all their lives." The captain was from South Boston, where a different clique of Irishmen lived, the kind who are old before their time, at the age of six.

Getting back to the business in hand, Ryan glared at Wilson, who looked back at him as impersonally as if he were stuffed and mounted. "Who told your landlady to ask you to substitute?" Ryan barked.

"She didn't say."

"You didn't ask?"

"Not I. I was glad of a chance to play over here, and earn a dollar. I substitute in plenty of spots."

"No regular job?"

"I promised myself, when I got out of the Army I'd never take another job that was the same, day after day," Wilson said.

"When did you see Jellyroll last?" asked the Sergeant.

"I haven't seen Jellyroll in weeks, I couldn't even estimate how long," Wilson answered.

"Get on back to the platform, and play soft," Sergeant Ryan said. He turned to Leverett Bengay.

"Now you. Have you got a lawyer?" the Sergeant began.

St. Clair Endicott bowed and gestured again. "Same counsel," he said. "You'll admit that I've made few objections."

"Could that be because you don't think fast enough?" suggested Ryan.

"I've seen interrogators who talk so volubly that they have no time to think at all," the lawyer said gently.

"O.K. Bengay. What was your relationship to the deceased, Blaise Lancer?"

"I never met the unfortunate man, I never saw him except in this room, and on a slab in the medical examiner's quarters. Between the moment of my first glimpse of him, and my last, he then being dead, I never communicated with him, directly or indirectly," Bengay said, warmed by the realization that Solange's lustrous eyes were burning with a kind of pride, narrowing only when they turned aside for a scornful glance across Finke's face.

"That sounds great, Mr. Bengay. And still, you tagged after him when he left this room just after 12 last night, tried to pump half a dozen employees about him, sneaked into his apartment house to spy on him."

Unruffled, Bengay said, "I did all that on a bet. A friendly wager between friends around this table."

"I heard something about the bet," Sergeant Ryan admitted. "May I ask you just a few questions, to complete the pattern?"

"Fire away," Bengay said.

"I understand somebody handed you a detective-story magazine, in which a correspondent criticized the editor for leading his public to believe that shadowing a stranger was easy. Right?"

"Right."

"Who was the party who handed you that piece?"

"Mr. Morton, I believe."

"Jellyroll?"

"The same."

"After you and your friends talked over the question, who selected the party to be tailed?"

"Jellyroll," Bengay said.

"Who left his post to follow the murdered man just before you got going?"

"I can't say, for sure, that anybody did," Bengay answered.

"This morning, just after 8 o'clock, did you pose as a salesman, and inquire about Jellyroll from a girl he's been seeing?"

"I did not mention Jellyroll to any girl who rooms in this hotel."

"Did you phone the San Diego police, to ask about a girl who roomed in this hotel?"

St. Clair Endicott wagged a forefinger. "We're not in Russia, Sergeant, so let's keep out of Southern California, too. And spare all the girls, as a matter of unwritten principle."

"You may not be aware that Jellyroll *and* his girl disappeared from this hotel just after Blaise Laneer was murdered. We know where they are, have the area blocked off, and will arrest them any minute," the Sergeant announced.

"In that event, you can question them directly, if I approve what you ask. I shall represent them, too," said Lawyer Endicott.

"The thinner you spread yourself, the better I like it," Ryan said. He turned on Angus Ferguson.

"All right, Brighten-the-Corner. Move over here to the witness chair."

"I prefer to sit here," the Scot said. "I know my rights, without retaining counsel."

"Your Sitz-rights," Sergeant Ryan said.

"I'll stay where I am," Ferguson said, doggedly.

"For a while," said the sergeant. He had taken some scribbled notes from his pocket. Nonchalantly he replaced them, leaned on his elbows, and looked contemptuously at the Scot.

"Where were you last night?" Ryan demanded.

"That's none of your business," Ferguson answered. "Nobody was killed until this afternoon. Between 2 o'clock and 6 P.M. today I was attending to my office work and making some calls on customers. I can account for every minute, with reputable witnesses, but I don't intend to."

"So you didn't murder Laneer," the sergeant commented. He beckoned a uniformed cop, and said to the latter, "Bring in Dr. Abel Deyo."

A few minutes later, a wise and weary-looking man of medium height, with a Latin dark complexion and gentle manner, entered and was guided to the sergeant. Ryan pointed across the table toward Ferguson. "Know this man?"

The doctor swallowed, hesitated, then said, softly, "Am I obliged to answer?"

"All right. So you've treated him, and are all bound round with ethics. To all intents and purposes you've answered my question with a 'Yes'."

Dr. Deyo shrugged.

"You're a specialist on concussion of the brain," Ryan declared.

"Head injuries, generally," Dr. Deyo replied.

"How many patients do you treat in a day, on the average?" Ryan asked.

"Between ten and sixty," Dr. Deyo replied.

"Good memory for faces?"

"Unusually retentive," said Dr. Deyo. He was not modest.

"How about names?"

"Those are a matter of record. One does not try to remember them," the doctor said, as if he were addressing a class.

"I'm asking because this man (thumbing toward Ferguson) has committed a grave offense. We're taking him with us, when we go, and charging him, formally. That means you'll be subpoenaed, Doctor, and will have to tell us what you know. Between ten and sixty guys who've bumped their heads will suffer every day you're in court," Sergeant Ryan said.

"I have competent colleagues and assistants I have trained, myself. No one, in a properly conducted clinic, is indispensable," Dr. Deyo said calmly.

Ryan almost grinned. "You may not know it, but you've one assistant less than you think."

"One less?" repeated the doctor, bewildered.

"A Dr. Gonzalez. He bumped himself off, with poison, earlier this evening. Any comment?"

Solange de Lassigny, who had found Ryan and his manner odious from the start, could not restrain herself any longer. Her eyes flashed fire, her cheeks flushed. "You are a stupid, insensitive pig!" she declared, glaring at the sergeant. Meanwhile Dr. Deyo was showing genuine regret and bewilderment.

"Dr. Gonzalez a suicide? Ridiculous!" he said, at last.

"Precisely. Fantastic!" agreed Homer Evans. All eyes turned on him. The sergeant bristled.

"What do you know about it?"

"Nothing much, as yet," Homer said, smoothly. "I'll look into Dr. Gonzalez's demise forthwith, and set you right, in so far as that seems feasible."

A nervous little laugh escaped Flossie Bunter, which caused Ryan to turn blue and red. Somehow, however, he managed to concentrate his spleen on Ferguson. Angus did not flinch.

"You're not taking me anywhere," Ferguson asserted, grimly.

The sergeant grabbed Jason Snor, the hotel proprietor, by the sleeve. "Was somebody assaulted with a dangerous weapon and robbed in this hotel last night?"

"So I understand. I was not informed—until this afternoon," the hotel owner said.

"Call in the help!" Sergeant Ryan ordered. "The whole kit and kaboodle."

Subdued modulations from the Hammond organ and the piano continued while everybody waited in tense silence. Employees of the Dorsetshire were herded in, single file, and ranged before the platform. They included Bozo, the house detective, Daisy, Clothhead and Wallyo, the desk clerks, the bell captain, bell boys and Elsa, the sixth-floor maid.

Ryan, now standing, instructed Jason Snor to "look over this bunch." The proprietor did so, to the discomfort of the help.

"Tell me which of these reported last night that Ferguson had been assaulted and robbed, on these premises," Ryan ordered.

"None of them did," the proprietor said.

"How many of them knew about the incident?"

"My sainted old aunt," protested St. Clair Endicott, rising reproachfully.

"All right. I'll ask them one by one."

"You already have asked them, one by one," the aristocratic lawyer asserted. "And each and severally, most likely, they denied having witnessed any such assault as you have described."

"That's right, Counsellor," said Daisy.

"You told us Mr. Ferguson did not call for the topcoat and hat he left with you early last evening until sometime this afternoon," Ryan said.

"Really, Sergeant," Homer interposed. "Miss Daisy was under no obligation to report an oversight like that."

"Let the sergeant get himself in deeper and deeper," suggested Finke. He faced around toward Captain Moriarty. "I'll outbid all comers for his stripes, as souvenirs, if you'll put them up at auction."

"Muldoon," roared the sergeant, and Clothhead stepped one pace front. "What time yesterday did Ferguson leave his jalopy with you?"

"Early last evening," answered Clothhead.

"When did he reclaim it?"

"Late this afternoon."

Again Flossie could not hold back a contribution: "He did no such thing. The car was obtained by someone else—acting for Mr. Ferguson."

Both Ferguson and Ryan blazed with indignation. The Scot beat the Celt to the question. "What do you know about it?" he snapped. "Who are you, anyway?"

Flossie, in consternation, appealed to Finke. "Please help me!" she begged. "I was only thinking out loud."

Lawyer Endicott spoke oracularly, "Miss Bunter, my client, stands on her constitutional rights. She will answer no questions. I will state, categorically, that she has no connection with either of the murders."

"There's only one murder," Ryan insisted. "And we know who did that, and what his motive was."

Homer bypassed Ryan, and spoke directly to the captain.

"May I ask a few questions, which may prove helpful?"

"Sure, Mr. Evans. As I said, co-operation is our watchword. And the night is young," Captain Moriarty replied. To Sergeant Ryan he added, "Pipe down for a while, Aloysius. Would you mind?"

"I assume that you have in the offing, certain taxi drivers, Captain, who carried passengers in whom we all have an interest. Could I speak with them—here?" Homer asked.

"Glad to have you," the captain said, and an officer was dispatched. He returned with three taxi drivers.

Greeting them pleasantly, Homer began, "Gentlemen. Do any of you know a piano player named Jellyroll Morton?"

"I do," said No. 3, from left to right.

"Did you drive him anywhere this morning, just after 4 o'clock?"

"I did."

"Where?"

"From in front of this hotel to the South Station," the cabman said.

"Mr. Jellyroll Morton descended there, and entered the railroad terminal?"

"I don't know. At that hour, there was almost no traffic, so I drove away without noticing which way he went."

"Thank you," Evans said. "You may go to the room in which you've been kept waiting, and order whatever refreshments you want—at our expense. Tell all the others that the invitation holds good for them."

Two taxi drivers remained. Homer continued, "Were either of you stationed near the Lehigh Clinic this afternoon, about 2:30 o'clock?"

Both of them said, "Yes, sir."

"Which of you was on the same side of the street as the clinic?"

No. 1 spoke up. "I was."

"And a passenger you have identified from a photograph came out of the clinic rather hastily, and got into your cab, asking you to drive him to No. 14 Newbury Street?" Homer asked.

"The officers didn't show me no photograph. I recognized the passenger's description. And his face, in Doc Ford's morgue," the chauffeur said.

"Good appetite," Homer said, and dismissed No. 1. The sole remaining cabman held himself in readiness.

"Were you instructed to follow the lead cab, on the haul we've just described?" asked Homer.

"Yes, sir. A tall dark man in a terrible hurry breezed out of the clinic, crossed the street against traffic—I thought more than once he was a goner, that he'd got himself clipped. He hops into my cab and says 'Don't let that one get out of sight,' meaning the cab my friend was driving with the deceased, who was then alive. My tall, dark passenger stopped me a short distance from No. 14 Newbury, watched the dead man get out, alive, of course. My passenger sat tight until after the other guy went into the house, then he stepped out, on the wrong side, paid me, and started away."

"In which direction?" asked Homer.

"Toward Newbury Street and the railroad tracks beyond," the cab driver said.

"You watched him go all the way to the railroad property?"

"No. I only got the impression he was headed that way," the taxi man said.

Ryan started to growl, but the captain restrained him.

"Thank you," Evans said, and the last of the cabmen withdrew.

Mirakian, who had been sitting bug-eyed, as if he had expected the roof to cave in upon him, tried to relax without attracting attention. Solange let a cigarette slip from her fingers to the tablecloth, and Bengay retrieved it with almost ludicrous dispatch.

Sergeant Ryan wheeled on Finke. "Where were you between 2:30 and 3, False Bottom?"

"I was smelling some imported perfume. That's a hobby of mine," Finke volunteered. "Then I dropped in, somewhere, and had eight or ten drinks."

"Chanel No. 5?"

"No. Old Ripey."

"Did you see any of these taxis or characters your guardian just asked about?" Ryan asked.

"I close my eyes when I'm smelling, and drinks go to my head so I can't notice anything worth remembering," said Finke.

Flossie let out another involuntary laugh.

"What do you do?" demanded Ryan of her.

"Defend myself," Flossie replied.

Homer interposed, gently. "How did you know, Miss Bunter, that Mr. Ferguson did not call for his car in person this afternoon, and that he did not show up at his lodging house last night?"

"This is an outrage," Ferguson bawled.

Homer continued, paying scant attention to the Scot's reaction. "You are fairly intimate with a girl friend who works for Mr. Ferguson, perhaps?"

"Priscilla never mentions Mr. Ferguson's name," Flossie said, positively.

"Many thanks," Homer said. He next singled out the bank clerk named Hector Deal, whom Poole had brought along.

"Mr. Deal," said Homer. "You devote most of your time, as an employee of the Pequot National Bank, Kenmore Branch, to the registration and sale of travelers' checks?"

"I cash them, too, Mr. Evans," answered Deal.

"Ah. You're an expert on signatures?"

"No forgeries have got by me, yet," said Deal, knocking superstitiously on wood.

"Do American customers who buy travelers' checks, of the world-wide agencies, frequently cash in those they have left over, on returning from a foreign voyage, or a trip through other States?"

Hector Deal hesitated, as if the question had disturbed him. "Sometimes," he admitted.

"Have you sold American Express checks lately to a Doctor Hoff, who speaks English with a pronounced German accent?"

"Yes, Mr. Evans. I believe so," Deal said.

Suavely, Evans switched to Edgy Gerry and continued, "How many express checks did Dr. Hoff buy? For his trip to Buenos Aires? The total amount, I mean."

"Now Mr. Evans," objected Edgy Gerry. "I couldn't tell anyone about our customers' affairs without permission." Gerry looked deferentially toward Quincy Cabot.

"Was the amount eleven thousand dollars, five in thousands, fifty in hundreds, and the rest in twenties and tens?" Homer asked, including Cabot, Gerry and Hector Deal in his interrogatory glance.

Deal said, "No. That sale was to another party, day *before* yesterday."

That seemed to satisfy Homer completely. He beamed at Ferguson, who was bristling like a goaded badger. But the Scot could not conceal that he was stunned by Homer's mention of the amount and denomination of the express checks purchased on Monday.

Homer launched into a brief explanation to the Captain. "When Americans set out with funds to visit other countries where currency regulations are strict, the amount they carry with them is noted on a certain leaf of their passport."

To Ferguson, Homer said, glibly, "Mr. Ferguson. Would you mind lending me your passport a moment, so I can show the captain the annotations that were made on your last trip to the Argentine?"

When Ferguson recoiled Homer made haste to offer his amends.

"A thousand pardons," Homer said. "I'd forgotten that your identification papers were stolen last night."

"We've got to get moving," Ryan insisted. "Can't you cut this short?"

"I won't detain you much longer," Homer promised. "Just a word with Mr. Cleaves. Mr. Jed Cleaves is the manager of the Boston branch of the United Fruit Company. He was kind enough to join us, at my suggestion, this evening."

"Pleasure's all mine," Jed Cleaves said, tersely.

"Your company, Mr. Cleaves, operates a steamship line or network?"

"Mostly for bananas. A few passengers," Cleaves answered.

"One of your vessels now in the port of Boston is the *Cecilie?*"

"Yep."

"Bound for Guayaquil, Valparaiso, and around the Horn?"

"Right."

"As I understand it, the *Cecilie* was scheduled to depart from Boston day after tomorrow, that is to say, late Friday afternoon. A change of plans resulted in moving the sailing date back twenty-four hours, so that actually the *Cecilie* will leave tomorrow, or Thursday afternoon," Homer said.

"Correct. Couldn't be helped. Happens often," Cleaves said.

"Is there a Dr. Helmut Hoff on your passenger list?"

"There is," Cleaves said.

Bengay exclaimed in surprise. "That name wasn't on there at noon today."

"No, it wasn't. He was booked this P.M.," Cleaves said.

"Any other late bookings, today?"

Cleaves looked pained, waited, then said, reluctantly, "Can't say."

Homer did not seem disappointed. "Could you look around this table and tell us if any of our companions have traveled on your liners before, several voyages, to various South American ports? From which a flight to Buenos Aires is bumpy but otherwise easy?"

"'Tain't my place to do a thing like that," Cleaves said.

"No matter. There are records—authorities of the port of Boston, returns to Immigration authorities, State Department's passport files. We can do it the hard way."

"Sorry," said Cleaves.

"Just one more question," Homer said. "Did anybody in your organization telephone Mr. Ferguson, or try to telephone him, last night, or early this morning, about the change in the *Cecilie's* sailing date?"

"I didn't," Cleaves said.

"Did you instruct or suggest to anyone that such a message should be communicated to listed passengers, and prospective last-minute bookings?"

"Wouldn't have to," said Cleaves. "Any of my help has sense enough for that."

"Much obliged," Evans said.

"And much obliged to you, sir," Captain Moriarty said to Homer.

"You're magnanimous," Homer said. "Could I make a last request?"

"Just name it," the Captain said, expansively.

"Your Sergeant Ryan," said Homer, "has it in mind to take our friend, Ferguson, into custody, and charge him with failing to report an assault with a dangerous weapon, and a robbery. Since he, himself, was the only victim, and because of his business affairs any publicity or scandal would do him irreparable injury, won't you stretch a point, and leave him at large?"

Ryan stormed and protested. "He's all ready to fly the coop!"

"I'll guarantee that he'll come back, without delay, from wherever he goes to swell our foreign trade, and improve our economy— as well as his own. Our honest businessmen are unofficial ambassadors."

"Will Mr. Ferguson co-operate, and help us catch the hold-up man, who swings spittoons?" the captain asked, with a twinkle in his eye.

"Privately," Homer said. "You won't say a word to the press?"

"If you won't lift your finger to hide this Jellyroll," the Captain said.

"He doesn't value my advice," Homer said, regretfully.

The police departed, the hotel employees went back to their duties, recreations or repose. And the company around the large round tables in the Lantern Room settled down to make a fitting finale, of some hours' duration, that would blot out the interruption of a memorable social evening.

13
Woman, in Her Hours of Ease

AFTER THE MUSIC, low and insidious, and the liquor, hazy and high; the police, light and heavy; shocks, contradictions and companionships; alliances, forward and back; there were three or four, or maybe more of our characters who tossed or smarted in their beds, or, possumlike, dissembled motionless. The questioning had not been disastrous, the festivities had been rare. No one had been jailed, or accused of murder, among those who had met in the Lantern Room.

In their suite, before and after Finke's tardy return, Homer walked to and fro, not too far from the phone, and what he expected failed to happen. No message. The Boston *Herald*, according to his arrangements, would come out with a sensational front page and, without disclosures embarrassing to Angus Ferguson, would tell much of the lurid tale involving the death of Blaise Laneer and Dr. Rodolfo Gonzalez. It would be made clear that the police were sure that Laneer had been stabbed by Jellyroll Morton, and even clearer that the *Herald*, on the highest authority, would not buy the official solution. Señorita Erica Strella would be described as the "phantom brunette," who had no decipherable past.

Concerning the death of Dr. Gonzalez, Homer had persuaded Dr. Abel Deyo to be quoted as asserting categorically that the young Argentine visitor had been "psychologically incapable of self-destruction."

"Jellyroll hasn't called, or sent word?" Finke asked.

"Not yet. This makes little sense," Homer said.

"Sure. I understand," Finke said, insidiously. "You don't care what happens to a pair of lovers, as long as they agonize logically."

"Precisely," Homer agreed, absentmindedly. Then he added, more lucidly, "He can't have spirited her out of town. The police have sewed up the exits."

Impatiently, considering his even temperament, Homer added, "Jellyroll is playing straight into Ryan's hand. He's building up a case against himself. We know, and possibly Ryan has found out, that Laneer was somehow involved with Señorita Strella. We know that Jellyroll might have misconstrued the situation, and probably was consuming himself with jealousy. From Ryan's angle, the perfect motive for murder. Our Missouri jazz man is not the intellectual type. Away from a keyboard, he is more likely to be wrong than right," Homer said.

"Nevertheless and notwithstanding, I'm going to bed," said Finke.

Just after Leverett Bengay had said a fond, inconclusive good night to Solange, Mirakian had reported to Lever in detail, and of all Mirak had added to what Bengay already knew, one factor outweighed all the rest. The *La Prensa* man, to whom the late Dr. Gonzalez had introduced Blaise Laneer, had been the "tall, dark stranger" described by the taxi man. *La Prensa*, whose name was Julio Etchegaray, had followed Laneer from the clinic to within sight of No. 14 Newbury Street. The name "Etchegaray" was lettered on a card on a door in the brownstone death house.

Back in his comfortable quarters at the Mayflower Club, Bengay could not sleep. He wanted Solange. He wouldn't hesitate an instant, if, in order to have her, he had to marry her. Such was his desperation. He didn't care how it came about, one way or the other, if he could hold out for unconditional surrender. How much he loved her was beside the point. He longed for *her* to love *him*. He was candid enough with himself to admit that such a development seemed highly unlikely. Perhaps if he could solve the murder case, or cases, outwitting Finke Maguire, he would not be a dead duck as far as Solange was concerned. He could not throw up the sponge, no matter how long the odds were against him. He decided that, first thing in the morning, he would have to consult the janitor at 14 about Etchegaray, then somehow question Etchegaray in person. Failing direct contact with the *La Prensa* man, Bengay would take a morning plane to New York, where the exiled editor-in-chief of the stricken South American daily was. The editor-in-chief would surely have a wealth of information about his Boston representative, and the Boston colony of visiting Argentines.

In her high suite on the Commonwealth Avenue side of the Dorsetshire, Solange was "the prey of conflicting emotions." She was bewildered as well as piqued. How could she have been so mistaken about Finke? When her tender sensibilities allowed her thoughts to crystallize, she was determined to prove that she was not a fool.

Just how? By saving and exonerating the helpless Señorita Strella, and, incidentally, her thick-headed Jellyroll. That meant finding Miss Strella. Solange resolved to devote to a weak woman's problem a strong woman's approach and resourcefulness.

Homer Evans? Her heart thumped off the beat when she thought of Homer. The great man, the Topside Joss of mayhem and plot, had shown all too plainly that he was content to toss the Mademoiselle from Montreal, riches, responsibilities, attributes and all, to his leg man, Finke Maguire.

She tried to get into "something comfortable." Stripped or strapped, made-up, greased, nightgowned, robed or slippered, Solange was hot and furious.

"Superb vacation," she groaned.

Up to a certain point, the line of her reasoning followed that which Homer Evans had projected, independently. The police of Boston were too well organized to let a suspect slip out of the city. The chances would appear too high against success for the fugitive. A hiding place within the police dragnet would have to be a hideout most skillfully prearranged.

Then came the flash of inspiration. Señorita Strella had an olive complexion, satin smooth, and long wavy hair bleached from childhood to a blondness. Would not Erica and Jellyroll think of camouflage? Not the false hair, charm swellers and bustles of yore, sufficient unto Baker Street. But modern advance guard progress of the beautician's art.

Solange came alive again, and shed her morbid feelings of frustration. Now that her mind had a springboard, she could elaborate. Jellyroll most certainly had quarters in the Negro district. He would appeal in his frightening emergency to a colored beautician.

How could Solange contact a beautician from around Lafayette Square, who would be sharp enough to trust her, and to understand that she was acting for Erica's own good?

Her self-confidence restored, Solange was able to order and eat a nourishing breakfast. As soon as the Boston department stores were open, she taxied to Filene's, to consult with a friend of long standing, who sold cosmetics and beauticians' supplies. The veteran saleslady was pleased to recommend an expert operator, call the girl on the telephone and arrange for her to go to Solange's suite in the Dorsetshire, bringing the necessary equipment for a "cold wave" with trimmings, at 9:30 o'clock.

Not more than a quarter of an hour past the appointed time, a stylish, trim and somewhat wistful coffee-colored young woman, about five years younger than Solange, presented herself. Her name was Evelina Boulanjay. The beauty shop in which she worked was on the lower end of Columbus Avenue, and was named The Capillary Castle. With her Tonkinese hairdo, Evelina had a certain resemblance to Josephine Baker. Her voice was soft, and her movements rhythmic. Her eyes glowed with frustrated spirit.

First, Solange submitted to Evelina's ministrations, and found that she was pleasant company and very dextrous and competent.

"Do you often have clients whose hair has been bleached, who change their minds and ask you to make it black, again?" Solange asked. She had tried not to make the transition abrupt, but Evelina was demoralized. She realized she had gone too far to retain Evelina's confidence, unless she took the plunge.

"Please believe that I'm Jellyroll's friend," she said.

Evelina turned a pale lavender, and dropped an expensive implement. She did not look resentful, but deeply afraid.

"Don't be frightened," Solange began.

"You just couldn't be the law. You *couldn't*," Evelina said.

"Thanks. I'm not. I'm exactly what I represented myself to be."

"Then how could you guess it was me who did the job?" asked Evelina.

"I'm trying to help," said Solange.

"Help who?"

"That nice foreign girl Jellyroll's trying to hide. He's got himself and her into trouble, big trouble," said Solange.

"So what do we do?" asked Evelina. "They didn't tell me what they were wanted for. I liked to fainted when I saw the *Herald* this morning."

The wave and hair-do were finished, so Solange insisted that Evelina put her apparatus and tools aside and relax. "I want you to listen, carefully," she said. "I want you to go back to your district, find Jellyroll's sweetheart, Miss Erica Strella, and bring her with you to the Arnold Arboretum. Taxi to the entrance on Route 138. Take the pathway to the grove of lindens, sit on a bench, in the shade if you can, and wait. I'll meet you there at noon."

The dazed beautician was anxious and tremulous. "But how can I sell that foreign refugee on such a proposition? She's afraid of her own shadow."

"You'll have to make her believe we've been in touch with Jellyroll, and he wants her to stick with you and me, and follow our advice."

"Suppose she's had a chance to check with Jellyroll?"

"You know better than that. Once Jellyroll, who's what you call 'hot,' got her safely disguised, he wouldn't go near her or risk trying to communicate with her, directly, until they're in the clear. Unless Jellyroll's dumber than I think he is."

"I've never seen a man so love-sprung," Evelina said. She sighed. "I'll try," she promised. "How I'll try!"

"Exactly at noon. Dismiss your taxi. My car'll be waiting across the park, along Route 1. I'll be at the linden grove ahead of you. You'll find me, all right."

14
An Arrest at Last

W‌HEN F‌INKE AWOKE, about 9 o'clock that morning, refreshed and ready for anything not too strenuous or boring, he found that Homer had departed for the Arboretum on the dot of 5, and had left him a note.

"Would you mind checking on Etchegaray, and conferring with Poole at the bank? I look forward to seeing you this evening," the note read.

"The s.o.b.," grunted Finke, but he was not displeased. By the time he got over to No. 14 Newbury Street, the janitor told him Mr. Bengay already had been there, but that Mr. Etchegaray had left, sometime yesterday evening, "on a trip."

"Did he take any baggage, an overnight bag . . . ?"

"What he took was in his pockets," the janitor said.

"How did Bengay feel about that? Did you open up the room for him to case?"

"Who wouldn't, in my position, for money?" the janitor asked. "The way I look at it, if a tenant's got nothing to hide, of a criminal nature, he's got nothing to lose if some nosy party verifies his innocence. And if a tenant's been up to something wrong, and is exposed, that's only justice."

"What's the fee? For casing an apartment?" asked Finke.

"Whatever you can spare," the janitor said. "It's all velvet."

Finke slipped the Cockney a dix, and added the amount to his unwritten expense account. The janitor went up with him, and stood inside the doorway.

"I like to watch," he said.

Finke set to work, methodically. The janitor was intrigued, then impressed, then flabbergasted.

"There's tricks to every trade," he said, in praise.

Finke did not bother to answer. What he was finding added up to zero—just personal effects. But items he had expected would be there, and he missed, gave him food for thought, in quite a number of courses.

"Is he clean?" the janitor asked.

"You can say that again and again," Finke grunted, and made ready to depart.

"You haven't had any questions from the police, about this Etchegaray?"

"Not a peep. Should I have? Say, Mr. Maguire. I hope I'm not going to have any more vacancies just now. I've had two, already, in less than twenty-four hours."

"Think nothing of it," said Finke. "Apartments like these can't be hard to rent, at two hundred a month, to the class of people this joint seems to attract." Finke touched his temple and rotated his forefinger.

"I read that 17 per cent of all of us will wind up in some kind of a bughouse. That gives a man pause."

Nodding, Finke was again about to set out for the bank. "So long, Compos Mentis," he said.

"Don't forget the pass-key's always out," the janitor said. "Is this call of yours top-secret, or just confidential?"

"Better let it slip your mind," admonished Finke.

On his way to the Kenmore Branch of the Pequot National, Finke spotted, in a dim doorway on the shady side of Beacon Street, two men whose silhouettes corresponded with those of Sergeant Aloysius Ryan and Captain Moriarty. Pretending not to have noticed them, he entered the bank by the customers' arched marble door. Inside, he found Ephraim Poole in Cabot's fenced-off enclosure. The accountant had spent the night in Daisy's apartment, poring over the documents he had collected. She had slumbered, half-smiling, in the stillness of her boudoir. When he had joined Vice President Cabot at 9 o'clock, just before the police and district attorney's accountants had descended on them, he had in his commodious sconce much information. To Cabot he reiterated what he had prophesied the evening before. The late Blaise Laneer had stolen nothing from the bank, but he had used its facilities, and his position there, to carry on private operations.

"What kind of private operations?" asked Finke.

The accountant was puzzled. "Something unlike any I've encountered before. Laneer cashed, put through this bank and the clearing house, any number of small personal checks that had been held months beyond a reasonable period. Practically all of them had been written by Americans in Buenos Aires, and had been endorsed by Argentines, individuals or firms, down there. None of them seemed to have been endorsed by parties who cashed them here. Laneer didn't put his name or initials on any of them. They did not pass through any regular account, and disturbed no balance sheets."

"How many of them bounced?"

"None of them. Not one, that's on record."

"So what's the harm?" asked Cabot, relieved.

Poole looked pained. "That's what's so fantastic," he groaned.

Their act was interrupted by the entrance of Sergeant Ryan, who forged ahead belligerently as Captain Moriarty seemed content to lag behind.

When Ryan came abreast, Finke unceremoniously thumbed him to the rear. "Your fumblers are out back," he said. "They've found no deficit, no defalcation, no nothing. You ought to give them a hand."

Instead, Ryan and the captain came into Cabot's enclosure and sat down. Ryan was grinning. "That fits," he said. "With jealousy the motive, why dig for complications?"

"You may have something there, since you can't produce your man. Maybe you shouldn't waste time here, with us. You ought to be tightening your dragnet," Finke said.

Ryan deadpanned. To Cabot he said, "You're a gentleman, Mr. Cabot. Know anything about Bengay? Where he might be found this morning?"

"You've got me. Haven't heard a word from Bengay," Vice President Cabot said.

The sergeant looked inquiringly at Poole, who had nothing to offer on the subject. Finke wasn't even asked. So he guessed that Bengay must have hopped into the void, and that Ryan was sore about his disappearance.

"I thought you had the exits from the city covered, as a matter of routine. What's gone wrong? Or did somebody get careless?" said Finke.

"Those crêpe hangers at the Mayflower Club claim Mr. Bengay's gone to New York," Ryan said, sullenly. "Just because we were decent enough not to order you all not to leave town, that dude takes advantage . . ."

"You still don't tell us about his means of transportation. He sure as hell didn't walk," said Finke.

"And he didn't ride no train, or drive a car, or fly. We're not too dumb to cover the airports and permits for private flights," the sergeant said.

Finke grinned. "You didn't take a look at Bengay's coat lapel. The modest insignia, I mean."

"So he was in the war!" Ryan sneered.

Poole interposed laconically. "Mr. Bengay was in the air force, with desk space in Washington, Cairo, Ankara, Bangkok—spots like those."

The light that dawned over Sergeant Ryan's face revealed a kind of no man's land. "A military plane," he grunted. "What can policemen do about that?"

"Many thanks—for the co-operation," the captain said.

"They probably gave Bengay the idea," Ryan said.

The right-hand phone on Cabot's desk rang discreetly. The correct vice president took the instrument from the cradle, held the receiver to his ear, and was rewarded by blurts and cracklings. "This is what happens when Gerry's not here. The minutest details get confused. . . . Hello. Hello. Cabot, here. Whom did you want?" With a discomfited "Oh" he proffered the phone to Captain Moriarty.

That distinguished-looking officer who held his temper, remembered his manners, and left most of the tumult and the shouting to his subordinate in rank, listened. Words entered his ear. His tolerant smile persisted.

"Now, isn't that fine!" he said, into the transmitter.

More words from the receiver, intelligible only to Moriarty.

"No, not there. Here. I'm at the Pequot National Bank, in Kenmore Square. With (he glanced merrily at Ryan) three guesses who, or whom."

The phone transmitted more words, spaced like dots and dashes.

"Bring everything," the captain said. He replaced the phone, and sat expectantly, waiting for someone else to sustain the interrupted conversation.

"May I ask a question?" Finke said, after raising his hand and appealing to Sergeant Ryan.

The sergeant, who seemed reassured and less unhappy because of the Captain's self-satisfied behavior, replied, "You can always ask. It's what you get that counts."

"O.K. I'll ask the higher level. Captain," Finke said. "Would you tell a shamus about the contents of Gonzalez' stomach? You must have had a report from Doc Ford."

"There was a strong dose of . . ." the captain referred to a slip of paper he took from a vest pocket. "Of *hyoscyamos niger*," he said.

"What's that in English?" asked Finke, but, to the surprise of them all, Quincy Cabot, Harvard '38, let out a chuckle.

"My word," he said. "Not *hyoscyamos niger?*"

"That's what the doc called it," said the captain.

"It just happens," Cabot said, "that to get my diploma from Harvard—the necessary credits, I mean—I was obliged to write a thesis. English A."

"And so?" encouraged the captain.

"I was given an idea by one of my classmates. A new angle on Shakespeare. I put in some hours at the Harvard Library, and jotted down the Shakespearean characters who were murdered—you get my drift—the weapons, opportunities, motives. It was a cinch. Naturally I padded out the piece with technical terms, and that's how I happened to remember about *hyoscyamos niger*."

"Well. What about it?" demanded Ryan. It was apparent that both officers were not clear about the nature of the poison Gonzalez had swallowed.

"You'll recall that Hamlet's father—who shows up in Scene I, Act I, as a ghost—had been murdered by a brother who thus had usurped the throne, and the queen, Hamlet's mother, in the bargain," said Cabot. "The dead king, gentlemen, had been poisoned with *hyoscyamos niger*, or henbane, which is rough on humans as well as chicks. It grows wild, in any temperate climate. A child could gather it, steep it, and dispense it."

"Not make it into tablets like aspirin pills," Ryan said. "Unless the kid was a prodigy. What's the difference whether this Gonzalez killed himself on purpose, or picked up the wrong bottle somewhere in that clinic? We're giving him the benefit of the doubt" (he crossed himself) "on account of his religion."

Just then the door revolved, the doorman stiffened disapprovingly, and two uniformed patrolmen came in, with Jellyroll Morton between them. As they approached the Cabot enclosure, Finke said, disgustedly, to the piano player, "Good morning."

Jellyroll made no answer. He did not act worried at all.

Ryan, gloating, asked the cops, "Where'd you find him, boys?"

One cop said, uneasily. "In a pastry shop, right smack in Lafayette Square. Eating those cones chuck full of whipped cream. *Charlotte Russe* they call 'em."

Before they got much further, another surprise entrance occurred, that of St. Clair Endicott. The sight of the famous lawyer caused Ryan to bristle. "Did you saps let him phone his lawyer?" the sergeant demanded of the cops.

"I haven't any lawyer. Don't need one," Jellyroll said.

The big corporation attorney shrugged. "Most probably you don't need counsel. Unless you get tired of a cell, and want someone to dash around with a writ of *habeas corpus*."

"Don't worry. I'll sit it out," said Jellyroll. "Providing these mugs let me have my meals sent in." He touched his middle gingerly. "The old gut," he said.

"Ask 'em to keep you in the old Charles Street jail," advised Finke. "You can have anything sent in to you, there, so I hear: women, wine, forbidden books, reefers, even Coke if you like it."

"Milk and the white meat of chicken," Jellyroll specified, doggedly.

"If you need a few doctor's certificates . . ." St. Clair Endicott suggested.

"You heard him say he didn't want counsel," Ryan said. "What are you, all of a sudden? A patrol-wagon chaser? First thing you know, you'll be the first of the Endicotts ever to come up for censure before the Bar Association."

"Let me tell you about the old Chinese philosopher, Lao-tse, who fished with straight hooks, so the fish having bitten, could hold on or not, as they pleased," said Endicott.

"An officer gets a liberal education around here," Ryan said. "Shakespeare, Confucius, Freud. Can't we ring in Einstein and Holy Moses, somehow?"

"Now never mind Moses," Captain Moriarty said, with that special blank expression reserved for disapproving cracks of a sacrilegious nature.

"He broke the Tablets of the Law," remarked Poole.

"Well, I wasn't on the force then," the captain said, severely. He rose to go. "Come on, Aloysius. We've got the murderer, although, so help me, he doesn't look as if he'd kill a mouse. If it weren't for that green-eyed goddess, our job would be a pipe."

With his most disarming expression, Finke made a last appeal. "I'm pleading with you to think this over, Captain. You're a good scout, at heart, no matter what kind of flunkeys you have under you. Don't bring discredit on yourself, and the force. You must know something of Mr. Evans' reputation. Somewhere in the back of your brain, all fogged with officialdom, you must have a core of hard common sense. This suspect of yours is not guilty. This Dr. Gonzalez could not have scrambled bottles, or poisoned himself on purpose. The deaths are connected. Why don't you get on to yourself, and slide out from under, while there's time?"

"Nuts to all this. Let's go," said Jellyroll, impatiently.

"See? He asks for it," the captain said, and the police, plus Jellyroll, departed.

Cabot faced Finke and Poole questioningly. "Well, gentlemen," he said. "I may as well admit that I'm deeper in the fog than before. Could you heave me a line?"

Finke and Poole looked at each other, like Alphonse and Gaston. The accountant was the first to speak.

"Jellyroll gave himself up, when it pleased him, and wants to stay in quod."

"The opposite of claustrophobia," St. Clair Endicott said. "Comparatively rare."

"He's afraid," said Finke, "that if they turn him loose, he'll be unable to control his yen, and lead them to where he's cached away La Strella."

They bought that.

Without delay, Finke grabbed the nearest phone and got Daisy on the wire. "Sorry to break your sleep. I'll make it up someday," said Finke.

She was still drowsy, but not too far gone to retort, "I'll hold you to that, if Mr. Evans gives the O.K."

"I'll tell him you'd rather have him. He's naïf about those things," said Finke. "Now, to business. I want you to check with everybody around the hotel, everyone you can trust. I've got to know, and soon, whether any cop, plain-clothes man, stool pigeon, or shamus has questioned the bartender who was on duty last night, just off the Lantern Room, between 6 and 8 o'clock."

As Finke hung up, Poole nodded. "Evans told me you and he were drinking there sometime between those limits, last evening, with Dr. Gonzalez and this man representing *La Prensa*. It's about that fellow, by the way, that Bengay's flown to New York. It seems Lever couldn't locate the man at his lodgings early this A.M."

The phone rang. Daisy already was prepared to report.

"Only one investigator has questioned the bartender," she said.

"And who was he? The bright one?" Finke asked, crestfallen.

She laughed. "The top of them all. What a man!" she said, rapturously.

Abruptly Finke replaced his phone and faced Endicott, Poole and Quincy Cabot. "Well?" demanded the accountant.

"The master mind," Finke said. "I might have known."

15

In Which Finke Strays Out of His Element

WHEN EVELINA BOULANJAY had passed outward, through the lobby of the Dorsetshire, carrying her neat waving, shampooing and drying kit, she had not noticed that a tall man with dark hair had peered at her, surreptitiously, over the top edge of a newspaper. Had she known that this man had risen leisurely and followed her, she would have gone into a panic. As things were, she was serene, although excited. She was clear about what was expected of her, and how to proceed.

Some time later, Solange rode down in the front elevator, and asked that her car be sent around front. It would take her twenty minutes to reach the entrance of the Arboretum. She allowed herself ten more to walk from there to the bench nearest the linden grove. She had ample time to drive around the Fenway, and the green-shaded thoroughfares and byways. That anyone might be tailing her did not enter her mind.

Exactly at noon, Solange was approaching the bench near the grove of linden trees. She was happy to see, standing close together, in the shade of one of the tallest and shapeliest trees, Evelina and another girl who, making allowances for recent transformations, seemed to answer the description of Erica Strella. Coincidentally, Evelina recognized Solange, so the beautician was beaming when the latter joined her and her trembling charge.

From that point on, things happened so inexorably that Solange felt as if she were performing a spectral role in some incredible play. From the direction of the gate near which she had parked her sedan, she saw a man approaching and realized, almost too late, that he was Edgy Gerry. Knowing that Gerry was working with Homer Evans, Solange was nonplussed. Should the cautious little man, so fond of routine, see her with two colored girls, beneath a linden tree, he would become inquisitive. She wanted to back away, into a thicket, but her indecision rooted her where she stood. She sighed with relief, when the busy bank clerk failed to spot her, and shunted off along a pathway through rushes, luxuriant weeds, cat o' nine tails, milk floss, and wild flowers. So she was not forewarned when a tall dark-haired man moved ominously toward them from the other direction along the pathway, pausing casually from time to time to gaze at an unusual tree or scan a Latin label. The horrible realization, the certainty that he was pretending, grew in the pit of her stomach. And Erica Strella, as supersensitive as a Geiger counter, began to vibrate with fear.

"I'm lost. He's from my country," the señorita gasped.

"Shucks, gal. Pull yourself together," Evelina told her, crossly.

"How can you tell?" asked Solange, in a strained whisper.

"His shoes. His vest," the señorita moaned.

"So what?"

Solange was trying to regain her composure. The summer sunshine was balmy, the hunched shadows indicated noon. Within plain sight stood the Arboretum headquarters, as legal and official as could be. A few scattered wanderers were moving along the pathways or were seated on benches, but none within call. The man, malevolence personified in Latin style, was three yards from them, now, and somehow, after a movement Solange could not follow, an automatic was in his hand, the short barrel pointed first at one of them, then another.

He spoke, in a low tone carrying the maximum of threat and desperate purpose. "One sound, from any of you, and I'll drill that one (indicating Erica) right through the middle, where it hurts the most, and longest."

"What do you want?" asked Solange. "I'm not afraid of your gun."

Something like admiration gleamed in the eyes of the man, and there passed through Solange a dim awareness she had glimpsed

him before. "Your courage is magnificent, but I don't plan to shoot
you. This one!" And again he pointed the automatic toward Erica's
shapely body, exactly centered and a few inches above the waist-
line. "All three of you turn around and walk quietly toward that
small oak."

The three young women complied, and the man followed close
behind them. Solange wheeled, at the end of her temper and patience. "You won't dare shoot," she said. It seemed to her that she
started to scream, realizing that the automatic had been reversed
and raised. She felt an impact, hands clutched her. She fluttered
through a spiral descent into darkness, leaving consciousness behind.

It was just after 12 noon when Finke again tried to telephone
Solange. She had just gone out, alone, he was told. He decided, for
want of another diversion, to taxi out to the Arboretum he had
never seen. He would chat with Evans about gnats and buttercups,
being careful to make no reference to the case. From past experience he knew that he could never get Homer's goat, but maybe he
could cause the creature to fret within its pen.

His taxi driver, who was not too familiar with the outskirts of
town, took him to the Route 1 entrance, and when Finke caught
sight of a certain parked car with a Canada license, he grinned and
warmed as spontaneously as if he had planned the coincidence himself. So that was it.

When he continued along the transverse pathway, the linden
grove attracted him. He decided to leave the path, which originally
must have been a wagon road, and take a short cut to the lindens,
through a corner of some woods of oaks and maples. Once "inside"
he felt more nervous than ever he had in a dangerous city flat entered by means of a skeleton key. Finke thanked whatever gods
there be that a private eye is seldom called upon to case a patch of
wilderness.

He heard a noise. Not the hum of insects or faint rustle of
leaves. Someone was moving, nearby, but out of sight. Finke
stopped short. He heard the sounds again, as if some prowler were

stalking through the brush. Only then it struck him that, maybe, in this Arboretum wild animals might roam.

A twig or two snapped, some pine needles crunched, but ever so lightly. Something was moving, but whatever or whoever it might be, he, she or it was receding. His instinct, which apparently was operating out of doors as it did in city blocks, told him he was alone again. He barged on a few steps, cocksure that his sense of direction was leading him to those linden trees. At the age when Finke might, under other circumstances, have been a Boy Scout, he was acting as waterboy on construction jobs in the slum sections of Boston. For that, he had no regrets. Rubbing sticks together to light Sweet Caporals, when one is twelve years old, is a bit silly if sulphur matches can be pinched at neighborhood groceries.

Suddenly Finke jumped and reared back, like a scared cat. He had almost stepped on a gunnysack. The sack was knotted loosely at the top. Finke stared at it, realized it had contents which took up little of its capacity. He hopped and gasped again when the contents moved. They did not wriggle or undulate, exactly, but, unpracticed as he was in woods lore, and in spite of the crude burlap that screened them, those movements had a meaning of their own. Somehow, their message was so preposterous that it snapped Finke back to his normal courage and presence of mind.

"A bag of snakes," he said. "Now that just can't be beat."

He had an atavistic fear of snakes, although he had hardly ever seen one except through plate glass in a showcase, and to be afraid of anything made him ashamed and resentful. Also, he had such an insatiable curiosity about anything incongruous, he could not be content with merely bypassing the sack and continuing his amble toward the linden trees, and later the swamps where Homer would be browsing around. Resolutely, Finke lifted the knotted end of the large gunnysack and untied it. He held the open end high and peered in. The greenish golden sunlight sifted through foliage and burlap weirdly to reveal at the bottom of the limp container three snakes. No two were alike, in size, coloration, pattern or conformation. The only one which assumed the alert position, uncringing and threatening, was black, with wide open jaws and goo-goo eyes. It was between two and three feet long, and about as thick as a black-skinned knackwurst. Next, Finke made out a kind of sleeping beauty, whose eyes, none the less, were beady and open. The colors were pale ochre, garnet and sienna and the design so harmonious that Finke wished he could buy it on a scarf for Solange. It was somewhat subdued for Flossie Bunter.

Then Finke recoiled again and almost dropped his end of the sack. For he saw what at first glance had been indistinct, almost invisible, because of the greenish-yellow quality of sifted light.

"Hell's bells," muttered Finke. "It must be five yards long." He was referring to a thin, leaf-colored serpent, no bigger around than medium macaroni, and phenomenally long, as if nature had tried to be absurd. That was the one Finke realized he would not touch, directly, for any number of department stores or legacies.

His saner judgment prompted him to knot up the top of the long sack and leave it, and the three snakes, as he had found them. But Finke got stubborn. When he resumed his trek toward the linden grove, he carried the sack by the top end, and held gingerly away from his body. The master mind had urged him, time and time again, never to ignore, while a case was in progress, anything out of the ordinary. If finding a green snake, a piebald one, and a black one, all together in a burlap bag was not odd, then he was Slapsie Maxie.

Again something caused Finke to halt. He saw, just ahead, where trees were spaced more loosely, a small tree with rough bark and gnarled branches. Behind the six-inch trunk, somebody seemed to be hiding. Must be a woman, because of the color of the clothes.

"Hi!" called Finke. "Come on out from behind. I won't bite you." A closer look at the tree and the figure made Finke realize that the woman was tied there, with ropes around her chest and ankles, and her hands bound behind the trunk. Before he could get a close look he was sure the victim was Solange. He gasped with relief when she opened her eyes. While those were unclouding, their beauty tinged with misery, he carefully removed the gag. The size of it, and the way it had been applied with intentional cruelty, made him fighting mad.

"Who did this?" he asked.

Her tongue was swollen and her jaws so stiff she could not in-stantly recover her powers of speech. Finke held himself in check long enough to sketch the knot of the rope that bound her ankles. Ordinary clothesline had been used, but in an unusually skillful way. Evans would know about knots. How soon could Finke find him?

"My handbag," Solange said, with effort. Those were her open-ing words, and she seemed to realize they were empty and auto-matic.

Glancing around, Finke said, "It's gone? That doesn't matter. You're not wounded, or hurt?"

As he spoke he was freeing her arms. Still somewhat dazed, she touched her head, on the top, toward the back.

"Who hit you?"

She couldn't answer directly, but she said, "An automatic."

He nodded. "The butt." He was, meanwhile, lifting her and seat-ing her carefully on a tuffet of dry moss, with the tree trunk for a back rest. He examined the wound, and by that time she was con-scious and clear enough to realize that he was gentle, even tender. A tear escaped from each eye and coursed down her cheeks.

"None of that," he said.

"I've been such a fool," she moaned.

"You must have been trying to help," he said.

"And two nice girls suffer, maybe die, as a result," she said, bitterly.

"The quicker you can brief me, straight," Finke said, "the more of us will stay alive." Seeing how his harsh manner affected her, he added, "Nobody's dead? Nobody new, I mean?"

She told him, then, suffused with shame, about her sleepless night, and her line of reasoning which led her to Evelina, who pro-duced Erica Strella; and then about the tall South American, whose threats had been aimed at Jellyroll's timid sweetheart.

"Good work," Finke said, "as far as it went. Where you muffed your chance was failing to get in touch with me."

"You'd tricked me, and Mr. Bengay."

"Is that what you thought?" asked Finke. He was too obstinate to explain that he had not known when he sent her on her errand, that Laneer was dead, or that 784 Massachusetts Avenue was the medical examiner's office and emergency morgue.

"Never mind me. Finke! Find those girls, before it's too late, if it isn't already . . ."

"It isn't too late, the way I figure," he said.

"What can I possibly do now, to save Evelina and Erica? You didn't see that man, his evil brown eyes, the way he moved and threatened. There's nothing that man wouldn't do. He's desperate!"

"He's never had it really tough," Finke said, grimly. "He'll learn, the hard way, how it feels to take what he tries to dish out. You can count on Homer, I give you my word. He got you into this, and he won't let you down."

"I'm counting on you," she said. "But what can *I* do? I'll go crazy, just waiting around."

"Listen," he said, "You beat it back to that hotel, call Mirakian and tell him I said for you two to stick together. At least, till Bengay gets back. If that tough Latin has snatched those girls, he'll be expecting money. From you." Finke gestured, opening and extending his hands. "That means you've got to hold yourself available."

"You don't think we should notify the police?" she asked, hesitantly.

"Let Evans decide things like that," said Finke.

"What shall I do, if I hear from that man—or anyone else who says he's in with him?" she asked.

"Phone Evans and me, through the director's office out here. We'll be in touch. Now run along. And I'm not tossing you into anybody's arms. This jam is serious. We all started out having fun, like a bunch of kids, and now—we got to grow up, for a while."

He stood there, on the rim of the park exit, and watched her try the door of her car. The car key must also have been taken by the Latin. Then he sighed with relief as she produced a duplicate key from a neat St. Christopher locket she wore on a chain around her neck. He waved as the car started off, but she did not turn back.

"So she's one up," he grunted, and made a dash along the transverse pathway toward Route 138 and the group of headquarters buildings which included Dr. Holz's snug bungalow, a public museum, and other facilities. His first thought had been to consult the director, then second judgment came to his rescue. A man in Dr. Holz's position, informed that a woman had been assaulted with a dangerous weapon, gagged and bound, and that two other girls had been, presumably, kidnapped, would be forced by all standards of ethics and prudence to phone the police authorities without delay. No. Finke must locate Homer. He remembered that Solange had mentioned Edgy Gerry, and that just before the South American ladykiller had arrived, the busy little bank clerk had veered into the woods and fens, taking a north-easterly direction. Finke tossed his bag of snakes for safe keeping into a commodious crotch of one of the fragrant linden trees. He continued along the edge of the transverse path until he stumbled on a smaller pathway which he believed Gerry must have followed.

What irked Finke most, in the dappled shade of the summer afternoon—it was not later than 2 o'clock—was his own uncertainty. In almost any kind of surroundings inhabited by his fellow-men, he could make up his mind, and act. As often as not, he might pull a boner, but at least he could make decisions. Here, where nature had been encouraged by Ph.D.'s with manure, tools and funds, he was nowhere. Also, it was up to him to be silent and wary. If the South American heavy should spot him, and be forewarned, it would be next to impossible even for Homer to save the situation. Two men had died already. Laneer evidently had been up to some hanky-panky involving easy money. Gonzalez, Finke believed, had been a good fellow quite innocent of guile. Now it was a question of two girls. Also Solange's peace of mind.

Whatever he seemed to use for a footing turned out soft and soggy, or made him sound like a rambling rhino. He could not refrain from looking for blacksnakes underfoot, and tree snakes, those vile long thin monstrosities, overhead. Faint sounds of traffic along one or both of the automobile routes, north or south, mingled with the scolding of jays, the tap-tap of peckers, the rustle of thrushes and the racket he was making, himself. When he halted, trying to determine from which direction sounds came, he got more mixed up than before. Some paces back, the trodden pathway had taken a bend he did not care for, and he had forsaken it. Later, when he tried to refind it, he got tangled up in briers and poison ivy. The nature of his errand made it unwise for him to shout or whistle. His shirt and union suit were wet with sweat, his eyes were sore from straining. He felt, not angry, but aggrieved, as if the other side was getting all the breaks. Finke was out of his element, out of sorts, and on top of that he itched and ached. Also he smarted and dripped.

Infrequently Finke had eaten woodcock, but he had never seen one uncooked. So when, at a moment he and all his verdant and animate surroundings were achieving an approximation of silence, a vicious sudden rustle and whirring in the brush a few feet ahead of him caused him to recoil, his back hair prickling. The swift bird catapulted upward and away on a slant. Finke, tough as he was, was startled and confused. That instant off-guard was enough. He felt hands clasping him across the eyes from behind—hands filled with a substance which got into his eyes while they still were wide open, and transformed the sylvan world into a stickiness and dark-ness. Instinctively his hands clutched where his sight had been and he kicked backwards, only to find that his assailant had got around front, booted him in one shin, and as he fell flat on his face, hit him hard on the back of the head with a heavy, rough weapon. Finke was stunned, but not completely out, so he clutched for a leg hold, got a small tree trunk instead, and rocked his head to one side. The second blow caught him on the collar bone and his hunched shoulder. The third landed on the side of his head, across the face. Finke went out.

16

More Blessed to Give Than Receive

AT 11:30 THAT MORNING, Homer Evans, squatting amid flags and sweet grass to watch certain detached sun- and butter-worts afloat on an evaporating pool, had to acknowledge that his mind was wandering. The perverse little plants were snaring, for sport, the tiniest insects (called by the native Redskins, No-see-'ums) although they did not need them for nourishment. Homer's attention was divided, so that he was not doing full justice, either to his scientific research or the best interest of his friends. The death of Blaise Laneer, whatever bearing it might have on international currency exchange, had not moved him deeply. The sad fate of. Dr. Gonzalez was on his conscience. Evans had liked Gonzalez, on short acquaintance.

So Homer, always honest with himself, rose, shrugged and forsook the northeastern area of the Arboretum. He headed straight for Dr. Holz's bungalow and was relieved to find that the genial director had not yet come in for lunch. Homer at once availed himself of the doctor's telephone. He dialed the Dorsetshire and inquired for Finke, only to be informed that Finke "had gone out." Evans tried the Pequot National, and got Poole on the line. It was thus he learned that traces of henbane, or *hyoscyamos niger*, had been found in Dr. Gonzalez' stomach, along with the salycilic acid which is a component of aspirin. He telephoned Dr. Abel Deyo and the Lehigh Clinic, ascertained that henbane was not among the multitudinous drugs, poisons and elixirs in stock there, and had never been used, as far as records showed. So Homer arranged with

Dr. Deyo to have certain experiments made, to establish how easy or difficult it might be to combine the deadly poison which had killed Hamlet's father with drugstore aspirin.

The next on Homer's telephone list was a certain assistant secretary of state, in Washington. From him he ascertained that Angus Ferguson had reported, by emergency call, the loss of his passport, with visas permitting him to travel in Ecuador, Chile and the Peron-styled Argentine "republic." Ferguson had requested that a duplicate be issued, and delivered to him aboard the United Fruiter *Cecilie* when she touched New York tomorrow (Friday) noon.

"Can you possibly arrange that, in time?" Homer asked. The assistant secretary answered, "In a pinch. He's in excellent standing. Legitimate business reasons for the voyage."

"Thanks," Homer said. "Will you send me a letter establishing that he lost the original?"

"If you say so," the key man of the State Department agreed.

"And advise Mr. Jed Cleaves, Boston manager of the United Fruit Company, to issue Ferguson a ticket," continued Evans.

Homer dialed again, and talked with Flossie Bunter. She had not told Priscilla Appleby where she had been last night.

"Good girl," Evans said.

"I couldn't," Flossie said. "She'd hate me. She'd be so jealous she would die."

"Fine," said Homer.

Because no taxi could possibly weave through the maze of Boston traffic at that hour, fast enough to suit him, he took the liberty of borrowing the director's coupe. At the entrance of the Museum building, in which Edgy Gerry was working on statistics, Homer paused long enough to inform the displaced bank clerk that he would be "in the western section of the woods" all afternoon, in search of *hyoscyamos niger*. The term apparently meant nothing to Gerry.

An hour later, Homer arrived at Ferguson's office building in Essex Street. He was received by Miss Appleby, who raised her unpenciled eyebrows. "Well?"

"I want to ask a few questions about your employer's affairs," Homer said.

"He doesn't confide in me."

"He's sailing, as you know, this afternoon," Homer said. "I tried to reach him at his lodgings."

"He's sailing! This afternoon?"

"Oh, come now. You're his private secretary. You don't mean, seriously, that he goes on business trips without telling you," Homer suggested, suavely.

The flower of old New England was quivering with wrath and resentment. "Mr. Ferguson, because of the stiff competition in his business, cannot announce his plans. Some other wool man might get ahead of him," she said.

"No need to get excited," Homer said, soothingly, and then remembered to introduce himself. "I'm Homer Evans."

"A detective!"

"Skip technicalities, which, by the way, I scrupulously observe. Just tell Mr. Ferguson that before he writes any personal checks, down where he's going, he'd better read the papers. And that if he doesn't want you questioned, officially, in his absence, he'd better take you along."

"You're not only a snooper, you're a panderer!" she said.

"A traitor to my sex, I fear," admitted Homer. "In short, a friend. Sorry I shan't be seeing you both at the pier."

In the ground-floor lobby, Homer entered a phone booth. He called the Dorsetshire. Finke was still out of touch. He asked for Solange. The unbelievable promptness with which she replied startled him.

"Oh. Thank God! It's Mr. Evans!" she said.

"What's so wonderful about that?" Homer asked, bewildered.

"I'm so relieved that Finke found you," she gasped.

"Finke? He hasn't found me, nor I him. What's all this about?"

"Where are you?"

"Downtown."

"Please come here, quick!" she begged.

Homer knew that Solange was not one to go off the deep end for trifles. He was at the Dorsetshire in no time. Once in Solange's suite, Homer learned of her adventures since morning, of her rescue by Finke, and of Finke's eagerness to get co-operation.

"You've been here, all the time?" Homer asked Solange.

"Sitting here with Mirak, trying not to go crazy. Just waiting. And nothing happening," she said. Mirakian, who seemed quite at ease, as if mild worry were his normal state, shrugged.

It took Homer only an instant to phone Dr. Holz. The director reported that all was quiet on the tree front, except that one of his men seemed to have misplaced a burlap bag containing some snakes.

"No word from a Mr. Finke Maguire?"

"Not a peep," the director said. "But where are you? Your statistics chap, Gerry, said you were picking something or other in the western section this afternoon. How come? Your meat-eating varieties are all to the east of the central pathway, where our slopes fall away."

He told the director that he would be out there, shortly, and, instructing Solange to stand by, sped to the Arboretum.

When Finke regained enough consciousness to be aware that he had been unconscious for some time, he was careful, in spite of the smarting and pasty discomfort under his eyelids, not to open them. At first he was afraid he had been put in some kind of furnace because the back of his bruised head was exposed to the hot afternoon sun, a small patch of sunlight that filtered through vernal obstructions. As soon as he could be glad or sorry about anything, he was relieved because his headache was not acute. He seemed to feel it, dull like the plaster in his eyes, but somewhere a few inches above the dome of where his skull should be.

"Wait. Lie still, you chump," he said to himself. "You're not clicking, not half—not yet. You don't know who clamped what into your eyes, and—ah, now you remember. You were slugged about the head with . . . It doesn't matter. Find out where you are, somehow, and whether you're alone, or being watched."

He heard sounds, the rustle, click, tip tap, rub, swish, the snapping all pianissimo, all subdued. Nature's minor stirrings and perpetual nearly nothings, where things were growing, rooted, or meandering according to instincts, caprices, fears, cunning, or chronic stupidity. He could not figure out the details, any more than he could sort out ingredients from an already baked crust. Then, against the pointless accompaniment he sorted out faint noises in series and held his breath. Someone was approaching from behind him. Silence. The someone or something had stopped, and most of the other sounds. The heat, surrounding and blazing with concentration on the back of his head was uninterrupted. He realized, now, that he was flat on the ground. Because what was beneath him was neither wet nor dry, not hard, not soft.

He seemed to feel eyes boring into the back of his neck. He resisted the temptation to turn, but he did try to raise his own eyelids just a slip. Whether he succeeded or not he could not determine, since whatever pastelike substance was in his eyes resisted, and was opaque. Either that, or whoever had jumped him had blinded him. That, Finke would not even admit as a possibility. He would see again, sometime. He remembered fairly clearly, while waiting for X to do Y, about two girls who seemed to have long coffee-colored limbs, and, in time with the breeze, were combing long tresses, now flaxen, now kinky and black. And Solange, wrestling with a tree the way Jacob grappled with an angel.

Someone was standing over him, astraddle his back. Hands raised his head, by the forehead, bending back his neck, letting the face flop back and smack the ground. It was hard for Finke to remind himself that in his present state he would do better to lie doggo than try to put up a fight. That would come later, when he caught up with those guys. He checked his reason for using the plural. Then he was sure there were two of them. The party who had blinded, then kicked and clubbed him, had a different action, as it were, from the one leaning over him now. The experiment with his head, neck and face was repeated, but more uncertainly, or with less curiosity.

When the man—there was no smell or tactile sensation suggesting a woman—picked up Finke's feet and started dragging him, laboriously, face downward, he forced himself to remain relatively limp. Whoever was dragging him was not very strong, and surely not too smart. For the man had difficulty making progress, and evidently thought Finke was dead, or so far out he would not recover. Every few feet, the dragger paused to rest, breathing hard.

As a course of least resistance, Finke passed out again, recovering only when he felt hands across his face, and figured out he was being turned around, so that his head would be where his feet had been. Just as he felt his head lolling over emptiness, his temper flared. He grabbed one hand with both of his and bit as hard as he could into his tormentor's forearm, somewhere above the wrist. A squeal of surprise and fright sounded not six inches from Finke's ear, as he tasted blood, not his own. He was half-dragged, half-shoved over the edge of a slippery cut bank and landed in semi-stagnant water, face down. It took all the force of his will to hold on to what consciousness remained, and all his strained faculties to raise his head so that his nose was above the water surface. His elbows, he realized, were resting on a submerged snag.

This supreme effort took time—seconds, minutes, perhaps. He could not guess about that. He expected that whoever had found, dragged and dumped him into a pool, backwash or creek, would follow through, and finish him off. Nothing happened. His ears had been filled with water, when the man had left him, if he had. But the same water that had clogged his ears had washed some of the substance from his eyes, so he could see dimly at a limited range and distance.

Words he heard spoken brought back, in a rush, so much of his stamina and spirit that he was started along the way toward being himself again before he retraced them backward on the reel of his confused memory, and understood the text.

"Finke. Is that you?"

Finke felt he had swallowed half the creek when he tried to answer.

"What's holding you up?" Homer asked.

The master mind was wearing rubber boots. Finke's next lucid thought was tinged with resentment. Commend him to a criminologist who foresaw that a leg man would be dunked in a bog, and equipped himself with hip-length accessories. As this was sloshing through Finke's mind, he was being lifted out of the muck and placed in a sitting position on the edge of the cut bank, six feet or so above the water level. He puked up some muddy liquid he had swallowed and wondered if it contained pollywogs or mosquito roe.

"Excuse me," he muttered, then leaned too far to one side and lay down, in a brown-out, again.

When he snapped into it, finally, his stomach felt much relieved, although the taste of mud and slime lingered to disgust him. Ah, Evans was still around, for Homer's voice said, "We'll have a drink of Martel's in a few minutes. If you don't mind letting Dr. Holz believe that you bumped your head and fell into the creek accidentally. . . ."

"I didn't do it on purpose," Finke said.

"Any idea what was clapped into your eyes?" asked Homer.

"You're out in front. Have you?" demanded Finke.

"I should say, off-hand, green clay, or *terre verte*," Homer said. "I've taken a liberal sample." He smiled and cocked his head with satisfaction. "Finke, doesn't it beat all how criminals expose themselves by going just a little too far?"

"You mean, I shouldn't resent their treatment of me?" Finke said.

"You'll have to check in at the clinic, to make sure about eye membranes and cranial bones, and have your bruises and scratches touched up with brand-new drugs, and take a few shots against swamp infections."

"In a pig's valise," grunted Finke.

He was more hostile to the idea when he saw that Homer was in dead earnest.

"I'm going nowhere, until I find those guys who made an ass of me," asserted Finke.

"First we'd better locate the girls, *n'est-ce pas?*"

"Once I get my hands on one of those bastards, he'll direct us to the girls. Don't worry about that."

"Sure you can make the men talk, if we catch up with them?"

"I may be lousy on this Fenimore Cooper stuff, but I've doped out a new way to induce men to sing," Finke said, with utter confidence. "I ask just one favor. That you'll leave that to me."

"You've earned it," Homer granted. "From now on, you're Commissar of Persuasion, with absolute powers. But Finke, be reasonable. We can't waste our resources or scatter our endeavors. The girls and their kidnapper, and his colleague who dragged and doused you, are still in this park, or I shall turn in all my medals. They're foolhardy and amateurish, in certain respects, and have two murders against them, but they are not silly enough to try to leave this Arboretum before dark. Sunset will occur, in these parts, when the adjusted clocks read 8 o'clock. Can you stand up, yet, without too much discomfort?"

Finke tried, and almost toppled. "What the hell?" he complained. "They didn't break my legs." He submitted, in the interest of progress, and Homer carried him on his back to within a few yards of the central transverse pathway. From there on, Finke managed to walk as far as the director's bungalow, where a few slugs of brandy restored some of his strength and made him mellow enough to consent to a brief checkup at the clinic. Dr. Holz, who accepted the story of his "accident" without cavil, drove him to the Lehigh hospice, volunteering to wait and transport him back, because he was a sensitive Ph.D., M.S. and Bot.D. and had gathered that Homer wanted the run of the tree park for a while, unhampered by officialdom. Evans was not alone in the house many seconds before he unfurled the best map of the park and studied it, intensely. This he interrupted only to phone Edgy Gerry, briefly, and ask the clerk to present himself before he quit work for the day.

The phone rang. It was Finke on the line. "Say," Finke asked. "The doc just asked me a question I should have thought of, long ago. And it never came into my mind."

"The question?" prompted Homer.

"How was it you happened to find me?" In a much lower tone, which barely carried, he added, "These medicos are no dopes." His voice broke off, as if someone was approaching, to listen.

Homer carried on, in a tone that would not project itself beyond the ear pressed to the receiver. "Don't worry. I won't let them send you to a bug-ward, since it was I who insisted that you palm off an unconvincing story. Tell Dr. Deyo I chanced along luckily, while trailing a couple of eels. They journey overland, you know, between bodies of water. As who doesn't, when God pleases?"

Homer went back to his map, and then consulted the files concerning soil composition and distribution. To his satisfaction, he found that the area of this earth's crust comprising the Arnold Arboretum had been examined and catalogued as carefully as the plants whose roots were there embedded. His concentration was such that he did not hear, a couple of hours later, a set of double footsteps on the gravel drive outside until they were almost to the bungalow door. He looked out, and saw Bunny and Edgy Gerry, hand in hand.

"You asked me to report, Dr. Evans," the assiduous bank clerk said. Since Gerry had heard Dr. Holz address his fellow Ph.D. and Phi Beta as "doctor," Edgy followed suit. Bunny wrinkled her nose and sneezed.

"I just love the great outdoors," she explained. "But it gives me hay fever."

"You drove out to retrieve your husband? How nice," Homer said, patting her free hand as he held it.

"I had to try six times before they'd grant me a driving license, but I made it this spring. It's convenient for Edgy, sometimes, and I've never run into anybody, or anybody's car. I can't be the worst driver in Boston, because six others have run into me." With childish grace and naïveté, she touched gingerly her shapely behind. "The car, I mean. It's in my name."

Homer looked apologetically at Bunny. "Could you spare your husband a couple of hours this evening? If I need him out here?"

"Oh, yes," she said, unruffled. "Will he be late getting home? Lately he hasn't been getting his full eight hours. But he keeps account, in a notebook, so he can make up sleep that's lost."

"What time shall you want me, sir?" asked Gerry.

"I'll phone you," Homer said.

It was left that way. The Gerrys walked toward the Route 138 exit, after switching sides. Again they were hand in hand.

With the remarkable ability he had to wipe interruptions from his mind, and resume a former pattern of thought, Homer went back to his soil data and maps.

Again the phone rang. "Solange," a voice whispered.

"Evans, here."

"A note," she said.

"How delivered?"

"By bellboy. The desk clerk handed it to him," Solange answered.

"Did you make any inquiries about where the desk clerk got it, or how?"

"No," Solange said.

"Good girl," said Homer. "Now read it to me. Translate it into French and talk a mile a minute, just in case the phone has a leak."

Solange obeyed. Restored to the original English, the communication read:

> Mademoiselle de Montreal,
> Advertise in morning *Herald* your offer for dark pearls, imperfectly matched, also outline payment plan.
> (*Signed*) Mittag and Tilio.

17

Measure for Measure, and Then Some

As soon as Dr. Holz returned with Finke, Homer asked the director about his staff of night watchmen. Holz nearly blushed. "Our appropriations are so limited that we have to take chances," he admitted. "After the formal closing hour, which is fixed by custom and decree at the sunset hour, and therefore varies slightly day by day, we can afford only two."

"Could you ask the watchmen to confine their wanderings to the western half tonight?" asked Homer.

"Certainly. With pleasure," Dr. Holz said. Then he added, wistfully, "I assume that sometime soon you'll let me know what's going on?"

"Tomorrow morning, at the latest. Possibly early tonight," Homer said. Finke sat up and took notice.

"How are you feeling?" Homer inquired, but it was hardly necessary. With an ointment which had anesthetic as well as healing properties, Dr. Deyo had made Finke relatively comfortable about the eyes, and Finke could see quite well. His bruises, where they showed, had yielded to modern medication. After Dr. Holz withdrew to prepare a simple dinner of lobsters, smoked lamb, Manchega cheese, and Spanish red wine, Homer wrote out the text of the ransom note Solange had received. It was the signature that baffled Finke.

"Mittag and Tilio," he repeated.

Homer explained that "Mittag" means "noon" in German and that the scientific term for linden tree is *tilia*, of which the masculine form is *tilio*. "Noon by the lindens. Not bad," Homer remarked.

"There are two of them. I want first crack at the tall, dark one. You can save the one who shoved me into the drink until I get through with his buddy," Finke said.

"Exactly," Homer agreed. He unfurled the map and spread it. "I'm going to do some reconnoitering around there," he said, touching an area a quarter of a mile east of the central transverse pathway, near the boundary along Route 138.

"What did you tell Solange? What's she supposed to do?" asked Finke, "She must be sore. . . . Most likely at me."

"I told her the first edition of the morning *Herald* doesn't go to press before 1 A.M. and the city edition's put to bed much later. She and Mirak are to wait. You remember the song entitled: 'Do Nothing Till You Hear From Me.'"

The shades of night were falling, but not fast. In the twilight Homer and Finke having enjoyed, with their host, the excellent dinner, wine and liqueur, took leave of the director "for a while." They went through the Route 138 exit and crossed the broad divided highway to the other side, where some high-class suburban dwellings, lacking only surrounding space to be classified as estates, were ranged well back from the thoroughfare. Finke began to get mad.

"If you're counting on parking me out here, with these forgotten plutocrats . . ."

"Patience. Self-mastery!" softly cautioned Evans. "I haven't told you of the beauty of your assignment. Were our talents reversed, I'd relish it, myself." He halted, his hand on Finke's undamaged shoulder. "Here's the play," he said. "If you lurk here, in the shadow of these lilac bushes, you will see, before long, an automobile slow down and halt by the Arboretum wire fence." Homer pointed to indicate the approximate spot.

"So what do I do?" demanded Finke. "Fetch the guy some gas?"

"Your timing must be perfect. You'll see a tall man come out of the woods, and ease himself over the fence. He'll be more or less in a panic. Now, the man driving the automobile may lose his nerve and leave his tall colleague in the lurch, by starting up and driving south with all possible speed. Or he may wait for his partner, at his own peril."

"I'll plug 'em both," Finke promised.

"It's not as simple as that. We must take the tall dark chap alive, *à la* Frank Buck."

"And let the car driver get clean away, if he rats on the other?"

"That's the idea," Homer said.

"Couldn't I shoot the driver, and grab the other bozo?"

"Don't shoot anybody, unless you absolutely have to," urged Homer.

"I won't have to. Don't worry about that. If the tall one turns out to be the guy who gave me the works, I'll make him the sorriest unshot specimen on earth."

"We'll need his faculties," warned Homer.

"I'll show him some he didn't know he had," Finke said.

"The Romans used to say," Homer remarked, whimsically, "it's better for one to boast, taking off his armor, than while putting it on."

Finke's recommendation as to what should be done to the Romans was impractical.

Alone, after Homer's re-entry into the Arboretum, Finke started lurking in the lilacs.

While Finke was lurking, Homer attended to a few last-minute details. He talked by phone with Bengay, who had brought the exiled editor of *La Prensa* from New York to the Mayflower Club. Although Homer suggested that Bengay and his guest might join Solange and Mirakian at the Dorsetshire, Lever somehow conveyed that he would not be *persona grata* with Mlle de Lassigny until he had produced tangible results in solving the murder, or murders. Bengay, in fact, was going to take the editor to the Lehigh clinic, not for a checkup, but to find out what he could about local members of the Argentine colony, among whom the distinguished journalist was confident of finding many friends, and probably, some enemies.

Next, Homer dialed Gerry's number. Bunny answered but Edgy was close by.

"Would you consider it an imposition if I asked you to join me here about 10 o'clock?" Homer asked.

"Glad to, Doctor," Gerry said, quite eagerly. "Thanks for giving me plenty of time. We had *navajas* for dinner this evening."

"Better make it half-past 10. I won't keep you after midnight, unless we drop in at the Lantern Room on our way back," said Homer.

Dr. Holz, who overheard the last conversation, raised his eyebrows. "Extraordinary schedule of hours, Doctor," he remarked.

"Yes, isn't it," agreed Homer. He took off his oxfords and drew on a pair of rubber hip boots. "Just going out for another constitutional," he said.

It was 9 o'clock. He started out, thoughtfully, his head inclined slightly forward, his hands clasped behind his back. His attitude was contemplative rather than relentless, his gait was deliberate. From his front window, Dr. Holz watched him blend with the dusk and vanish into darkness.

"There, but for the grace of a small monthly salary check, go I," the great arborealist said. "Alas."

As Homer proceeded, parallel with Route 138, about twenty yards inside the Arboretum, he made little sound. Exactly opposite from Finke he halted to familiarize himself with the surroundings. Between the fence, and the creek into which Finke had been pushed, rose a knoll about fifteen feet higher than the roadway, readily accessible from the park's contiguous area, dropping off somewhat sharply toward the boundary. A group of jutting rocks from the underlying ledge protruded from the soil, and offered cover. It would be the natural point of vantage for anyone who wished to scan the outbound traffic on Route 138, and keep watch at the same time over a considerable area of scrub woodland, dominated on the Route 1 side by a tremendous dead and ancient oak overgrown with wild grapevine.

With the utmost caution, Homer descended into the creek. When one of his booted feet sank into the mud, he had to draw it out in such a way that no sucking or gurgling noises resulted. What troubled him most was the sickly malodorous vapors he stirred from the slime. The barely perceptible breeze, no more than a zephyr, was moving from the creek toward those protruding rocks atop the knoll. Could anyone hiding there detect the faint stench? And, if so, would it mean anything to the party in question?

Step by step, Homer continued up the creek until he saw, dimly—his remarkable eyes had adjusted themselves to the paucity of light so that he could make out shapes and patches—a rustic footbridge for the convenience of the Arboretum help. When he was directly under the old boardwalk, he waited. Was he on time? Or just too late? It was not yet half-past 9.

He stood there, knee deep in the water, on treacherous footing, and envied Finke his wholesome lilac clump. Seconds passed. Then minutes, a few of them. Homer was about decided to abandon his dank station, and scout around the rock-tipped knoll, when a muffled sound, suggestive of movement in the undergrowth, caused him to relax with satisfaction. Someone was approaching the bridge with practiced stealth. Homer could not see the person, because the planks of the bridge intervened, but he realized that whoever it was stopped before stepping on the bridge to try the boards. Having satisfied himself, the man above started to cross the old wooden structure. Halfway across, two yards from either side, he was panicked by the sudden, even sound of Homer's voice, issuing from the darkness below.

"*Pobre loco!*" ("Poor fool") Homer said, in Spanish.

The man made such a dash toward the sheltering rocks on the knoll that some sleeping wood creatures stirred, an owl flew, and Homer, making plenty of noise, scrambled up to the bridge, and stood near the center.

He heard the man descending the steep decline toward the park fence along Route 138. There was a twang of fence wire. Then a hair-raising rasp from an automobile horn, as if the driver had seen a ghost. Shrugging fatalistically, Homer started back toward, the administration buildings.

From Finke's point of view, the sequence unreeled in this fashion. He was aroused from his resentful reverie among the lilac bushes

by a dim precipitous movement of something, and the twang of
the fence wire, just as a pair of headlights wobbled and hesitated,
and the car which must have been attached to them veered toward
the gravel border of Route 138, approximately where Homer had
asked Finke to expect a car to halt. Even with his attention so rudely
divided, he muttered something to himself to the effect that the
driver must be inexpert and drunk. He was dashing across Route
138 at top speed, unhampered much by traffic, when he realized
that the driver of the car had abandoned it, with a pathetic scream,
and was running with an awkward stagger back toward the Arboretum entrance.

Meanwhile a man had heaved himself into the car and was trying to roll up the window and simultaneously start the machine.
Finke smashed the window with the butt of his automatic, reversed
it, and took a shot at the ignition switch, dodging as he did so a
rigid forefinger jabbing for his eyes. Whatever he hit or did not hit
with the bullet from his .45 had discouraged the man from trying
to start the car. He was using both hands, now, on Finke, who had
clutched him by the shirt and coat lapels. With all his force, the
man lunged backwards and broke loose. Finke realized how long
and strong his arms were and the frenzied expression of his
strained face. That was about all.

The man—Finke now saw he was tall—got out of the car on the
opposite side and started to run, along the cindered border of the
route, in the opposite direction the driver of the car had taken.
"Made to order," grunted Finke as he set out in pursuit. No South
American lounge lizard could outrun him, he thought, yet at full
speed he saw that he was not gaining. O.K. So it's a question of
endurance, Finke thought, grimly. The beating he had taken that
afternoon had weakened him. The longer the chase, the less chance
for Finke. Just as he was saying to himself, "I've got to shoot him
in the legs," he was caught in the glare of an extra bright headlight
from behind. The tall man, at that moment, caught a fence post,
wheeled and fired. He missed, by such a close margin that Finke
felt the breeze of the bullet.

The same headlight that had spotlighted Finke for the Argentine left Finke in blackness and illumined the Argentine. Finke drew, fired on the dead run, at the man's knees, and knocked off his felt hat. By the time the man had decided it was safer to risk a hand-to-hand fight, Finke was upon him. The tall Argentine, emitting a noise like a sink whose plug has been yanked, went over backward, reversed as they fell, entangled, and was on top as they hit the ground. But Finke had the enemy gun, which he had tossed through the wire fence, at the same time retaining his own. He flailed out from under the Argentine, and, either to avoid temptation, or to intimidate his opponent, tossed his automatic well beyond reach. They were standing, face to face, two feet apart.

"Now," Finke said. "We'll settle this."

"Understood," the Argentine said, quite calmly. He had two or three inches advantage in reach, and had not been blinded, kicked or clubbed.

Dr. Holz, bored with his bungalow, had wandered into the museum and was staring at framed sketches of prehistoric swamps and forests, inhabited by giant reptiles. At 9:30 Edgy Gerry stepped in and apologized for being an hour early.

"Doctor Evans took a walk, after dinner," the director told him. "Make yourself at home."

They chatted a while until both were aroused by Bunny's entrance. She was frightened, quite shaken, but penitent.

"What's wrong?" Edgy said, putting a protective arm around her shoulders.

"I did it again," she said.

"Did what?"

"I lost my head when I parked the car. I heard a noise and saw something come out of the woods. That scared me out of my wits and I started to run—and here I am."

She was panting, but no longer trembling.

"Adrenalin," Dr. Holz said, understandingly. "Your glands."

"Oh, *they're* all right," said Bunny.

"Do you suppose Dr. Evans would mind if I took a quick look at the car?" Edgy asked.

"I've never met a man more reasonable," Dr. Holz assured him. "I'll talk with Bunny about her glands."

Bunny giggled, and Edgy made his exit.

A few minutes later, Homer came in. He had stopped at the bungalow, taken off his rubber boots, and was conventionally if not elegantly shod.

"Why, Bunny," Homer said to the accountant's little wife. "This is an unexpected pleasure. Where's Edgy?"

She blushed and bridled again. "You know me. I made a messy job of parking. Dr. Holz says it's my adrenalin. In glands." She made motions with both hands as if squeezing soft bulbs.

"That's nothing," Homer said. He greeted Gerry as the little clerk returned, handed him a huge packet of manuscript and asked him to count the words, one by one, of the first hundred pages, then try to work out a satisfactory method of estimating them. Dr. Holz glanced at Evans questioningly, and restrained himself from sighing.

"Was the car all right?" Homer asked.

Edgy looked reproachfully at Bunny. "Somebody broke a window glass," he said, and sighed.

Leaving Gerry at a desk, and Bunny with Dr. Holz, still discussing girls' glands, Homer excused himself once more. He walked eastward along Route 138, keeping to the unpaved border near the wire fence.

In all his career, Finke had never been up against a similar or comparable problem. He had been struggling with the Argentine, no holds barred, for a time which stretched back so far he did not try to guess about it. He could hit him, within reason, when he had to, but he could not knock him out. When they wrestled, he had to rely on cunning, since his strength was not nearly normal. And the Argentine had as much, or more cunning, because he was out to kill Finke, and Finke was under instructions to bring him in alive.

As badly off as he was, Finke was depressed by the possibility that Homer, who evidently had flushed this bird from the woods for him, might join them in time to intervene. If he could not pull this off by himself, after the way the Argentine had treated him that afternoon, he did not care about surviving.

As the two men had fought, they had worked their way eastward, since Finke, the aggressor, was facing that way. So Homey, before he caught sight of them, had come upon Finke's automatic, by the roadside. That was hard to account for. If the other had disarmed Finke and retained a gun, himself, he would have fired it and escaped. Could that mean that Finke had deliberately discarded the weapon? To take the man alive?

Homer thought that over, and reluctantly accepted the implications. Finke's feelings would be hurt, perhaps irrevocably, if he were "rescued" from the man toward whom he bore such a justifiable grudge. On the other hand, Finke was under a frightful handicap. Hurrying along in the direction the combatants must have taken, Homer was aware that the situation called for the utmost in tact. Meanwhile, he had picked up Finke's .45 and slipped it into a side pocket. With the automatic he carried in his shoulder holster, that made two.

His senses keyed by his danger, Finke thought he detected a shift of mood in the Argentine. He had reached a point, unless Finke was mistaken, where he would settle for a getaway. For the Argentine had made a feint as if to dash across Route 138 and run for it. As Finke had countered, the Argentine had dodged back and succeeded in vaulting the fence. How he managed, Finke never knew, but he also found himself within the wooded park. That gave the guy two strikes against him, on top of the advantages he already had.

"Here goes nothing," Finke murmured, and waded in, none too cautiously. The Argentine clouted him on his right ear and tried to tear it off, as he struck also with his thumb into the left ear. Deaf, Finke realized he was temporarily cut off from sound. As he backpedaled, for the first time the Argentine's triumphant grunt was stifled by something Finke was unable to hear. An even, derisive deadly voice had spoken two words.

"*Pobre loco!*"

Finke's superhuman recovery and the Argentine's frantic hesitation coincided. That was the beginning of the end. Finke got his fingers on both sides of the Argentine's windpipe, pressed, and brought his knee up into the choking man's crotch. Finke backed him against a tree and slammed him flush on the jaw. If it hadn't put the man out, Finke would have been finished, because of the jar to his wrist, and the numbing shock to his knuckles.

After a decent interval, Evans approached, making plenty of noise. He was now outside the fence. In the act of climbing over he pretended to discover Finke and said, "Nice work. Are you quite all right?"

"So so," said Finke. "Here's your party, mostly alive, unless he croaks just to make a sucker out of me."

"Let's tie him up," Homer said, taking a length of clothesline from under his arm.

"Remember your promise? I'm the one to make him talk," Finke said.

"The sooner the better," Homer said, securing the limp Argentine to a tree.

"Let me adjust the gag," Finke asked, and Homer acquiesced. He was pleased to see that, at the last moment, Finke thought better of his first intentions and gagged the fellow humanely. Wherever one tested him, Finke rang true.

"Shall you need any props?" Evans ventured. "We've got to locate those girls."

"I'll need a few things," said Finke, "but I know where they are. Can we spare five, ten minutes?"

"Let's hope the unmatched pearls are mercifully unconscious," Homer said, and they started back, together, toward the Route 32 entrance. When they got to where the damaged car was standing, Finke halted and frowned, questioningly.

"Something screwy about this. The driver who beat it was either a woman, or a female impersonator," Finke said. "I wasn't too rattled to register that."

"Our little friend, Bunny, caused our plan to misfire," Homer said. "She drove Edgy out here, and tried to park in our selected area. So she got frightened by our Argentine, ran back to Edgy's protecting arms."

"So we missed our other guy?"

"Those things happen," Homer said.

They joined Dr. Holz in the living room of his bungalow. Finke lost no time in borrowing a pair of rubber boots. The Director looked so puzzled that Homer relented.

"You can see the finale of our mysterious adventure, Doctor," he said. "You've been most considerate and patient. Now you're entitled to be fully informed. Come along, if you like."

Finke looked pained. "You mean, the doctor's going to act as a witness?"

"That needn't cramp your style or zeal," said Homer.

"If that's the way you want it—you asked for it," Finke said, grimly. Once out of doors, Finke led them to the bag of snakes in the crotch of a linden tree. In the glare of a pocket flashlight he trained into the open sack, he let Homer take a peep. Director Holz did likewise. The two Ph.D.'s saw snake shapes and undulations, and three contrasting pairs of beady eyes.

During all the ensuing years, no matter how often he thought of that tableau, Finke was overcome with admiration for his chief. Homer did not as much as flicker an eyelash. And Director Holz, once he saw that Homer seemed content, said merely that the snakes belonged to the Arboretum, and he hoped to have them back when Finke was through with them. By the time the trio, two of whom were adept at nocturnal wanderings through woods, and Finke, who followed, bearing rubber boots and the burlap bag drew near to where the Argentine had been trussed up, Homer said, "In all my travels, doctor, I've never had experience with any people quite like the Spanish, or their colonial descendants. They have no fear of death, and torture wrings nothing from them."

"So it was with our redskins, they say," agreed Dr. Holz.

"This guy'll talk," Finke said.

"Ah. You're conducting an experiment?" the director asked, with anticipation.

"So it appears," Homer said.

18

Of Punishment That Fits But One Crime

WHEN HOMER, FINKE AND THE DIRECTOR drew near the tree to which the Argentine had been fastened, Dr. Holz's hitherto placid expression showed concern.

"This is Señor Tilio—that's his *nom de crime*. We were obliged to tie him up and deprive him of the use of his voice in our absence," explained Homer.

As the captive's dark eyes stared at them scornfully, Dr. Holz asked, rather feebly, "May I ask why?"

"Had he yelled and hallooed, he would have disturbed the sleep of your birds and animals," said Homer.

"Is this the first time he was caught loitering here after dark?"

Removing the gag from the Argentine's mouth, Homer addressed him. "Did you hear the director's question?"

The contemptuous look on the Argentine's face deepened. He made no answer.

"After all, that doesn't matter. It's the first time he was caught. He'd merit, at the most, a sharp warning not to come here after twilight again," Dr. Holz said.

"He's been here since noon," observed Homer. "Haven't you, Señor Tilio? Since Mittag."

Again the Argentine remained silent, and glared.

"Speak up, you," said Finke, in an ominous tone. "And be quick about it."

"I'm not in a hurry," the Argentine said. "None of you have anything on me, or any right to question me. I'm saying nothing at all."

Restraining Finke, Homer said, suavely. "Whether you know it or not, señor, you have very little time. I" (Homer showed his U.S. badge) "have every right to question you. Furthermore, I have proof that you assaulted a young woman with a dangerous weapon on these public premises just after noon today, and kidnapped at the point of a gun two other young women. They are, at present, in this park. Your treatment of them, when we learn about it, will determine our policy in dealing with you. It is dark. This area is difficult and extensive. We could find the girls, without your co-operation, but we might waste precious time. So I'd advise you to talk, without delay."

The Argentine shrugged. "You're trying to avoid raising a general alarm. Go ahead. Call all your 57 kinds of police, city, county, metropolitan, state, and your colleagues in the federal service."

This was too much for Finke. He stepped up to Homer and the director. "Would you mind retiring for about five minutes?" he asked.

"You mustn't mutilate him beyond recognition. His editor-in-chief has come all the way from New York to consult with him to-night. We don't want any mistake about the identification."

"I won't leave a mark where a jury could find it," promised Finke.

"In that case," said Homer, "perhaps Dr. Holz, who has missed so much adventure lately, would prefer to stay."

"Ra*ther!*" the director agreed, readily.

"Our specimen, Señor Tilio, né Etchegaray, has facial control to a certain point, but he gave himself away when I mentioned his editor," Homer observed.

Finke had got past the talking stage and was making preparations. He untied the rope that held Tilio to the tree trunk, and pushed the Argentine, impersonally, flat on his face, his ankles still attached and his wrists firmly bound. He picked up Tilio and stood him erect. The Argentine tottered and wavered, but he maintained the standing position. Tilio appeared not to notice when Finke gathered sticks and cones and made a crude circle with stones. His lack of address was too much for Director Holz.

"You're not going to burn him!" the director said, in awe.

"No," said Homer. "He'd endure that."

Finke made a small fire, Indian fashion, contained in a ring of damp stones and moved the bag of snakes fairly close, so his reptiles, sluggish with cold, would respond to the warmth. They did, and the sensual undulations beneath the rough burlap were almost indecent to behold. The Argentine stared, his jaw set, but something of the sheen had dulled in his agate eyes.

Finke grabbed one of Tilio's legs below the knee, and sat him down so hard his perfect white teeth came near to rattling.

"Easy does it," Homer cautioned.

The Argentine spoke to the director, but there was a touch of hysteria in his threat. "You, Doctor, in responsible charge of this park, will be called as a witness when I bring suit. Remind these amateur inquisitors that you cannot lie, under oath."

Urbanely Dr. Holz smiled. "I've never tried," he said. Meanwhile Finke was procuring from the shadows one long rubber boot. Against the sole of Tilio's sharp Oxford, he tried it for size. It was roomy and large, as to the foot, and could be buckled snugly around the leg. The firelight shed a weird glow on the scene and the proceedings.

"Want to talk?" Finke asked the Argentine.

No answer.

"O.K. You asked for it," said Finke. He sat across the Argentine's outstretched legs and unbound the rope around the ankles. He tied the left ankle to a stout protruding loop of tree root. He took off Tilio's right shoe, then flipped him under the chin to induce him to stand up again. There was Tilio, his left foot attached, his right foot unshod and free, his hands firmly bound.

So Finke peeled back the pliable rubber boot, leaving the inside of the boot exposed from the knee downward. The sole was broad, so the boot stood stably in the flickering firelight. Picking up the bag of snakes, Finke opened it, summoned all the will power he ever had, and then some. He forced his hand downward, inch by inch. Then slowly, fighting nausea and cramps in his arm, plus giddiness in his head and firefly spots beneath his eyelids, he drew out what proved to be the garter snake.

It must have been the solicitous expression on Dr. Holz's face that caused him to deliberately release the anxious little creature, with flicking double tongue, more colors than a tortoise shell, and a one-way glide. But he was rewarded by hearing a gasp from the Argentine, rather a series of gulping sounds above a mumble of prayer.

"That's right. The little fellow's fagged," said Dr. Holz approving.

A hiss from within the burlap sack indicated that another exhibit was, on the contrary, raring to go.

"Ah, Blackie," murmured Finke, surprised and pleased with himself because he was able to talk at all. Homer was humming the Argentine national anthem, by far the longest in the world.

Finke reached into the sack. He brought Blackie into the open, jaws working prodigiously on elastic hinges, body lashing and writhing, goo-goo eyes bulging with a malice antedating the development of man. A constrictor Blackie was, and a constrictor he remained, clamping tight on Finke's wrist and forearm, bravely squeezing. With his left hand, Finke had to pry off Blackie, inch by inch.

A hoarse whisper came from the Argentine as, finally, Finke dropped Blackie into the open rubber boot, where the thumping and hissing sounds he made transcended the imagination of any sorcerer's apprentice of skeletons cavorting on a Walpurgis Night. It was all so soft and fiendishly cozy.

Tilio addressed Dr. Holz, "I appeal to you, señor. There are things to which you, a scholar and a gentleman, could never consent."

Trying to hold himself together, Finke was saying to himself, "When you've handled two snakes, you've handled them all." At heart he knew better. His test was still before him. That long one, sickly green, abnormally thin, obscenely long. The tree snake. He forced his hand into the sack again, and it refused at first to function. Working over yards of that green freak was beyond his scope. He lunged, grabbed a handful of loops so complicated that he hardly was aware of their resistance, and drew forth the tree snake. With his left hand, he made a quick grab, secured a hold around the neck and, standing between the demoralized Tilio and the fire-light, untangled foot after foot of green reptile, until the tail came along. Then, inserting the tail into the rubber boot he let the snake, proper, slither downward into the boot, so the fungus-colored shoe-button head was uppermost.

The Argentine, too far gone to think of nobility, or even dig-nity, was babbling and pleading.

"Too late," Finke said, implacably. "You had your chance to talk."

"The girls are in that big dead oak, halfway toward Route 1," the Argentine said, wildly.

Homer already was on his way. Dr. Holz was unable to decide whether to follow Evans or stay where he was. He stayed. He watched, spellbound, as Finke slipped the Argentine's right foot into the rubber boot with the writhing, ill-assorted occupants. He did not haul the boot on tightly, so the snakes would be crushed, but left room, as he strapped the boot tight above Tilio's knee, for Blackie and Long Greeno to operate.

From Tilio's mouth came hideous frothing and laughter, out of control. He was like one who was being tickled beyond torture.

"He'll lose his mind," the director objected. "Many men are like that, about snakes."

"I'll take 'em off, now he's had a taste of what's coming," Finke said. He removed the charged boot and dumped the snakes back into the sack. The Argentine, deprived of qualities essentially hu-man, fell flat on his face, writhing and blubbering, in a slow decre-scendo and ritard, like a fish losing strength against convulsions.

"I'm amazed," the director said. "Should we dash over to the oak?"

"Sure. This man'll come around, but he'll never be the same," Finke said. "He's lost his nerve, and, brother, he'll wish he had it back when it's time for him to fry."

"You mean he'll have to face electrocution?" asked Dr. Holz.

"Too bad they can only do it to him once. That doesn't apply to me, and my new technique," said Finke.

The doctor smiled. "I'm not unobserving," he ventured. "Next time you'd better let me handle the snakes."

"With pleasure," Finke said.

Homer, who had preceded them, had gently lifted Evelina and Erica Strella from the hollow of the giant old oak. He had found them in a pitiable condition. Tilio had bound them, stuffed them in, with limbs entangled, knees down, heads up, and plastered them over with greenish clay which had baked in the sun. They were breathing, dimly conscious, having suffered as long as they were able all discomforts, pains and tortures conceivable. They had been gagged with deliberate cruelty, as Solange had been. By the time Finke and the director arrived, they were able to react and utter inarticulate sounds, but their stiffened limbs were still rigid and grotesque. Little by little, encouraged by Homer's words and his help, they were able to straighten their legs a little, and to bend their arms. Circulation was restored slowly, to the parts which had been bound too tightly.

"This is an outrage. . . . A double outrage," roared the director, forsaking all pretense of calm. "Why was this not reported promptly? You, yourself, Dr. Evans, inferred that these young women were kidnapped at noon, or slightly after."

"Had you caused the police to start stamping around the Arboretum, Señor Tilio would have killed Señorita Strella and Miss Boulanjay, and made an easy escape. At the moment you sounded the alarm, he would have been warned," Homer said. He turned to the young women who were reviving, and said, "You've both had to suffer, because of my decision. I had to assume you'd rather take chances on surviving. Was I right?"

In spite of her disheveled plight, Evelina's eyes glowed.

"Now it's over, anything's better than being dead," she said.

"And you, Miss Strella?" asked Homer.

The Argentine girl, converted *en négresse*, was not reassured. The better she felt, physically, the more worried she became.

"If you please, señor. Where's Señor Morton?"

"Quite safe," Homer said.

"If he were safe, he'd be here," the señorita said, fearfully.

"It's fairly safe in jail. He gave himself up, soon after you were safely camouflaged," Homer told her.

"He didn't kill Mr. Laneer, or anyone," the señorita insisted.

"I'm glad," Homer said, simply. He turned to Finke. "Think you can find your way back to the doctor's headquarters? The bungalow, I mean?"

"I guess so," answered Finke.

"You should call Mlle de Lassigny, to relieve her mind. Tell her we've found the girls, alive and without permanent damage. Also, that we caught the chap who kidnapped them."

Evelina exclaimed, "She's alive? I didn't dare to ask."

"What about Ryan, the dope?" demanded Finke.

"Give him a ring, and let him have Tilio. It won't take long to write out a confession, and get Tilio to sign it, if we do it—your way—before officialdom takes over," said Homer.

Señorita Strella, overhearing, was aghast. "Shall I have to testify? Once the police get their hands on me, I'm lost," she said.

"We'll give you a quick trip to Canada, and provide you with legitimate entrance papers valid in these states."

When Finke set out to perform his clean-up missions, Homer had a talk with him, aside. "Better write out two confessions, on separate sheets of paper. One will cover the assault on Mlle de Lassigny and the theft of her C notes. The amount of money she had on her will involve Señor Tilio in a grand larceny charge, along with the others. Include also in the first document, the one we'll give Sergeant Ryan tonight, the kidnapping of the two girls."

"I begin to get wise—about the other confession," Finke said, doubtfully. "But can we get away with it? Won't Ryan have a legitimate beef, if we withhold pertinent information in a murder case?"

"Two murders," Homer said. "Make that plain, in the document we withhold. Have Tilio sign a statement that he killed Blaise Laneer with an ice pick, and poisoned Dr. Gonzalez by means of *hyoscyamos niger*."

"He had a confederate," Finke insisted. "I want him, too. Don't forget the bird who dragged me and threw me in the drink."

"One step at a time," Homer said.

19

What's in a Name? Plenty

THE SPACIOUS DIRECTORS' ROOM of the Pequot National Bank was chosen as the final meeting place, and because the two kidnapped girls
required a full night's rest, the hour was set for 10 A.M. on Friday
morning. All those who had been involved, however slightly, in the
succession of events beginning with the bet and about to culmi-
nate in Homer Evans' elucidation, were present, save only Angus
Ferguson, Priscilla Appleby, the late Blaise Laneer and Dr. Rodolfo
Gonzalez, also defunct. The law was represented by Captain
Moriarty, Dr. Thaddeus U. Ford, the medical examiner, and Sergeant Ryan, besides a couple of uniformed policemen who guarded
Jellyroll Morton and the Argentine booked as Señor Tilio.

The distinguished editor-in-exile of *La Prensa*, the Cockney
janitor of No. 14 Newbury Street, and several others formally identified him as Julio Etchegaray. The renowned editor denied indignantly that the man had ever had authority to represent *La Prensa*,
at home or abroad.

At the same time, when Sergeant Ryan and the cops had herded
in their prisoners, the girl called Erica Strella, who had removed
the stain from her skin, but whose hair was still black, and not
flaxen, threw aside all restraint and embraced Jellyroll, whose
manacles prevented him from responding, and whose face showed
the utmost dismay. It did not take Ryan an instant to discover who
she was, and he had a pair of handcuffs clapped on her.

The editor of *La Prensa* objected. "She is not guilty of anything
grave, and her name is not Erica Strella," he declared. "She is the

daughter of a colleague of mine who's been imprisoned by Peron and stripped of his estate."

"Whatever her name is, she's an accomplice of a murderer. That's good enough for me," Ryan stated.

"You seem determined to make an exhibition of yourself," Evans said, resignedly. "The señorita will not mind a few minutes in handcuffs, after what she has been through. She's the fiancée, if that's an accomplice, of Jellyroll. We've assured you from the first that he has never murdered anyone."

"Laneer was carrying on with this girl. Morton was jealous. We can place him at the scene of Laneer's murder at the time Laneer must have died. He was seen entering the house, and leaving. And right afterward, he and this girl cleared out of the hotel room where she'd been staying, and receiving him at all hours, and hid out."

"As usual, you are wrong on every count. Laneer was not 'carrying on' with the señorita, whom we shall still call Strella, for her protection, until she's Mrs. Morton. The late Laneer, in fact, was rather considerate with Señorita Strella. In Buenos Aires he offered to help her out of the country with 180,000 pesos, to be converted into dollars here in Boston. He was a passenger on the same United Fruit liner that carried her from Buenos Aires around the Horn to San Diego. He installed her there, without intruding unduly, preceded her to Boston, got a job in this ultra-respectable bank, arranged her transportation from California here, reserved a room for her at the Dorsetshire, and has supplied her with money, from her own funds, as she has needed it. Her balance, Mr. Poole informs me, is intact."

Jellyroll was struggling and fuming, as if he were out of his head. "I would have killed him," he shouted.

"Put it more mildly. You went to No. 14 Newbury Street Wednesday afternoon, to demand an explanation, banged on his door, pressed his bell, then peered through the keyhole and saw that he was lying on his own hearth rug, dead, with a gas fire burning in the hot afternoon," Homer suggested.

"Prove it!" Sergeant Ryan demanded.

Homer took from an inside pocket Julio Etchegaray's written and signed confession and handed it over to Captain Moriarty. Ryan read over the captain's shoulder and choked. The captain glared at Etchegaray.

"I killed them both," the Argentine said. "You know very well that I followed Laneer in a taxi from the Lehigh Clinic to No. 14 Newbury Street. I was on the scene. I lived in the same house, for a week, and my key would fit his apartment. I got the ice pick in a store."

"And what about Dr. Gonzalez? I know you killed the doctor," Evans said, suavely. "And how, and why? Two witnesses saw you switch aspirin bottles unbeknown to him, as you were entering the bar just off the Lantern Room."

"It wasn't when we entered the bar," Etchegaray said, sullenly.

Finke spoke up. "No, you chump. It was when you jostled Dr. Gonzalez, to make room for some customers who crowded in. You knew the doctor was subject to headaches."

Ryan interposed obstinately. "Those confessions may not be worth the paper they're written on."

"Señor Etchegaray and Sergeant Ryan are equally mistaken if they think I have relied solely on a confession to prove a murder charge. How do they think a jury would be impressed if I should prove that within the last few days, Señor Etchegaray has been studying for hours in the public library and elsewhere, the rare poison, *hyoscyamos niger*, that was used to kill Hamlet's father and Dr. Gonzalez?" Homer asked.

"Who told you that?" the Argentine asked.

"A cousin of yours," Homer said.

There was a movement, like a reflex, somewhere behind Homer, in the room. "Finke! See that the doors are closed, locked and guarded. And discourage anyone who should try to bolt, or use a weapon, please."

Finke arose, moved until his back was to the wall, drew his .45 automatic. Captain Moriarty, puzzled but taking no chances, issued orders to his cops to lock and guard the doors.

At the word "cousin," a baleful black look had crossed the shackled Argentine's hitherto impassive countenance. Homer felt a twinge of satisfaction.

"I haven't any cousins up here," Etchegaray said.

"Is it true that you planned to submit a thesis to your university in Buenos Aires, on a certain aspect of Shakespeare's immortal work?" Homer persisted.

"The more school credits one gets, in our country, the more he can travel abroad, and the more privileges he gets at home, if he stays out of politics," said Etchegaray.

The editor nodded. "Peron wants to boast about his subjects' scholastic standing, and maneuver all the politics, himself."

"Can't we ever cut out this baloney, and get down to work?" Sergeant Ryan objected.

"Before I set you right, I'd better explain briefly how the black-money market operates in Argentina. An understanding of the financial pattern is essential to this whole riddle. Under Peron, the Argentine so-called republic is starved for dollars, economically speaking. It is hard for an Argentine to get permission to travel, and harder for a prospective traveler to take out of the country sufficient funds. So a system has developed, whereby visiting North Americans, or others with checking accounts in the United States, are encouraged by a clique of merchants, industrialists and dealers to pay for their purchases with checks on United States banks, rather than the standard travelers' checks the Peron gang can easily trace."

"What does that get any of them?" Ryan asked, skeptically.

"In effect, dollars," Homer said. "The black-market exchange operators known to the Argentine merchants cash the United States checks (personal checks, in small denominations, always) at such a generous rate in pesos that the Argentine dealers make a larger profit than could be realized on a domestic transaction at the legal ceiling for exchange. The black-market middlemen, who have acquired the checks payable in the United States in dollars, sell them, at a large discount, to prospective travelers. There is no record, no

check-up by Peron. Dr. Deyo, for instance, has told me that he arrived here with about one hundred small checks worth $3000, more
or less."

The editor spoke up. "I don't mind admitting that I took advantage of the plan, myself, since it enabled me to escape, and helps
undermine the Peron regime."

Dr. Deyo spoke up. "The black market is nonpolitical. That is,
it does not discriminate against patriots like the editor, or
Peronistas who could be denounced if they proved indiscreet. Still,
every dollar that gets out of the country makes it harder for Peron
to continue, and eventually his farcical economy will defeat him."

"I understand," Homer said, smiling, "why an operator like the
late Blaise Laneer would be extra careful to be fair with Señorita
Strella. To the extent of getting her a false passport, and a steamship booking under an assumed name."

"He pretended to love me," the señorita said. "All men in
Buenos Aires say that, to any woman, as a matter of course, like
'Good day' or 'Excuse me'."

Jellyroll struggled and roared.

"We must have order," said Homer, indulgently. "Laneer, poor
chap, had always been inclined to make easy money. He was not
long content on establishing contacts between American buyers
and Argentine sellers in Buenos Aires. He foresaw the immense
advantage in establishing himself in a solid conservative bank in
the United States, located in a city frequented by Argentines, and
readily accessible to New York. The chief of the black-market operators in Buenos Aires was able to carry on his business on a larger
scale, and with more convenience and security, having a Boston
outlet for assorted personal checks dated weeks or months back."

Sergeant Ryan was restless and disgusted. "You don't make
sense, Professor," he said. "Supposing this Laneer was helping
Argentines collect money that belonged to them? You said yourself he didn't play favorites, for or against the political factions, in
or out of the government down there. Who'd want to kill him for
doing his countrymen a service?"

"Wherever there are good pickings, from an illegal enterprise, hijackers develop. You've heard about hijackers?" Homer asked the sergeant.

Ryan grunted, not quite so sure of himself.

"That brings us to Etchegaray, alias Tilio," Homer said.

The editor looked doubtful. "I've know Julio all of his life," the editor said. "You can't tell me he worked out any kind of complicated plan, legal or otherwise."

"Exactly," Homer said. "That's where his cousin comes in. And his cousin, being smarter than he is noble, has been perfectly willing for Julio to take the whole rap."

Etchegaray, suspicious as a turtle, withdrew into his shell. He might not be clever, but he had heard about traps, and was determined that no high-sounding questioner was going to show him up.

"Let's go back to the principal outline of the black-market setup. Laneer was the Boston outlet. An inconspicuous Argentine who loitered near the American Express and Thomas Cook and Sons' places in Buenos Aires exchanged pesos for the U.S. personal checks. There was a rake-off from the dealers in goods, another from those who wanted the checks, to cash in North America in terms of dollars, and Laneer took a modest percentage here in Boston, where the dollars were paid. Still, the customers all were better off with whatever dollars they received, however they were shortchanged. An Argentine peso was of little use to them, at Peron's artificial rate of exchange."

"Could you tell us about the hijackers?" Captain Moriarty asked, politely. "If they figure in our murder case."

"Simple enough. Etchegaray came to Boston at his cousin's invitation, hoping to improve his fortune without work. Before he left Buenos Aires, he converted all his money into personal checks on U.S. banks. These he obtained, as others did, from the black-market operator who frequented the travel-agency district down there. His cousin wanted Laneer out of the way, so that he could run the North American end of the racket, and advised Etchegaray to horn in at Buenos Aires. Senor Etchegaray, too fond of his leisure to work on the sidewalks of his native capital, intended to let the experienced black-market chief pay him off, and then was going to settle in Paris and enjoy the proceeds."

Ryan sneered. "Still you claim that Etchegaray had energy enough to icepick Laneer and poison Dr. Gonzalez. Not to mention kidnapping Miss Montreal and the other two babies. Not very consistent, Professor."

"One thing led to another," Homer said. "Besides, it was the cousin who killed Laneer. Señor Etchegaray, who's made a blanket confession, realizes that we can convict him of enough crimes to justify the extreme penalty. He's willing to cover up for his cousin, and let him go free. Family ties among Latins are strong, you know."

"So you grab the stooge and let the one who planned the murders get clean away," Ryan said.

"The cousin who supplied the brains is in this room," Homer said. "We'll come to him, directly."

The members of the company stirred and looked at one another uncomfortably. Homer went smoothly on. "Let me tell you about the cousin."

"Pray do," urged Captain Moriarty.

"The cousin has circulated freely in local Argentine circles for a long time, and found out much about the late Laneer, enough to envy him and to dream of replacing him. Once the prospect of amassing wealth took root in his mind, he became obsessed. The cousin made extensive plans, in which all the rough work was to be executed by Julio, but the latter was afraid that if his cousin did not commit the major crime, he might not carry out the bargain, and insure that Etchegaray would receive funds in Paris, when he was established there. Out of sight, out of mind, is a proverb common to all races. Furthermore, Etchegaray lived in the same house with Laneer, and therefore might be suspected, or involved in an investigation. So the cousin had to get up courage to kill Laneer, and worked out the details in his methodical way. Etchegaray could furnish a key to Laneer's apartment. The cousin would slip in, while

Laneer was out, and stab him with the ice pick when he returned. The appointed day was last Wednesday."

"This is all talk," Ryan said. "We've got the goods on Jellyroll. To hell with high finance. The prisoner's in love. Laneer tried to cut in." The sergeant made vivid icepicking motions.

"This is as good a time as any to describe Jellyroll's part in this affair," agreed Homer, pleasantly. "You all know about the bet that was made in the Lantern Room Tuesday evening. Jellyroll had been trying to find out what he could about Laneer and was getting nowhere. The article in the detective-story magazine gave him an idea. Naturally, when Jellyroll had a chance to choose the party to be followed, and Laneer happened in . . ."

"Come now," said Ryan. "You want us to think it was a coincidence that Laneer happened in?"

Jellyroll spoke up. "I never said so. I knew Laneer was coming in that night. He'd told Erica that he was going to explain things to me. He thought I'd swallow anything he said."

Homer nodded doubtfully. "Did it occur to you that Laneer was afraid that if you stirred up a fuss, his employers at the bank might get curious? Miss Strella's 180,000 pesos had also been converted into small personal checks, before they left Buenos Aires," he said.

"I didn't care about her money. I didn't want to hear about it. I wanted proof of how he was trying to two-time me. I'd read the article in the magazine days before, and figured that Mr. Bengay and his crowd might take it up, and bet. They bet about anything at all, evening after evening. I hear them. Well. It worked, up to a point," said Jellyroll.

"Up to the hilt," grunted Sergeant Ryan.

"What you say about Laneer is understandable," objected the editor. "But why should anyone murder Rodolfo Gonzalez, a gifted young doctor and a gentleman?"

"I regretted that," said Julio Etchegaray quite earnestly. "It became necessary by the most unlucky chance."

"Unlucky for whom?" asked Captain Moriarty.

"For me. If there's a life after the Hot Squat, as you call it, I shall be held accountable," said Etchegaray.

"Now, now," admonished the captain. "No sacrilege in any case of mine."

The manacled Argentine shrugged, as if, in view of graver sins he had committed, small technical ones were of little importance. "I sincerely regret Gonzalez," he repeated. "It had to be done."

"May I explain why?" suggested Homer.

"Please do," begged Solange. "I've seldom permitted myself to feel so nervous, even on vacations."

Evans nodded, understandingly. "On the day, last Tuesday, when Laneer, completely unaware of the fact, was slated for extinction, he rose before noon. Mirakian followed him to breakfast, then to the clinic. At the clinic he met Dr. Gonzalez and took from him small checks, of the kind I've described, in the amount of about $3,600. So far so good. But before he went his way, Laneer was introduced to Señor Etchegaray, who had been passing himself off as a reporter for *La Prensa*, in order to cover his real machinations. In the course of the three-cornered conversation between the late Dr. Gonzalez, Señor Etchegaray and the late Laneer, Etchegaray learned that Laneer had the checks belonging to Gonzalez in his possession. If Laneer should be murdered before those checks were cashed, Gonzalez would be sure to talk, and the true motive for the murder would be exposed, or, at least, the clew would lead to an investigation at the bank."

"I did my best to save him," Etchegaray insisted.

"I know," agreed Homer. "But Laneer became suspicious, and tried to get away from the clinic so he could check on your status with *La Prensa*. Knowing your reputation in Buenos Aires as a young man who loathed steady work, Laneer was pardonably skeptical. He thought you might be an agent of Peron, an occupation that would not involve monotonous effort. So he made an excuse to elude you and took a taxi back to his quarters. You followed, to warn your cousin that the murder must be postponed. You left your taxi half a block from No. 14 Newbury, entered by the back way, rushed to Laneer's apartment and found that he was already dead, and your cousin had departed, with the checks and all Laneer's papers. Of course, the murderer had gathered up all the papers except the checks Laneer brought in with him before Laneer arrived. Probably the cousin stood behind the door, ice pick in hand, did the job in an instant, stretched Laneer's body on the hearthrug, went through the pockets, and bolted. It was your idea, I assume, to turn on the gas and delay rigor mortis."

"I'd read about that," said Etchegaray. "But, alas . . ."

"Alas, there was nothing to do but erase Dr. Gonzalez. You had been preparing your thesis on Shakespearean crimes, by translating Mr. Cabot's into Spanish. You prepared some tablets with henbane, and my associate, Mr. Maguire, saw you jostle the late Dr. Gonzalez at the bar and then make a quick exit," said Homer.

Finke, embarrassed, said, "I didn't attach any significance to what I saw, until too late. Who could?"

"Unfortunately I was too intent on my talk with Dr. Gonzalez about head injuries," Homer said. "I was at fault."

Ryan looked at them, belligerent as a turkey. "Cut the Alphonse-Gaston act. You say the bird who killed Laneer's right here with us?"

"Still with us," Homer agreed.

Solange spoke up. "Please, Mr. Evans. What part in this tragedy did poor Mr. Ferguson play? Or was he just coincidental?"

"Ferguson," said Homer, "had expected to leave Boston on Friday afternoon, aboard the United Fruiter, *Cecilie*, with the object of buying wool in the Argentine. He had learned, previously, that he could get a sizable discount if he paid in small personal checks instead of U.S. currency or travelers' checks. The Argentine dealers, of course, turned in Ferguson's checks on Boston banks to the black-market chief in Buenos Aires, who exchanged them for pesos offered by Argentines who wished to travel in style."

Lawyer Endicott spoke up. "Off-hand I can't see anything illegal about that, from Ferguson's angle," he said.

"The maneuver gave Ferguson a splendid advantage over his competitors," Homer said. "Now when Ferguson covered the bets in the Lantern Room on Tuesday night, he expected to sail on Friday. The time limit of the bet would expire at midnight Thursday. Not long after the wager was laid, Ferguson was informed by telephone that the *Cecilie* was to sail Thursday afternoon. To avoid any risk of publicity about his having bet so heavily, and then disappearing without trace, Ferguson tried to call off the wager. Bengay refused. On his way back to the Lantern Room, Ferguson was waylaid in an obscure men's room, deprived of his passport and other papers, and some cash. He couldn't get a steamship ticket without a passport. He had to phone the State Department. And all the time he was on pins and needles for fear his competitors would find out he was planning the voyage and take steps to have his movements watched in South America."

"Who knocked him on the head and took his passport? That passport makes it a federal offense," Ryan said.

"The same party who killed Blaise Laneer. He saw a chance to pinch a passport, which he might need, and took advantage of it on the spot," Homer said.

Solange gasped. "You said 'he'! One of these men?" she made a comprehensive gesture to include the company.

"All right," Homer said. "We'll narrow the field to the men."

Vice President Cabot had a question. "If Ferguson was going to pay for his wool in South America with personal checks, why did he buy $11,000 worth of American Express checks? You brought that out in the Lantern Room, rather cleverly."

"On entering Argentina, he wished to have the American Express checks to put on record. Otherwise Peron's crew might wonder how he came into the country with no money, and paid for wool in wholesale quantities. On returning, sometime later, at his convenience, he would turn in his unused travelers' checks, and deposit them in one of his accounts," Homer answered.

Ryan was boiling. "If you don't produce that murderer without more stalling, Jellyroll goes back to jail," the Sergeant said. "And into another goes the señorita."

"Naturally you're anxious to clear up this affair," Homer said. "Our murderer made the mistake of abusing Finke, when the latter was relatively helpless. Finke marked him for us. If everyone here will expose his or her wrists, and forearms half way to the elbow . . ."

"Are you serious?" asked Solange.

"Oh, come now," echoed Bengay.

There was a motion, then a mild commotion behind Homer. A little man dashed like a scared rabbit, butting a corpulent policeman in the stomach, somehow pushing the huge cop's bulk aside, and turning the latch of the door.

Sergeant Ryan caught up with the man and held him. It was almost too easy. There was a chorus of gasping in the room and a wail of grief from Bunny. Vice President Cabot was staring incredulously.

"Not Edgy Gerry. There must be some mistake," Cabot said.

Etchegaray, in irons, said something in Basque, then, when Ryan rebuked him, translated the remark into English. "Sorry, cousin. I did my best."

"Am I the only one who noticed the similarity between Edgy Gerry and Etchegaray?" Homer asked.

"What put you wise?" demanded Finke. He and Ryan had examined Gerry's right forearm and found the tooth marks which corresponded with Finke's excellent teeth. It was clear that Edgy would make no further resistance, or try to evade the painful truth.

Homer smiled, then saddened as he saw Bunny, racked with sobs. "The Basque cooking I smelled in their apartment was my first real clue. Bunny said she had learned from Edgy's mother, and I found that his father, too, was a Basque. Etchegaray, among the Basques, is a name renowned as well as common. When our amateur criminal found it convenient to simplify his name to Gerry, he quite naturally took the first name Elbridge, after the former Massachusetts statesman who conducted his questionable operations on a larger scale. The nickname for Elbridge is Edgy."

The former bank clerk, unhappy but resigned, turned to Jellyroll. "I wouldn't have let you go to the chair—I don't think. I've got more brains than my cousin Julio, but not his kind of courage. Since he was going to be electrocuted, anyway, I felt that I could hold back."

Ryan was facing Julio Etchegaray, tapping the double murder confession on his palm and glowering. "You realize this is perjury," he growled.

The manacled Argentine laughed. "I ran up quite a string. What's perjury? Where I made my mistake was kidnapping those girls, to get money from the rich Mademoiselle from Canada. That was my idea, on the spur of the moment, and once I got started on it, Edgy, as you call him, had to help. My cousin, I'm ashamed to say, has become thoroughly North Americanized. He's afraid to die."

Gerry, white as paper, his teeth chattering, tried to pull himself together. Bunny wailed.

"Continue," suggested Homer, to Julio Etchegaray.

"I didn't dare try to leave Boston while the authorities were guarding all the exits. So I checked into the Y.M.C.A. on Wednesday night and hung around the lobby of the Dorsetshire yesterday morning. Who would have thought of looking for me so near the scene of the crime? In such a busy lobby, with nearby writing rooms, libraries, bars and corridors?" explained Etchegaray.

"Who, indeed?" agreed Finke, with a glance at Sergeant Ryan.

"The rest was easy, until it got too hard," the Argentine said. "When I saw Mlle de Lassigny hurry out, before nine o'clock yesterday morning, and then re-enter, more excited, a half hour later, I felt sure something was afoot. I started thinking about her fortune, her appearance of generosity, the naïveté in other practical or sentimental matters that all females who consider themselves 'businesswomen' are sure to have. Then I saw the beautician come in, inquire for Mlle de Lassigny's room, and ascend with her kit. I waited, not thinking, exactly. My mind was groping for a quick way to get a share of that department-store money. When the beautician departed, I followed her. She led me to Señorita Strella, and then the pair of them went to the Arboretum. I trailed along. I witnessed their rendezvous with the rich Mademoiselle. My plan formed itself. Mademoiselle evidently was about to rescue my timid countrywoman. She was committing a crime, in the eyes of the law. Therefore she was vulnerable. I could blackmail her for enough to keep me in comfort in Paris, forever. The plans for hijacking the black-money market showed signs of going wrong. I acted. My cousin had to help me."

Finke spoke up hotly. "You didn't have to be so rough and put those women through hell," he said.

"I was excited," Etchegaray said. "And in South America one hears so much rot about chivalry that I reacted against it. That's the way I am. I can't conform. That's why I've never tried to do any regular work. But, Señor Maguire. It is not for you to assume this pious attitude. You're no slouch as a sadist, yourself. If not toward women, when it comes to men."

"Now, now," cautioned Captain Moriarty. "Let's keep this clean, while I'm in charge."

Ryan wheeled to face Gerry. "So you can claim only one murder? Don't get the idea you can wiggle out of that."

"Oh, no, sir. I shouldn't have let ambition corrupt me. I was happy, in my job and at home, with my wife. If only I hadn't been so curious about Mr. Laneer, and the extra money he seemed to enjoy," Gerry said.

"Was it you who suggested that your cousin Julio copy Mr. Cabot's thesis about Shakespeare, for his credits at the university?"

Gerry hung his head. "Cheating!" he admitted. "Yes. I put Julio up to that. Cheating, theft and first-degree murder. I'm really ashamed. You must believe me, Sergeant. When a man leads a life as regular and restricted as mine, the least deviation leads to chaos and disruption."

"How did you know I'd written that thesis about crimes in Shakespeare's works?" Cabot asked.

Gerry smiled apologetically. "I found out everything about everybody in the bank, Mr. Cabot."

"You did!" exclaimed Cabot, uneasily.

"It will all die with me," Gerry said, and Bunny howled piteously. Solange hurried to her side and put an arm around her. "You shall come to Canada with Erica and me. You can start life anew."

"I don't want to start life anew," Bunny sobbed, but she clung to Solange.

"Now Bunny," pleaded Edgy. "Upsy Daisy!"

Reluctantly, Ryan was taking the handcuffs from Jellyroll's wrists.

"Do I get in on this Canadian trip?" the piano player asked.

Erica, eyes shining, took one of his hands, shyly.

"Somehow, if I can go to Canada and re-enter, I can become a United States citizen—and wife. What a country!" she said, and sighed, but joyfully.

"What about me?" Bengay asked, wistfully, looking straight at Solange. She glanced at Finke. "I'll be back," she said.

COACHWHIP PUBLICATIONS

COACHWHIPBOOKS.COM

The Mysterious Mickey Finn
Elliot Paul

The Mysterious Mickey Finn
ISBN 1-61646-293-0

COACHWHIP PUBLICATIONS

ALSO AVAILABLE

Hugger Mugger in the Louvre

Elliot Paul

Hugger Mugger in the Louvre
ISBN 1-61646-294-9

COACHWHIP PUBLICATIONS

COACHWHIPBOOKS.COM

Mayhem in B-Flat

Elliot Paul

Mayhem in B-Flat
ISBN 1-61646-295-7

COACHWHIP PUBLICATIONS
ALSO AVAILABLE

Fracas in the Foothills

Elliot Paul

Fracas in the Foothills
ISBN 1-61646-296-5

COACHWHIP PUBLICATIONS

COACHWHIPBOOKS.COM

I'll Hate Myself in the Morning

Murder on the Left Bank

Elliot Paul

Murder on the Left Bank
ISBN 1-61646-312-0

COACHWHIP PUBLICATIONS

ALSO AVAILABLE

The Black Gardenia
Elliot Paul

The Black Gardenia
ISBN 1-61646-313-9

Murder Ends the Song
ISBN 1-61646-298-1

MURDER
IN A WALLED TOWN
KATHERINE WOODS

Murder in a Walled Town
ISBN 1-61646-332-5

THE
DARTMOUTH
MURDERS

THE
WAILING ROCK
MURDERS

CLIFFORD
ORR

Clifford Orr Mysteries
ISBN 1-61646-323-6